WASPS
IN  THE
ICE CREAM

Tim McGregor

**RAW DOG
SCREAMING
PRESS**

Published by Raw Dog Screaming Press
Bowie, MD

First Edition

Cover: Elderlemon Design

Printed in the United States of America

ISBN: 9781947879522 / 9781947879539
Library of Congress Control Number:
2022951505

RawDogScreaming.com

Also by Tim McGregor

Taboo in Four Colors

Lure

Hearts Strange and Dreadful

The Spookshow series (books 1-11)

Just Like Jesse James

Old Flames, Burned Hands

Killing Down the Roman Line

Bad Wolf trilogy

For Jeff,
This shit ain't the same without you.

ANY HOUSE THAT stands empty too long becomes haunted. That's just the way it is in small towns. The old house out on Merrily Road certainly looked the part with its sagging veranda and rotting roof, a withered husk of lichen and dry rot timbers. A storybook mansion fallen into ruin, it reeked of ghosts and secrets.

It wasn't always deserted. The family that lived there were the town oddballs—an eccentric clan that had lost its fortune but still clung to its lofty airs. No one liked them, and they didn't like us, but that all changed the summer the Farrow sisters began skulking into town. The family car had broken down and the three daughters were sent on foot to the grocery store or the library, heads down and avoiding eye contact. Always after sundown, like the brides of Dracula. They were pale and looked underfed. Folks whispered that it was scurvy brought on by their disturbed parents' strange diet.

Gossip ran deep every time the sisters were spotted. It was the local pastime. Depraved, said one. Inbred, claimed another. The sisters were accused of poisoning the water supply or loosening lug nuts on parked cars. Slipping razor blades into unpicked apples in the orchard or stealing cats to sacrifice in black mass rituals. It was the 1980s and, according to the news, Satanists lurked in every school, every daycare.

As outrageous as the gossip was, it really just masked the venom of the people doing the tongue-wagging. We projected our own worst nature on those three girls. And all that crazy talk about devil worship and wicked deeds was nothing compared to the cruelty we inflicted on them. Me, worst of all.

But here's the kicker; the Farrow house really was haunted back then. A ghost watched over it, protecting the family from harm. That ghost is gone now. It left when the family moved away. I know this because I fell for one of the weird sisters when I was sixteen. It was the middle sister, the one who practiced witchcraft. Hand over my heart, the following is all eyewitness and nothing but.

AUGUST 1987

IF ALL YOUR FRIENDS JUMPED OFF A BRIDGE, WOULD YOU FOLLOW?

MY OLD MAN loves that saying. He dredges it up every time I do something stupid. Which happens a lot. How disappointed would he be with me right now, standing on the wrong side of the bridge that spans the river? There isn't much of a foothold, a few inches of slippery iron at most. Below me, the river rolls past in slow muddy ripples. It's a thirty-foot drop. A wrong splashdown could mean a snapped neck.

It's midsummer, another hazy afternoon with nothing to do. Boredom breeds trouble, which is why the three of us are clinging to the guardrail, trying to make ourselves jump.

Eric is white-knuckling it, refusing to look down. He hates this kind of daredevil stuff. A recent growth spurt has left him clumsy and awkward, barely able to cross a room without knocking into something, let alone climb the guardrail of the bridge. The clumsiness has left him even shyer, almost mute some days.

Kevin White is the opposite, laughing in the face of death or possible mutilation like the maniac he is. Kombat Kevin, we call him, because every stitch of clothing he owns is camouflage. Kevin is all ropey muscle and hair-trigger temper. He dangles by one hand, tempting fate, and scolds us for being pussies. These are my two best friends. Sometimes I hate them.

"Time to die, ladies!" Kevin hollers at us. "Ready? On the count of three."

"Screw this," Eric barks back. His heel slips on the thin ledge, and he hugs the rail for life. "This is stupid. I'm not doing it."

"Too late now," Kevin laughs. "Everybody's watching."

There's a crowd on the riverbank below. A few from our grade, some older. Like us, they're hungry for something, anything, to break the boredom of a humid afternoon. I spot Stacy Gibbons with her friends. She's a year older, one of the cool kids. She'll talk to me if no one is around.

Kevin is right. There's no way to chicken out now. I hate when Kevin's right. And then the crazy bastard jumps. No warning, just a howling "Bonzai!" as he launches himself from the iron ledge. It seems like a long time before he hits the water, and even longer before his head bobs up. The kids on the riverbank hoot and holler. Stacy even claps. Still laughing, Kevin swims to the bank and barks at us to quit stalling.

Eric says it's suicide and refuses to do it. I concede his point. That's a hell of a long way down.

"Screw this," he says again. "I'm not dying today. You coming?"

Eric climbs back up the guardrail, but the guy is all gangly legs and orangutan arms. He slips, bounces off the ledge, and spins all the way down. A big splash and then nothing. He's underwater for a long time, long enough for Kevin to dive in and save him. When Eric finally pops to the surface, coughing up a lung, Kevin hauls him to safety.

Eric's fine. Worse than that, he jumped. He didn't mean to, but that doesn't matter. He did it. That leaves me. The crowd on the bank are looking up, waiting. Stacy too. Backing out now isn't an option. I'll be branded a chickenshit loser. I couldn't live with that. Drowning, I can live with.

I jump. But I jump all wrong and I'm cartwheeling worse than Eric. Hitting the water is like slapping into concrete. I've had the wind knocked out of me before. It's scary, but this time I'm underwater. I can't tell which way is up. I'm going to die down here in the polluted water of Carthage River. Out of nowhere comes air. I can breathe. Kevin's hauling my stupid carcass to the muddy bank.

"Nice dive, asshole," he says.

The river water tastes like sulfur and algae as I hack it up.

Eric is kneeling over me, shaking his head. "Jesus, Mark. I thought you bought it that time."

The pain across my stomach is so intense, I think my guts are spilling out. "Am I bleeding?"

Both of them laugh at me. "Maybe internally," Eric says.

"That was the stupidest dive ever," Kevin adds. He shakes the water from his hair like a dog. "Typical Mark, always needing to be saved from himself."

We stagger out of the sucking mud to the grass. I look down the riverbank at the others, but the older kids have already lost interest. Stacy and her friends are smoking and tossing pop bottles into the river, back to being bored.

I almost died, and for what? The passing amusement of others? It's only the end of July. This is going to be one slow summer.

DEAD WASPS

A VOICE HOLLERS at me to get up. Kicks the bed for good measure. He does this every morning and then goes on about how when he was a kid, he got up at dawn every morning, Sundays in summertime too. In the kitchen, he drones on about the chores he used to do and how much easier kids have it these days. Listening to him, you'd think my dad was raised in a Victorian poorhouse, worked to death for slave wages.

He's not a liar exactly, my old man. More of an elaborate exaggerator. Every dumb story grows larger with each telling. He assumes I want to hear these stories, that they are somehow educational to me. The worst is when he tries to underline each tale with a moral instruction or note of wisdom.

"And that," he says, wrapping up yet another dull story, "is why you never go ice fishing with an Irishman."

Bill Prewitt, my dad, snaps the morning newspaper, turns the page. A crisp short-sleeve shirt with a tie that's as lame as his wisdom. As far as I know, he's never once gone ice fishing.

I've missed his story entirely. Mornings are not my thing, and I despise chitchat over the breakfast table. The old man is the exact opposite—brimming with conversation and optimism for the day ahead. His mood goes dark as the day winds down. He sometimes wonders how we're related.

"Great story, Dad." I say this, hoping it will shut him up.

"You know, I was talking to Jimmy Reeves yesterday. You know Officer Reeves?"

Like every other small Ontario town, everyone in Brandenburg knows everyone else. Including the cops. Dad is buddies with all of them.

He goes on. "He said some kids were jumping off the bridge yesterday. You wouldn't know anything about that, would you?"

I look him in the eye and lie to his face. "Not me."

He seems satisfied with this answer. "What kind of mental defect jumps off a bridge?"

The mood changes when Liz whooshes into the kitchen, her face freshly scrubbed and daubed with a minimum of make-up. "You're both going to be late."

Dad pours a cup of coffee and slides it across the counter to her. "You look nice."

He's not wrong. Liz doesn't overdo it, the way other women do. She doesn't need to. She turns in my direction as if waiting for me to agree, but I don't say anything. Liz Pembry is seven years younger than he is and nowhere near as buttoned-down.

They look odd as a couple. I don't know if other people see that too or if it's just me.

"Morning, Mark," she says. "Sleep well?"

I shrug, put my bowl in the sink. Liz reminds Bill that she's going out with her girlfriends tonight, so he's in charge of dinner. She encourages him to cook something instead of picking up the usual bucket of fried chicken.

When she leaves the kitchen, Dad scowls at me. "Would it kill you to be nice?"

"I am nice."

"We're about done with this routine. Things need to change around here."

The sunlight coming through the window is already blinding. It's way too early for threats. "I gotta go to work." I have two summer jobs. Today I work both.

"Hold on, mister," he says. "Check the garage before you go. The Galaxie is leaking."

Another complaint about his precious garage. "Are you sure?"

"Saw it last night when I took the garbage out. Deal with it now. I don't want any oil stains on my garage floor."

The car is enormous, eating up most of the space in our narrow garage. A 1967 Ford Galaxie 500 two-door hardtop, candy apple red with matching vinyl interior. Rolled off the Detroit assembly line four years before I was born. It spent the last ten years moldering in my grandfather's barn. I used to play in it when I was little. Grandma Jean always complained about it, but Grandpa vowed he would get the Galaxie back on the road. He never did, and Grandma Jean still griped about it after he passed.

Last summer, she decided to clean out the barn, including the dusty Ford. I told her I wanted it, asked her how much. She said two hundred dollars—for a car that hadn't started in eight years. Dad refused to even hear me out, so I went around him. Cut out the middleman, he always says, so I did. He didn't find that very funny, but I remember Liz stifling a giggle behind his back.

Grandma Jean was willing to come down on her price if I got the car out of her barn by the end of the week. So Grandma made a hundred bucks (paid in installments), and I paid another twenty for a tow truck to haul it to our house. Dad was so miffed about having his garage hijacked that he charged me rent. My whole family are a bunch of gougers. When I complained, he just shrugged like it was beyond his control and said it was part of our Scots blood.

"You know how copper wire was invented?" he asked, never missing an opportunity to bore the living shit out of me with pearls of wisdom. He actually thinks I listen.

"Why would I know that?"

"Two Scotsmen fighting over a penny." Laughing at his own joke, he cuffed his hand over my shoulder and said, "The garage rental is five dollars a month. First of the month, every month. You miss a payment, that ugly car gets towed out of here."

I bought the Galaxie in April and got my driver's license in June. I failed my first test because of a rolling stop. What a jerk. The second time I just got lucky. The driving tester was an impatient dude more concerned about lunch than about me making a complete stop. He signed his little form, granting me a license, and ran off to get a meatball sub. Standards are clearly not very high at the Brandenburg Motor Vehicles Bureau. By the time school finishes, my savings are gone, so I hustled and got not one, but two summer jobs. Weekdays are spent at Dutton's Recreational Vehicle Emporium, where I mow the grass between trailers and wash Winnebagos. Four nights a week, I sling ice cream out of a shack on Main Street. All earnings go into fixing up the Galaxie 500 and covering the rent.

The candy apple paint is dull, but the body's in good condition. A little rust, but the chassis is solid and the brakes work. The problem is the engine. It turns over, but it won't run for more than ten seconds because of a faulty fuel pump. It's not an expensive fix, but it is hard to find a replacement part for a 20-year-old car. There's one junkyard in town and another five miles out. I check both on a regular basis, but there's never a matching Galaxie I can strip for parts.

I adore this car. It's huge and sleek with a pointed grill that looks like bared teeth—a shark on wheels. And one day, this shark will cruise again. For now, it rests quietly in the shade of the garage, awaiting resurrection.

But it does have a leak. The old man was right.

It's just the oil pan. I changed the oil two days ago and didn't tighten the drain plug properly. Easy fix, but it leaves a stain on the concrete. There's a box of kitty litter under the workbench for exactly this reason. I toss a handful of the stuff down to soak it up, then I grab my bike and ride off to work.

When my dad talks about the summer jobs he had, he goes on about how much fun he had—picking fruit, washing cars, running errands for the old men at the pool hall. It's hard to imagine because mine is not fun. It's slow and screamingly boring.

The Dairy Scoop has a great location, right on the main drag and across from the movie theater, but it's the shittiest ice cream stand in town. It's a plywood hut painted pastel pink and blue, and the roof leaks when it rains. Kevin calls it the Fairy Scoop, says scooping ice cream is a girl's job.

Kevin doesn't have a summer job. He always seems to have cash on him, but he won't tell us if his parents give it to him or if he steals it. He denies it's an allowance, because he knows Eric and I will crucify him for it. I have my two summer jobs and even Eric mows lawns for old people on his street. Kevin remains a gentleman of leisure. My old man doesn't like Kevin very much. He tells me the Devil has his work cut out for him keeping that boy's hands idle.

The ice cream here is pretty bad, cheap stuff bought at a discount from an outlet two towns over. There's a wasp nest wadded under the outside eave, and I've been watching it grow as the summer rolls on. Each afternoon when I open up the hut, I have to pluck the dead wasps out of the ice cream bins. They always go for the black cherry or strawberry. The bin of Tiger Tail, which is vile, they ignore.

Most people know the ice cream is bad and stay away, but some people stop in— older folks or dumb kids who don't know any better. I spend most of my time reading. Kitty-corner from the Dairy Scoop is the Palisades movie theater, which has been there since the time of Moses. On Thursdays, I watch the owner prop a ladder on the sidewalk and climb up to change the letters on the marquee. The movies are always four or five months stale. If you want to see something new, you have to drive all the way out to the Roxy over in Greenville. The Palisades is missing some of the letters, so the marquee often looks misleading or downright screwy. *Pack to the Future* or *Cremlins*. One time I saw Mr. Blurton, the owner, lean too far to stick the letter and the ladder went sideways, sending him to the pavement. Fuck, I laughed.

The best thing about the Palisades is Stacy Gibbons. She works the ticket booth and concession stand. Once the movie starts, she steps outside for a smoke. If it's a really dead night, she'll wander across the street to the Dairy Scoop. Stacy gets a kick out of seeing the dead wasps in the cream. She leans over the counter, bangles rattling against the glass, and grosses out as I lay the dead insects before her. Stacy wears the tightest jeans I've ever seen. Someone told me Stacy has to lie flat and hook a coat hanger into the zipper just to do them up all the way. I don't know if this is true or not. I've also heard that super tight jeans will squeeze a uterus and produce deformed babies, so there you go.

Tonight, I watch Stacy sell a total of five tickets for *Police Academy 4*. Bored, she wanders over to check the bug count. My hands are already sweaty as I pluck out a wasp and place it on the glass so she can see its alien-looking carcass slathered in black cherry ice cream. In my head, I'm saying something funny or clever, but what comes out is stammering blather. I sound like a turnip with vocal cords.

"Look," Stacy says, drawing her face close to a slowly unfolding wing. Her eye teeth bite down on a sparkly bottom lip. "It's still moving."

She squeals in satisfied disgust and runs back to the theater before her boss yells at her. Stacy's a grade ahead of me, but she only goes out with guys who've finished school. There's more than you'd think, circling Brandenburg High in their muscle cars with the windows down and music blaring. They prowl the parking lot and talk to girls like Stacy until a teacher comes out and chases them off.

That's the part I can't understand. If you managed to make it out of high school, why the hell would you ever come back?

HEADS IN THE ICEBOX

THE SIDE DOOR at Eric's house opens onto a landing, three steps up to the kitchen or eleven down to the basement. I walk in without knocking, without seeing his parents. The basement is a dim rec room of wood paneling and smelly shag carpeting, pictures of matadors on the wall, and his parents' first television, the old kind that takes forever to turn on. Kevin's on the floor and Eric's in the beanbag chair, which leaks white stuffing over the rancid carpet. The place stinks of boredom so bad that Eric's mom refuses to come down here anymore.

"He kept her head in the fridge," Kevin says. He's reading a trashy tabloid, his favorite, the kind they sell at the grocery store checkout. Kevin claims his mom buys them and he just reads the crazy stories, but I'm pretty sure this is a lie. He loves reading about serial killers, fugitive Nazis, and Bigfoot.

"Says here he buried the severed heads in his backyard, under the rose bush," he continues, lips moving as he skims the article. He lowers the paper to look at Eric and me. "He told the cops he wanted to feel close to his victims. How crazy is that?"

Eric isn't listening. The glassy look in his eyes tells me that Kevin's been droning on about serial killers for a while. Eric has a hard time concentrating on anything that doesn't involve spaceships or monsters. He struggles to keep up at school. At anything.

I prop my feet up on the chipped coffee table. "Sounds like a swell guy."

"Kinda looks like you, Eric."

Kevin holds up the photo for us to see and then chucks the paper at me. The headline on the front page warns that leaking radiation from Chernobyl will poison western Europe within the year. UFOs were spotted over Nevada again.

Kevin rams a handful of chips into his mouth. "Should I ask about the car or am I just going to be disappointed again?"

"Kind of answered your own question there, bub," I tell him.

He shakes his head in disgust. "You're never gonna get that thing on the road, are you?"

"I'm working on it."

"Like hell you are." Kevin says. "All that talk about us cruising down the strip in your wheels. What a joke."

"Enough squabbling, children," Eric says, reaching for the dial on the ancient TV. "It's wrestling time."

The television turns on with a *thunk* and the screen takes a minute to warm up so we can watch WWF. We are staggeringly bored. The three of us burned through most of our amusements in the first few weeks of summer break, swimming in the creek or wasting hours in the arcade downtown. We've rented every movie in the horror/action/sci-fi section of our video store. Multiple times. Eric still wants to go fishing or build a raft, but Kevin says that Huck Finn shit is lame. There's always blowing up stuff or burning shit. Kevin's always down for that.

Most of our friends are gone, off to visit cousins in faraway towns or their summer cottage. Brandenburg is boring at the best of times, but now it's completely dead. Nothing but dry August dust blowing hazily along Main Street. The summer will burn too fast like it always does, and when Labor Day comes, we'll all groan about it being over too soon. But here in this moment, in Eric's basement, summer drags. I mean, it fucking crawls.

The two of them start wrestling. Within seconds, Kevin has his much taller opponent on the mat. Kevin White is compact and wiry, but he's also vicious when provoked. He's like a mongoose on a cobra—lightning fast and brutal. With three older brothers, Kevin learned to fight before he learned to walk.

By the time Eric is suffocating in Kevin's chokehold, I have this terrible suspicion that I don't even like my own friends. But there's nowhere to go and nothing to do, so I just sit here until I notice how late it is. I've missed dinner, and there will be a discussion about that when I get home. I get up to leave, chip crumbs falling from my shirt to the rancid carpet.

"Later."

Kevin sits up. "Tomorrow. Eighteen hundred hours."

He talks like that a lot. Military jargon he's picked up from too many war movies. It matches his camouflage pants.

"Tomorrow?"

Eric wheezes at me, shocked. "Don't tell me you forgot? Jesus, Mark."

My brain is shooting blanks, and I must have a stupid look on my face because they both roar at me.

"*RoboCop!*"

The movie we're all dying to see. It came out months ago, but it's only now coming to the Palisades. We've talked about it endlessly, whooping at the TV whenever the commercial aired. How did I forget it was coming?

I high-five them both and head for the stairs. "Tomorrow, six o'clock."

"Does Stacy work Mondays?" Eric asks. I tell him I don't know.

Kevin laughs at that. "Bullshit you don't know."

Now they're both laughing at me. My face gets hot, but I guess it's pretty funny. I bang out the screen door, get my bike. The sun is low, and the cicadas are loud as I ride home. It feels good to finally have something to look forward to.

The kitchen's dark when I get home. Dad and Liz are in the living room watching the Sunday night movie which, from the racket of gunfire and horses, sounds like a western. My old man is such a cliche. On the kitchen table is a plate wrapped in foil.

Dad's already in the doorway, hands on his hips. It's too late to think up an excuse. He nods at the table.

"Sit."

"I'm sorry—"

His hand shoots up like a referee to stop me. Dad's idea of parenting isn't that different from dog training—single word commands and hand gestures. Liz stands behind him and the look on her face is pure sympathy, but that only makes me like her less.

"Unwrap that," he says.

The foil comes away with a crinkly sound. Roast beef with mashed potatoes, a side of green beans—the smell of it has me drooling. I guess I am a dog after all. I'm wondering how long the lecture is going to take before I can tuck into this.

"We don't need to go over the rules about Sunday dinner, do we? You're clear on those?"

"I lost track of time, that's all."

The hand goes up again. Penalty. "Yes or no."

"Yes."

"Do you know how much work goes into making dinner?" When I shake my head, he carries on. "Do you know how long it took Liz to make this? Or how long it takes to earn the money to buy the groceries?"

He's in form tonight. He gets like this nowadays. I think it's for Liz's sake, putting on this show of discipline. Why is he trying to impress her? They're already married.

"No, sir."

He seems pleased with the "sir" part. He folds his arms, nods at the food again. "Pick up the plate. Bring it here."

I do as I'm told. His foot goes down on the pedal that pops open the garbage lid. "Chuck it in."

The old man's upped his game tonight. Maybe he's feeling inspired by the western they were watching. Dad's big on John Wayne. God knows why.

I hesitate. "That's kind of a waste, isn't it?"

"Yes, Mark. It is a waste. Go on."

"Bill—"

His upshot hand cuts her off. I scrape the food into the bin, set the plate in the sink.

"Wash that and put it away," he says. "No food, no snacking. Straight to your room when you're done."

He's gone back to the living room, leaving Liz in the doorway and me standing at the sink. She's trying to make eye contact, but I won't give her the satisfaction. There's a wine glass in her hand. She goes to the fridge to hit the pour spout on the box. I wash the plate.

"Sorry," she says. She means it too. "That was a bit harsh."

"It's the only way I'll learn." I recite this part from heart.

She frowns, leans her hip against the counter. "I know it's easy to lose track of time when you're having fun with your friends."

"We didn't have any fun."

"Sunday dinner is a big deal with your dad," she says. "One day a week. Just be home on time for it, that's all."

She's trying so hard, but it's a thin line—trying to be my friend, walking the tightrope of neutrality. And all I do is throw it back at her, deflecting it with my invisible force field. Liz has a lot of patience, but everybody has their limits. Then she'll stop being nice and throw back as good as she gets. You know what the funny part will be? When that happens, I'll regret being so shitty to her all this time. I don't know why I do the things I do.

"Okay." She turns to leave, waits. "Life's tough enough as it is. You don't have to make it harder for yourself."

It would be so easy to just be nice to her. But I don't. I just let Liz dangle out there in the wind. She says goodnight. I grunt an unintelligible reply.

My bedroom ceiling is decorated with little stars and moons that are supposed to glow in the dark. They were put up there when I was eight, but the glow-in-the-dark part never worked. Stupid kid stuff I should have trashed a long time ago.

It's too hot to sleep, so I think about how cruel I am to Liz, and how easy it is to be cruel. It takes absolutely no effort. I wonder if there's something wrong with me—something deep that can't be fixed or cured or outgrown. When Liz was trying to be kind, all I could think about was the tabloid story Kevin was reading. I pictured Liz's severed head in the fridge. The eyes were open and blood was trickling from the neck stump through the wire rack. The expression on her chilled face wasn't shock or terror, just a mild disappointment. Like she always knew this would happen.

Yeah. I'm pretty sure this can't be fixed or medicated away. Years from now, Kevin will open up his favorite tabloid and see my picture there. He'll turn to his wife and say, "Holy shit. I used to know that guy."

WEIRD SISTERS

"THAT MOVIE ISN'T playing. Sorry, guys."

This doesn't compute, and it makes my heart hurt. "What do you mean? It's right there in the schedule. *RoboCop*."

Stacy blows a pink bubble, lets it pop. She's sitting inside the glass booth of the movie theater, stomping all over our little hearts. "Misprint. Happens all the time."

I look up at the marquee, but it's empty. I look back at Stacy chewing her gum like nothing's happened, like our world hasn't just been blown to smithereens. "Then what's playing?"

"Tender Mercies."

Pop.

A vein is pulsing on Kevin's temple. Eric's bottom lip quivers. We've been looking forward to this for months. The anticipation of it had me so giddy at work that my boss asked if I was high. I biked home from the RV yard and broke into my sacred car fund. It's more than enough for a ticket and an armload of junk food, but now I have nothing to spend it on.

Eric's lumpy Adam's apple bobs up and down. "Well, what do we do now?" He addresses this question to Stacy as if she's supposed to have an answer.

Pop. "Maybe next week."

Kevin's vibrating, he's so angry. He can be a little scary when he gets like this, and I worry he's going to punch the glass. He glares at the naked marquee. "We ought to burn the place to the ground, watch all the rats escape down Main Street."

The Palisades is rumored to be infested with rats. Folks claim they scamper over their shoes, hunting the spilled popcorn on the sticky floor. Most girls won't wear sandals to the movies, even in summer.

Eric points out that we'll never see *RoboCop* if we torch the movie house. He suggests renting a movie and going back to his place, but he's quickly overruled. We're here and we're all keyed up for something big. I'm grateful we don't have any beers with us. That combination always leads to something catastrophically stupid.

We go to the arcade.

Lucky Penny isn't much of an arcade. Four games with scratched up screens and an air hockey table no one ever plays. A window in the back opens onto a repulsive kitchen where a flabby dude in a filthy apron chain-smokes over the deep fryer. We plug our quarters in and smash the buttons until the sweaty cook yells at us to go easy on his machines. That only prompts Kevin to hammer the console harder until I tell him to knock it off. If we get kicked out of here, we got fuck all else to do.

Eric settles into *Frogger*, blowing through the levels until his eyes bulge from his head. He's on a mission. His older sister, Christine, ruled this game like a ninja, getting her name into the fifth place ranking. This irks Eric to no end, and he's determined to knock her out of the top scores. He's deluded, but try telling him that. Christine's cool. She's fanatically competitive and punches harder than anyone I know. She's away at college now, so going to Eric's isn't half as fun as it used to be.

This gets stale pretty damn quick. I tell them I'm going to the grocery store to load up on junk food. The pair of them grunt in response, their eyes never leaving the cloudy video screens.

Greene's is a block away, the only grocery store downtown. It smells like overripe bananas and Irish Spring, one lone cashier at the register and a few shoppers haunting the aisles. I head straight to the aisle where the Ho Hos and Ding Dongs are, and that's when I see her.

The only soul in an otherwise empty aisle, hovering over the snack section. Her dark hair is flat and kinda greasy-looking, the clothes dingy and out of date. There's an open package of Twinkies in her hand, and she's wolfing these down like she hasn't eaten in days. She stops when she sees me, crumbs falling over those ugly nun shoes. Her face is hidden behind the fall of hair so I can't see her eyes. She puts the crinkly package back on the shelf, wipes a wrist over her mouth and walks away.

Everything slows down. I'm speechless, like one of those people who claimed to have seen Bigfoot or a UFO—mouth gaping, unable to believe my own eyes. She's one of the sisters, the weird ones that haunt town but are rarely ever spotted in the wild. Like narwhals: you know they exist, you just never expect to see one in real life.

The mysterious Farrow sisters. I spot the other two at the cash register, ringing up their groceries. The taller one is digging through a change purse. She looks older than me. The younger one looks about twelve. Their clothes are threadbare and odd, like they were ransacked from a donation bin.

The girl I caught wolfing Twinkies is at the spinning rack of cheap books. She has one of the paperbacks open, close to her face like she needs glasses. Something about her twitchy movements raises the hair on the back of my neck. She's waiting for a chance to slip the book under her shirt. I used to shoplift all the time. I recognize the tense body language of someone wanting to redeem the five-finger discount.

"George, put that back," says the older one, scolding the girl with the book. "You know the rules."

George? Then I remember her—the girl with the boy's name. She used to be in my class back in the seventh grade. Then she stopped going to school. She was weird back then, too.

Flustered, the girl jams the book clumsily back into the spinning rack and joins the other two. They each take a shopping bag and leave. I'm still in shock at a rare sighting of the Farrow sisters in public.

When they're gone, oxygen rushes back into the space and the paralysis drains from my limbs. I cross to the book collection and turn the rack until I find the one paperback rammed lopsided into the wire cage. The cover shows a gruesome face leering behind a broken window. It looks like trashy horror, but the author's name suggests otherwise. Lovecraft. A romance book?

"You ready?" says the cashier, making me jump. She nods at the big wall clock. "Store's closing."

She rings up my stuff and locks the door behind me. My palms are still slick, and there's a lump in my chest that won't go away.

I remember her from school, but not very well. She was a loner who plucked dandelions at the edge of the yard while the rest of us climbed over the monkey bars. No one liked her back then, especially the other girls. She had a younger sister a few grades behind, and two older ones in high school. Then something bad happened. The girls were pulled out of school and never came back. I thought the Farrows had moved away until recently when whispers started circulating about the sisters skulking through town at sunset. Just three of them, going to the grocery store or the library. I assumed it was dumb gossip until now.

Back at the arcade, I find Eric sitting on the curb, staring off into space like he's stoned. He gets like this when he plays video games.

"What happened to you?" he asks. "You're all pale and shit."

"Just saw a ghost."

"A what?"

"Nothing." I offer him the paper bag of junk food. "Did you add your name to the ranking?"

His face turns sulky as he reaches for the licorice. That means he failed to dislodge his sister's name from the game. "Next time."

There's a rumble of voices from inside the arcade. I see Kevin talking to two other guys—Jeremy and Dennis, both a grade ahead of us. Jeremy's a popular kid, a good hockey player. I've never liked Dennis.

The three of them are huddled at the air hockey table, talking rapidly about something. I nose my way in and Kevin reaches for the bag in my hand.

"What's going on?"

The question was directed at Kevin, but Jeremy replies. "Dude, we just saw the witch sisters."

So I didn't just imagine them. But what does Jeremy care about the weird sisters?

Kevin's shaking his head. "That's twice this month. The hell's going on with that freak show?"

"Maybe they killed their parents," Jeremy says, "and they're coming into town to forage for food."

"Rich creeps," Dennis adds. "Think they're better than everyone else."

"I don't think they're rich," I blurt out, recalling the girl's shabby clothes.

"How do you know?" Kevin snaps. He gets like this around older dudes. Tough, trying to impress. "My old man says they never go to the bank. Which means they're hoarding cash up there in that house. Probably stuffing it in a mattress."

A muscle in Jeremy's cheek flexes. "Where the hell are the parents? They just let those psychos loose after dark?"

"You know they carry knives on them?" Kevin adds.

Where he's gotten this information from is anyone's guess. Rumor becomes fact the moment it's said aloud. Something's been set off, a spark or something darker. There's a revulsion that turns all of them jittery and tense. Eric joins the huddle, and everyone's talking over each other.

"Somebody ought to teach them a lesson."

"The whole family ought to be locked up."

"Maybe we should have a little fun."

"That's not a good idea."

Dennis sneers at me. "Don't be a pussy, Mark."

Smirking grins all around, elbows nudging ribs, and then Jeremy and Dennis are out the door. Eric runs after them, not wanting to miss out. Kevin hesitates, but he's twitching to go. He lives for this kind of thing.

I shake my head. "No."

He takes off like a shot, hollering at me to get my butt in gear. Sprinting past the church, trying to catch up, I come to the bridge where the main road leads out of town. All I can hear is the river moving slowly down there in the dark.

I've lost them.

A noise to my left. They're scaling the wall of Tony's Auto Garage to get to the flat gravel roof. It's not the climb that makes me hesitate; it's the sense of disaster that I know is coming. Whatever this is, it's a bad idea, but Eric's already barking at me to haul ass and Kevin tells me to stop being a pussy and get up there. I clamber up and drop onto the pebbly rooftop.

It's already in motion, whatever the plan is. Jeremy peeks over the edge to where the road meets the bridge. Kevin's handing out firecrackers to everyone. He keeps firecrackers in his back pocket at all times, always prepared to sow a little mayhem. Like a Boy Scout eager to earn a badge of destruction.

My stomach curdles. "This is stupid."

The looks are all venomous. Someone produces a lighter and now the wicks are smoking. Jeremy's sounding out a countdown. Kevin thrusts a fizzing stick at me.

"Take it."

"Let's get the hell out of here."

"Take it!"

"Would you bitches shut up!" Jeremy hisses at us. Eyeballing the street below, he gives the signal.

"Fire in the hole!"

The incendiaries sail over the edge, leaving arcs of smoke in the night air. I'm still holding mine, and it's about to blow my hand off and everyone's snarling at me to just fucking throw it.

So I do.

Sharp pops ripple the air. Frightened shrieks. Kevin and the others lean over the edge and howl with laughter. I creep up and look too, expecting to see three girls dead on the pavement.

But that's not the case. The Farrow girls are still on their feet, but the grocery bags have hit the ground, cans rolling this way and lemons spilling that way. They don't react, don't even look up despite the howl of laughter from the roof of the garage. They just gather up the fallen groceries, put them back into the bags and walk to the bridge. The middle sister, the one I saw scarfing down Twinkies, clutches a hand to her ear. Then they melt into the shadows of the trestle bridge and vanish.

Everyone laughs like they've never seen anything so funny, thumping each other on the back and mimicking the screams they heard. But there's a strained note to the sounds, like they're insisting that this stunt is the funniest shit ever.

If I was any sort of decent human being, I'd tell these meatheads to go to hell. But I don't. They keep laughing, and now they're thumping my back too, insisting that I howl along with them. God help me, I laugh.

REIGN OF THE FARROWS

THE ALARM GOES off, but I just lie here staring up at those stupid stars on the ceiling, wondering if I can call in sick. Unlikely. There are no sick days on a summer job that's paid under the table by a guy who loves cheating the tax man. Mr. Dutton would just find some other kid for even lower wages. The funny thing is that I really do feel sick.

I went to bed with the sound of firecrackers popping in my ears, and when I wake up, the racket is still there. I keep seeing the sisters standing in the smoke, not scared or surprised or even mad. It was like they had expected it—the one sister covering her ear… What if she's deaf now?

Why did I just go along with it? Because they called me a pussy? Because I don't want them to hate me the way they hate those girls? What's wrong with us? Being destructive or cruel is like a fever that takes over. It brings a weird glee that makes us drunk, building momentum until we're all rolling with it. And then something bad happens. Something goes up in flames or someone gets hurt. Every time.

I don't want to think about this anymore because I have to go out to the kitchen and face Dad and Liz. So I lock it up like a rat in a cage and close the lid, suffocate it. I'm pretty adept at this, suffocating things I don't want to think about. It comes in handy. Standing under the shower faucet, I turn the hot water all the way up until it burns.

"You get sunburnt?" Dad looks up from his paper when I enter the kitchen. "You're all red."

I mumble that it's nothing and fill a bowl with cereal. Liz asks if I want any coffee, but I say no, needing to get out of here quickly. Fortunately, the two of them resume discussion about a camping trip they are planning and leave me out of the morning chitchat.

"What's the deal with the Farrows?"

It just blurts out of me, interrupting their camping plans.

Liz looks at me. "Who?"

"That family, the Farrows. Why are they so weird?"

My dad's brow breaks into deep lines. "Why are you asking?"

I shrug. "I saw them last night."

"The family?" Liz asks, looking surprised.

"The girls, at the grocery store. Jeremy said he saw them last week, too. Skulking around after dark." My mouth is running away from me, blabbing about stuff I had no intention of revealing.

Puzzled, Liz looks at Dad. He waves it away, tells me to pay them no mind. "They've always been strange. Stay away from them."

"Why?"

His eyes roll to the kitchen clock, noting that we are going to be late. He fishes his car keys from the bowl, kisses Liz goodbye and runs out the door.

Liz never rushes, no matter what the time. She gathers the cups and sets them in the sink. "They're kind of reclusive, that family," she says. "Can't say I blame them, losing a child and all that."

That triggers a memory, but it's fuzzy and unreliable. "One of them died."

"A few years ago, wasn't it? One of the daughters." Liz visibly shudders at the thought. "That poor family."

An abrupt nausea kills my appetite. I push the cereal away. "Did you know her?"

"No, I've never met any of them," she says. "They really keep to themselves."

"How did she die?"

"Car accident, I think." She takes her bag and roots around in it for her car keys. "I can't imagine what that would do to a family, losing a child like that."

Despite the morbid discussion, her smile beams, her mood brighter than usual because of our little exchange. She wishes me a good day and goes out to her car. This is the most conversation we've had since she moved in. Imagine something as pathetic as that making you happy?

Today is a double shift—a full day at the RV yard followed by a stint at the Dairy Scoop, an hour in between where I bike home to make a sandwich. I'm grateful for it since it leaves no time for my friends. I'm annoyed with them for pulling that stupid prank, but I'm more angry at myself for going along with it. It's like I have no willpower around other people. I fall in line and do what's expected, what's cool.

Work is slow at the RV Emporium, so Mr. Dutton lets me practice backing a travel trailer into the space between two double-wides. You have to use the side mirrors and turn the wheel opposite to the way you want the trailer to go. Mr. Dutton is patient while he sits in the passenger side, guiding me through it. Propping the hitch on cinderblocks, I ask him about the Farrow family.

"The ones out on Merrily Road?"

I nod. "You know them?"

"Nobody knows them."

The grit on the cement block makes it slippery. "What does that mean?"

"The Farrows always thought highly of themselves. Rich folks tend to do that. They put on airs like their shit don't stink."

"What happened to them?"

Mr. Dutton tugs the ballcap from his head, wipes his brow, and then squares the hat back on. "They lost everything somewhere along the way. When I was a kid, the Farrows owned half the town. Not anymore. Bad investments, lavish spending. They got wiped out. Funny thing is, they still act like they're rich. Hell, you seen that big house, haven't you? Falling to pieces around them and them still living there."

We walk back to the shop to get out of the sun. Mr. Dutton lowers his voice even though the shop is empty. "Kooky bunch, those Farrows. That happens when the breeding stock is kept too close, know what I mean?"

I don't have a clue what he's talking about. "Not really."

"They don't fraternize with anyone in town, you see. Never marry outside their circle." He underscores this by twirling an index finger next to his temple. "Inbreeding. Causes the wires to cross."

He shambles off to his office, leaving me to weigh this information against its possible truth. It's juicy gossip, which I can only conclude is horseshit.

At the ice cream hut, I count over a dozen wasps drowned in the black cherry bin. I pick them out and fling them out back. Two hours pass without a single customer, so I wander across the street to the glass booth of the Palisades movie house. Stacy's got her head down, reading a paperback. It's a slow night all around, and she's as bored as I am. When I ask her what she's reading, she lifts the book to show me the cover—*My Sweet Audrina*. I didn't know she likes horror novels, but she turns her nose up at the suggestion.

"Horror's trash," she says. "This is like a tragedy about a psycho family."

I check the poster for this week's movie—*Summer Heat*. "Is that any good?"

"Dunno."

"You haven't watched it?"

Stacy glances at the poster. "That's not what's playing. Sometimes the film reels get mislabeled. The cans said *Summer Heat*, but the movie we got is some Italian movie. Last month we were supposed to get *The Rescuers*, but they sent us a Traci Lords flick instead. Needless to say, the crowd wasn't happy."

Stacy goes back to her book, chewing loudly with aggressive, open-mouthed chomps. I can see the pink gum roll around her perfect teeth. No cars on the main drag, everything dead quiet in the humidity. I try not to stare at the silver cross dangling in her cleavage. I file the image away for later and grasp at small talk.

"Stacy, you know that family that lives across the river? The Farrows?"

She lowers the book, annoyed that I'm still here. "The weirdos? What about them?"

"The girl who died. Did you know her?"

"She was older than me." Stacy glances around. The street is empty, but she still leans closer to the louvered hole in the glass. "You know how she died, right?"

"Car accident?"

"It wasn't an accident." She whispers, her breath fogging the glass. "She killed herself."

"Get out of here."

"Swear to God," she says, underlining her point by making the sign of the cross. "She drove her car straight into a pole on purpose."

Suicide is a weird concept. We joke about it all the time, but death is abstract to Kevin and Eric. They've never witnessed it. The eyes turn to blank glass and the body sinks as if losing twenty pounds in an instant. It's bizarre.

"Why did she kill herself?"

"No one knows, but you hear stuff." She lets this statement hang there in the air.

"Like what?"

Stacy's eyes dart around again. "The dad was doing stuff. That's why she popped herself."

My eyes dip to the book cover as I say this. "And you believe that?"

"Like I said, they're weirdos. Why do you think the dad pulled the rest of the girls out of school after that? So no one else could get to them." I must have a skeptical look on my face because Stacy leans back and laughs at me. "You're such an innocent, Mark. All kinds of stuff goes on behind closed doors. But I guess you wouldn't know about that."

She thinks I'm just a kid, and this leaves a sour taste in my mouth. I turn to go, saying I should get back to my post. But Stacy's not done. She calls back, her tone a little softer now. I guess I'm sulking for being called innocent.

"You ever see that house they live in? Who wouldn't go crazy living in a place like that?"

THE LURKING FEAR

STACY ISN'T WRONG. The house is creepy and sad-looking. It's huge, one of the grand old houses in town, but it droops like it's lost its will to live. The veranda sags and lichen stains the clapboard like mold. Some of the scale-shaped roof shingles have blown off, and the paint is faded, peeling. The station wagon in the driveway matches the house, old and used-up.

Merrily Road is a twenty-minute bike ride across town, over the bridge and across the train tracks. There's a few other houses on this street, but they're normal-looking bungalow types. The Farrow property sticks out like a patch of dead grass on a pristine lawn. Twin gateposts guard the driveway, along with a wrought iron fence, the kind topped with spearheads meant to skewer intruders. It's all very Gothic drama. I roll my bike up behind the tall gateposts to gawk at the place without being seen.

One of the sisters is sitting on the front stoop.

A book perched on her knees, head down as she reads. I can't see her face through the fall of hair, but it's the same girl from the grocery store. One hand is cupped over her left ear. I can't tell if this is just how she normally sits or if her ear hurts from the firecrackers. My stomach curdles at the thought that she's deaf because of us.

I'm not making any noise, but her head bobs up suddenly as if startled. I retreat behind the gatepost. I don't think she sees me because her eyes roam the yard for whatever broke her attention from the book. This immediately feels wrong, but there's no way to leave without being seen, so I stay put. She closes the book and goes into the house. When it's safe, I pedal away, feeling like a creep.

Sundays are excruciatingly slow. The RV yard is closed, so I'm only working the ice cream stand, but that's not 'til this afternoon. I have the day to kill. Dad and Liz are home, so I avoid them and murder the day with my friends. Summer days blur together, with us shuffling through our tedious routines with no purpose, no meaning to anything.

I don't tell Eric or Kevin about spying on the Farrows. They'd crucify me for it. The three of us routinely engage in stupid debates about which supermodel is hotter than another. Kevin champions the cause of Daryl Hannah while Eric argues for Phoebe Cates. There is zero awareness of the irony of three fugly boys debating the looks of supermodels. I once made the fatal mistake of suggesting that Annie Lennox was weirdly hot. They reacted with revulsion.

"She looks like a boy," Eric had sneered. "Maybe you're secretly queer."

This is the sharpest of cruelties we can skewer each other with, to be called a "fag" or "gay." Even worse than being called a "pussy." To be queer is to be less than a man, which is the worst flaw to have. It implies insanity, somehow. An outcast, not unlike the weirdo sisters we had ambushed with our toy grenades.

Neither of them mention the firecracker incident. It's old news, and we only want what's now. Something, anything to lift the sticky boredom of another summer day. We ride up and down Main Street and see the same buildings, same pod people. Older guys in muscle cars trawl the strip, blasting Priest or Leppard from their kicked-out sound systems. A red Charger tries to scare us off the pavement by swerving hard as if to mow us down on our bikes, howls of laughter from the open windows. Everyone in this town is bored out of their minds.

We stop at the corner store to shoplift penny candy and check the paltry video rack. There's nothing new, nothing we haven't seen a dozen times. We sit on the curb and do nothing.

"How much damage can a firecracker do?"

Kevin looks at me. "What, like if it goes off in your hand?"

I take a loud slurp on my straw. "Last night, I saw one of those girls holding her ear."

Eric's eyes are glassy from the sugar rush. "And?"

"What if it popped her eardrum?"

Kevin is deadpan. "Am I supposed to care?"

"Don't tell me you feel sorry for them," Eric complains. "Fuck's sake, Mark."

"To Hell with them," Kevin says. He spits on the sidewalk with contempt. "They got what was coming to them."

The callousness is so breezy, so dismissive, it galls me. No one says anything for a while, and we sit here numbing our empty skulls with brain-freeze.

I toss my cup into the trash and pick up my bike.

"Where you going?"

"Work."

Kevin snorts with derision. "How does the Fairy Scoop stay open? No one goes there."

"Beats me," I say, coasting away.

"Say hi to Stacy for us," Eric hollers back, elbowing Kevin in the ribs.

Kevin responds with a fast punch to Eric's gut.

I count thirteen dead wasps when I open up the ice cream hut. An average number, but this time they're all in the vanilla, not the black cherry. They never go for that flavor. Maybe it's a sign, but of what? The world is about to end? The missiles are in the air? Someone in Washington will finally flip their wig and press the big red button? The US and the Soviets have enough nuclear warheads between them to vaporize the planet ten times over. It's weird to imagine everything reduced to a cinder.

One of the wasps wiggles when I pluck it out. It's smeared in cream, but still alive. I lift it by the wings, watching the stinger jab in and out of its abdomen, and lay it in the shade outside the hut. A sensible person would destroy the wasp nest to avoid this problem. Come back after dark when they're all in the nest and blast it with wasp-killer. But I don't do this. We came to an understanding, the wasps and me, years ago.

That incident might have also been an omen, but I was too stupid to heed it. We were twelve, bored, and up for anything. Kevin suggested hopping the fence to go explore the junkyard. It was a Sunday and the junkers would be closed, so we wouldn't get caught. Eric and I agreed it was a brilliant plan. We scaled the fence and roamed through the graveyard of old cars left to rot in the sunlight. We climbed over old Packards and rinky-dink Pintos until we hopped into the cab of an old dump truck and bounced on the seats like maniacs.

Eric stopped. What's that noise? Then Kevin screamed.

Yellow jackets swarmed over us in the stifling air of the car. The nest was under the seats we were jumping on. In our panic, we fumbled for the door handles as a squadron of angry wasps defended their home. I'd never felt pain like that, those piercing stings again and again. We bolted for the fence like lunatics. We were almost there when I felt one buzzing against my chest, trapped inside my shirt. One last sting before I could peel the shirt off.

My mom flipped out when I got home. I looked like something out of a monster movie, like Brundlefly—all freakshow red and swollen with stings. She slathered me with calamine lotion and called the doctor. When her initial panic settled down, she burst into tears for scaring her like that.

So the nest under the eave of the Dairy Scoop is left unmolested. The wasps and I stand by our agreement, not unlike the nuclear standoff between the superpowers.

Kevin's assessment of the ice cream hut proves true—not a single customer tonight, and I am bored out of my skull. The movie theater is closed, so I can't kill time with Stacy. I watch a rat dart across the Palisades doorway.

I still feel sick over the stunt we pulled on the sisters, about how callous my friends are about it. Kevin most of all. He should know better. The more I stew over it, the angrier I get until an idea bubbles up that is so stupid it makes me giddy. So, to hell with it. I turn out the lights, shut down the ice cream hut, and get the bike. Cycling to Greene's Groceries, I keep an eye peeled for anyone I know. The grocery store is quiet. The only other customer is Mr. Frid, my old math teacher, buying a case of tinned cat food. With the coast clear, I turn the spinning rack of cheap novels until I spot the book she tried to steal. *The Lurking Fear* is still sitting cockeyed in the wire rack where she left it.

Three bucks later, I'm back on the bike with the book tucked neatly in my back pocket.

Riding over the bridge, I remind myself how stupid this plan is, but I don't stop until I roll up before the gates of the Farrow house.

The sun's gone down, so I don't bother hiding. I stand my bike against the post and hustle up the pathway. I'm just going to leave the book on the front step for her and then scram. I have no idea why I'm doing this.

Actually, that's a lie. I know exactly why I'm doing this, but it's easier to lie. It's easier to convince myself that I simply feel bad about the stupid prank we pulled on the weird sisters and want to make amends. The truth is too awful to contemplate.

The house looms over me with its dark windows and dingy clapboard, an ugly and unwelcoming thing. It watches me as I lay the paperback on the wooden step and back away. I keep my eyes on the door, expecting Mr. Farrow to come bursting out with a shotgun in his hand. Rumor has it he shoots trespassers on sight.

When I turn to leave, she's there, blocking the path back to the gates.

I freeze and my hands go up, signaling that I mean no harm.

"I'm sorry," I say reflexively.

She doesn't move, doesn't speak. There's a knapsack on her shoulder and a shovel in her hand. Her eyes go to the book on the front step.

"That's for you," I say.

She tilts her head to one side like she can't hear what I'm saying. Her ear. Oh shit, she really is deaf.

I tap my ear in pantomime. "Are you hurt?"

No answer. She crosses to the veranda and wags her chin at my peace offering. "Why did you bring this?"

I don't have an answer to this. "I saw you reading it in the grocery store. You wanted to steal it."

She shakes her head. "No I didn't."

"You tried to slip it under your shirt, but you didn't get the chance."

"That's a lie." She lets the shovel fall to the grass and picks up the book. She cracks it open and then her mouth grimaces as she tears it right down the spine. The two halves are tossed at me, flopping to the flagstones at my feet.

I'm in shock. "Why did you do that?"

She doesn't answer. I gather up the two halves and fold it back together. When she picks up the shovel, I take a step back, thinking she'll take a swing at me.

"What do you want?"

"I don't really know." It's a lame answer, but it's honest. "I'm sorry about the other night. The stunt we pulled."

"Why did you try to hurt me?"

I don't know how to answer that, so I kick the blame down the line. "My friends. Uh, they're idiots."

"Your friends?"

I shrug. I always shrug when forced to confess the truth. "It was me, too. We're all idiots."

Her eyes finally let go, and she looks off down the street. There's no passing cars or kids playing road hockey. There's just nothing.

"I don't have any friends," she says.

No shit. I nod at the spade in her hand. "What's the shovel for?"

Her eyes go sharp on me again. "Stirring tea."

I go all mouth-breather, gaping like an idiot.

"It's a shovel, stupid," she says. "It's for digging."

This was a mistake. I need to get out of here, but she's standing between me and the bike.

She spins the spade up and props it against her shoulder. "Want to help dig?"

"Dig what?"

"A grave," she says. "We killed our parents. Gotta hide the evidence."

My jaw slackens again.

"That's a joke." She turns and retreats into the yard. Waves at me to follow. "Come on."

You hear people talk about listening to their instincts, about following their gut.

Mine's screaming to get the hell out of here. I ignore it and pass through the gates after her.

WITCH BOTTLES

I'M PICTURING AN ambush, dead leaves concealing a pit where I fall onto sharp stakes. Or the snap of a tripwire and a spring-loaded scythe whooshes in to lop my head clean off.

I follow her to a stand of trees behind the house. We march along a footpath barely visible in the moonlight until we come to a low stone wall. End of the property, I guess.

A toy pinwheel sticks out of the ground, but it's not spinning because there's no breeze. The girl plucks it out and hands me the shovel.

"Dig here," she says. "About a foot down. But go gentle."

"Why?"

"I don't want to damage it."

The ground is damp with leaves and pine needles. I picture the spade piercing the soft tissue of a dead body under the dirt. "What's down here?"

"Glass." She sets the knapsack on the ground and then waits for me to start. I'm waiting for her to elaborate, but she doesn't say anything.

"Any day," she says impatiently.

I ease the spade in and turn the earth. The ground is soft under the blanket of rotting leaves, making it easy to dig. I excavate a hole about a foot in diameter, trying to be gentle.

"What's your name?"

I stop digging. "Mark."

"Mark what?"

"Prewitt."

She nods at the ground. "We don't have all night, Mark Prewitt."

What is wrong with this kid? "Your name is George, isn't it?"

Her face darkens. "How do you know that?"

"That's a boy's name."

Her gaze turns harsher. "Maybe I'm a boy."

Is that supposed to be funny? Coming back here was a big mistake. I need to leave. It's dark out here, but I can hear bullfrogs nearby, which means the creek can't be far.

"It's Georgia. I just like George better, okay?" She sighs at me, annoyed. "It's not like Mark is such a great name."

I don't know what to say to that, so I go back to digging. Two more spadefuls and the blade knocks against something solid.

"I hit something."

She kneels down and digs her hands into the dirt, scooping it away until an object gleams in the weak light. The girl named George teases a bottle out of the earth and brushes the dirt from it. Whatever's inside is dark, alien.

"What is it?"

"Protection."

Maybe it's gasoline. Or even gunpowder. "Like a bomb or something?"

"Kind of." She brushes the soil from a cork stopper. Then she hands it up to me. "Open this."

Is this the trap I'm expecting? Sulfuric acid or nerve gas?

"Scared?" she asks.

"No."

"Go on then."

The cork comes out with a pop. I recoil from the stink. "Christ! What is that?"

"Dump it over there," she says, pointing at the stone wall.

I invert the bottle, and a thick sludge slops out in wet gurgles. I hold it at arm's length because it stinks so bad. "Smells like something died in here."

"That means it's not working anymore."

"What the hell is it?"

She holds out a hand. "Give it back."

I jam the lid tight and give it to her. I scrape my hands in the weeds, not wanting to wipe the smelly shit on my jeans. George puts the empty bottle in her knapsacks and pulls out another jar. It's filled with stuff, but I can't make out what it is.

She twists the lid off and holds it out to me. "Take this."

"Why?"

She frowns until I take it from her. Turning it to the light, I can see a few buttons and pebbles stuffed inside some darker material. Some razor blades, a few nails, and what I think is hair. I bring the jar closer to squint at something white. "Is that bone?"

"Snake bone," she says. "Spit in it and put the lid back on."

I try to return her hard stare. "Are you kidding me?"

"You're part of this now. So spit."

There's no way to spit politely. I hork into it and put the lid on. The jar goes into the hole, and she pulls the loose soil over it, patting the earth flat. She plants the pinwheel for a marker, takes up the knapsack and continues along the fence. "Three more to go."

I don't budge. I point to the buried jar. "What is this all about?"

"Come on, Mark Prewitt," she calls back without stopping. "Before it gets too dark."

So I march after her, feeling like an absolute dupe. I hear my dad's voice, asking again about following my friends off a bridge.

We follow the footpath through the brush until we come to another pinwheel tilting up from the weeds. I plunge the spade in and dig gingerly. Another buried bottle. The same routine plays out. She makes me empty the jar, and I almost puke at the stench. She pulls a fresh jar from the knapsack and makes me spit into it. She reaches out to take it back, but I hold it at bay.

"What is this for? All the pins and razor blades and God knows what?"

George Farrow kneels before the small pit, impatience drawn thin over her pale face. "I told you. It's protection."

"How is this protection?"

She wriggles her fingers, eager for the glass receptacle. "Don't you know a witch bottle when you see one?"

I wait for a laugh, but she's dead serious. The phrase should send me running for the hills.

"Witch bottles?" I don't know if she can see the disdain on my face, but it's there. "What does it protect you from?"

"People like you. People who want to hurt us."

Psycho alert. "So, it's like a spell or something?"

"To ward off evil." She holds up the excavated jar. "I buried these a long time ago. They worked for a while, but they've worn out now. Otherwise you and your friends wouldn't have hurt us. So they have to be replaced."

The reminder cuts the wind from my sails. I'm not following any of this, but I don't want to sound stupid. "Look, that was a dumb stunt to pull, and I'm sorry. But spells had nothing to do with it. We were just bored."

"It has everything to do with it," she says. "Cause and effect. You sensed our defenses were down, so you tried to hurt us."

I watch her bury the new jar, clawing the soil over it like this is the most normal thing in the world.

I stomp the spade into the soil and let it stand vertical. It's melodramatic, but I've had enough. "This is nuts. I don't even know why I'm doing this."

George stands, brushes the grit from her hands. "You're here because you're meant to be here. Cause and effect, like I said."

I walk away. "This is stupid."

"Stop."

"Bye, George."

"Stop!" She snatches my arm, digging her nails in. "You'll hit the tripwire."

She points at something in the weeds, an almost invisible run of fishing line strung tight between the trees. Dangling from it is a collection of tin cans and old spoons. A crude alarm system, the kind where you trip the wire and the cans all clang loudly, alerting everyone to an intruder. She stopped me before I blundered right into it.

"That's a bit paranoid, isn't it?"

"It's a warning system. It protects us against intruders."

She hooks the knapsack back onto her shoulder, and we march on for another twenty paces. The trees thin out, and the ground slopes down to a valley. Their property backs onto a marshy creek where bulrushes sway in the fading light. George has already pulled up the sad-looking pinwheel that marks another burial site.

"This one's important," she says, pointing to the open marsh below us. "There's no fence here at the creek. We're vulnerable."

I'm leaning on the shovel but haven't started to dig. "You honestly believe this stuff works?"

"It worked fine until now."

"And you think this will protect you?"

"There's also the bear trap," she adds. "Which might be overkill, I don't know."

"Bear trap?"

She blows on the plastic pinwheel to make it turn. "I guess I shouldn't call it that. I didn't set it to trap bears."

I can get behind a lot of crazy ideas, but even I have my limits. "Bullshit."

"Are you calling me a liar?"

Another dirt track winds through weeds to the creek below. George stops at a conspicuous tangle of dead leaves and twigs on the footpath. She drags the branches away and there it is. A spring-loaded monster with iron teeth, nasty enough to cleave your foot clean off rather than trap you. I've never seen one before, except on TV.

"Where the hell did you get that?"

"I found it out in the woods. So I pulled up the stake and brought it home."

I'm frowning. "You stole it."

"Are you going to tattle on me?" She pulls the branches over the device and strides back up the dirt track. "Come on. That hole isn't going to dig itself."

With the pinwheel marker pulled up, we've lost the exact spot and have to dig around until I feel the spade tip against the jar. We repeat the process, exhuming the old witch bottle and dumping out its rancid contents. She insists I spit into the new jar again. I refuse.

"Why not?"

"Because. I don't want my body fluids in this voodoo stuff."

"It's not voodoo."

"Whatever."

She folds her arms, glaring at me until I'm uncomfortable. Her hand comes out. "Where's that book?"

I pull the torn paperback from my back pocket, hand it to her. She takes a loose page and folds into a tight square. Stuffs it into the jar.

"Why are you doing that?"

"I told you, you're part of this now." She sounds impatient, like she's talking to a not-too-bright kid. "Something of you has to go into each jar."

"Why?"

"Because it has to. I don't make the rules."

Talking to this girl with the dirty fingernails is like blind man's bluff. I hear what she's saying, but I'm completely lost. "So you understand why I brought the book?"

She sits down on the carpet of pine needles and looks off to the creek. "Did you poison the pages, so I'd get sick and die while I read it?"

I'm still blind, but I just roll with it. "Why would I poison you?"

"Because you hate us," she says. "You all do."

"I don't hate you."

"It's okay. The feeling's mutual." She hands the jar to me. "Here. Bury it."

The grit on my dirty hands makes the glass slick. The jar slips, falls onto a rock. The glass breaks, spilling gunk everywhere.

"Whoops."

George doesn't think it's funny. Her face goes white with a look of horror. "Oh, my God. What have you done? What have you done?"

"Sorry."

She scrambles for the jar, but the hair and bone and nails have scattered everywhere. "Are you stupid or something?"

"It slipped."

Her eyes get this ferocious look that makes me back up. "You've ruined it. Now this whole side is unprotected. Do you know what that means?"

I've had enough crazy for one night and turn to leave. "This is stupid."

She shoves me. She's way stronger than she looks because I stumble backward, almost landing on my ass. Noise erupts all around us.

The tin cans are clanging up a storm. I've stumbled into the fishing line, triggering the ridiculous alarm system. George freezes like she's holding her breath. That's when we hear the voices coming through the trees from the direction of the house.

"Run," she says.

Panic makes my balls shrivel up. "Is that your dad?"

She shakes her head. "My sisters. They'll kill you."

"I'm not running from a bunch of girls."

George shoves me again. "Do you think this is funny? They will murder you if they catch you. Run."

I hear them racing through the trees, calling their sister's name. I don't want to be here when the lunatic mob shows up. George hustles me down the path to the creek.

"Come back tomorrow. After dark."

"Screw that," I holler at her. "I am *never* coming back here."

"You have to," she says, gesturing to the broken glass on the ground. "I can't leave it like this. We have to fix it."

I'm gone, bolting through the weeds like a frightened rabbit. At the last moment I remember the bear trap and leap over the iron teeth waiting to clamp down on my shin. I don't stop until I splash through the creek to the other side. When I glance back, I see the sisters, gathering stones and hurling them at me.

SCRATCH MARKS

GEORGE IS A dumb name for a girl. And she's clearly deranged. Witch bottles? Give me a break. That's the conclusion I come to looking up at the plastic stars on my ceiling. Last night is a little hazy—the girl with the dirt under her fingernails, the jars buried in the ground. An iron bear trap, waiting to sever a trespassing ankle. The rumors are true; the sisters are witches, practicing their dark art in the woods behind their dilapidated house.

There's a chance I dreamed the whole thing until I swing my feet off the bed and see the mutilated paperback on the floor. *The Lurking Fear*, or half of it anyway. I jammed it into my back pocket last night. God knows where the other half is. Probably drifting down the creek, bloated to twice its size. I thumb through the pages. Maybe I'll read this torn half of the book and never read the rest. Like a Choose Your Own Adventure, but I'll never know how the story turns out.

I shamble into the kitchen at precisely the wrong moment and stifle an urge to puke. Dad and Liz are wrapped tight into each other, giggling. Liz pulls away quickly, busying herself with the dishes. Dad just smirks, like he's proud or something. Barf.

"Morning, chief. You sleep okay?"

I grunt something and reach for the cereal, wanting them both to just ignore me. I should be so lucky.

Dad keeps eyeballing me. This usually means trouble. "What time did you get home last night?"

"Late."

"How late?"

The milk sloshes against the side of the bowl. "Criminally late."

Liz parachutes into the situation, as always. I don't understand why she feels the need to referee this nonsense. Sometimes I do stuff just to make him angry. To provoke him. I don't know why. And Liz always gets in the middle. She's a glutton for punishment.

"The coffee is still fresh," she says, setting a cup down beside my bowl. "Cream and sugar, right?"

I let her twist in the wind as usual. The kinder she is, the more cruel I become. Out of nowhere, Liz's smile drops away.

"Mark, what happened to your arm?"

Angry red marks, crosshatched over the skin. After splashing up the creek bank, I had to claw through brambles and wild raspberry to get back to the road. I look like I've been whipped.

"It's nothing."

Dad shakes his head with patented derision. "The hell were you doing last night?"

"Just got caught in some branches. It's nothing."

"Let me guess," he says. "Hanging out with those pinhead friends of yours? They jumped into a thorn bush and you followed right after them?"

Adults lose their shit over the stupidest things. Sure, the whole world is a hair away from being incinerated in a mushroom cloud, but never mind that—let's all freak out over a scratch on a dumb kid. My dad leaves the room, griping about the youth of today.

Liz takes the seat next to me. "That really looks painful. We should put some aloe on it."

"It's fine."

Concern pinches her moisturized face. "Did you clean it? It might get infected, it's so raw."

"I said, it's fine." My tone is too sharp. I see her wince, but it's only a flash before the polite smile returns. Why does she keep trying? The woman is a masochist.

She rinses her cup in the sink and then comes back for more, looking to get burned again. "Mark, you know I'm not trying to, well…"

Christ, here it comes. The speech I've been dreading for the last four months, the one that starts with *I'm not trying to be your mom, but…* Had to happen eventually, I suppose. My knuckles go white.

She takes a breath, carries on. "I'm not trying to be bossy. I just don't want that to get infected. I knew a guy who sliced his hand and didn't take care of it. It got so infected the doctors had to amputate."

That gets my attention. It's not the speech I was dreading, so small mercies and all that. I dial back the scorn. "That would suck being one-handed."

"No," she says. "What sucked was being no-handed. He'd lost the other hand in a thresher when he was twelve."

Despite every effort to appear not to give a shit, I'm impressed. "Jeez. Must have been a bitch to jerk off with no hands, huh?"

Liz scoops her car keys from the bowl on the counter. I wait for her to be shocked or offended, but she doesn't even blink. "Not really. He just had to get creative."

The screen door squeals as she goes out to her car. The starter in her Tercel is dying, and it cranks three times before kicking to life. I'm sure the expression on my dumb face was one of shock, but there was a slight smirk on the end, like a footnote.

Who goes around burying stuff in the ground thinking it will protect them? Magic. Witchcraft. Come on. If George was a little kid, I could understand, but she's the same age as me. She looks a little sick, the way people who had a childhood disease do. Twisted out in a certain way. Malformed.

All day at the RV yard, I keep going over last night and what she said. About how everyone hates them, and she needs to protect her family. How lonely would that feel to be hated by everyone? How crazy do you have to be to think a jar of fish hooks and snake bones are going to protect you?

Maybe it's not that crazy. There was a time when I used to think the same way, back at the hospital. Following the same orange stripe on the hallway floor every day, tapping the desk of the nurse's station three times as I passed, the door handle seven times. If I performed these little commandments exactly right, then everything would be fine when I got to the room. Magic. A ritualized spell that needed to be repeated precisely every time. And it worked.

Until one day, it didn't. That was when I realized there was no magic, no secret spell that could prevent catastrophe. The tapping ritual stopped that day. So I get it. I understand what George is trying to do.

I know I should leave George alone, but I can't stop thinking about her. Jesus, haven't I done enough already? She's deluded, that much is clear. But what if I could help her somehow?

There's also the matter of the smashed jar. She said it would leave them exposed because we didn't finish the ritual. I remember what it felt like to screw up the hospital routine and leave something untapped. Disaster looms over everything and all you can do is keep your head down, waiting for the guillotine to drop.

Biking home after work, I know I'm going back to the Farrow house. It's unavoidable at this point. There are too many mysteries to leave it alone. Cats and curiosity, I suppose. I stop at Tony's Auto Garage to pick up a few things for the Galaxie—a new air filter and replacement hose for the radiator. Minor stuff for today, but a small step closer to resurrecting this beast. That's going to be a glorious day, firing it up and rolling the Galaxie out of this garage. I'll be like Dr. Frankenstein, screaming, "It's alive! It's alive!"

Sometimes I talk to the car while I'm working on it, same way you talk to a dog or a horse. Cooing softly, reassuring it that everything will be okay. It's stupid and downright embarrassing when I'm caught doing it. Like now.

"Who the hell you talking to?"

I bonk my skull on the hood, looking to see who it is. Eric sits on his bike, arms draped over the handlebars like he's waiting for something.

"How long you been sitting there?"

Eric shrugs. "Long enough to hear you talking to yourself. You feeling okay?"

"Fine." I gather up the old rubber hose and pitch it into the trash. "What's going on?"

He rolls the bike closer and peers down into the engine. "You got this beast running yet?"

"Almost. A little closer every day."

Eric's not impressed. "Summer's half over, Mark. Are we ever gonna cruise in this clunker?"

"Easy," I warn him. I flatten my hand on the metal and pat the car like it's a pet. "She doesn't like being called names."

"It's just a car, man. Why are you so superstitious about it?"

I look at him like he's crazy. "I'm not superstitious."

"Yeah, right," he says, mimicking a wank motion.

I keep expecting Kevin to roll up on his bike, but it's clear that Eric is on his own. "Where's Kevin?"

Eric puckers his mouth in distaste. "He went to the Crafting Corner."

"Why the hell would he go there?"

"Angela Baker. She got a job there."

That makes me laugh. "Angela? He thinks she's gonna go out with him?"

"I told him he was crazy."

"How come you didn't go with him?"

Eric sneers at the thought. "I wouldn't be caught dead in that place."

This is new, Kevin's interest in Angela Baker. Or girls in general, really. Eric hates it because he doesn't like change. He hates trying new things. He only eats sandwiches with the crusts trimmed off, and he still has *Star Wars* sheets on his bed.

"Hey," he says, reaching into his backpack. "Check out what I got."

The cover of the VHS box pops up for me to see—*Basket Case*. A classic among the three of us. So bad, it's good. Eric loves movies, even more than I do. He memorizes his favorite lines and recites them when he's bored.

"It was in the second-hand bin at the video store. Three bucks." He jiggles the tape. "Time for a re-watch. Come by after dinner. Kevin's bringing beer."

"Can't."

"Why the hell not?" Eric's face sours. Same expression he's had since he was eight—sad dog eyes, bottom lip out. "Don't tell me you got something better to do, 'cause we both know that ain't true."

"My old man's on me about being out all the time. He wants us to do some family shit or something."

Eric glances at the house. "Because of Liz?"

"Who else?" It's weird how easily I can lie to my friends. To everyone, in fact. I even lie to myself sometimes. I'm the easiest person for me to fool.

"That's not so bad, hanging out with your step-mom." He nods, and for a second I think he'll let it go. But he doesn't. "She still wears those little Daisy Dukes?"

"Fuck off."

This topic never gets old with Eric and Kevin. When Liz first moved in, the two of them would come by all the time just to check out Liz in her cut-off jean shorts. The two of them would Eddy Haskell her all the way. Liz, wanting to make nice, went along with it. They even got her to bake cookies for them once.

I tug the hood down and it clangs home. "You guys have fun."

Eric frowns and rolls his bike across the grass. He looks back. "Well, when are we gonna do something? I'm bored."

"Soon."

Eric spits onto the gravel and pedals away. I think about why I lied to him and what he and Kevin would say if they knew where I was last night. It would be like the ending to that short story we read in English class last year, where the villagers throw stones at the unlucky lottery winner.

HAIR, BONE, HOOK, SPIT

I WAIT UNTIL sundown before riding back to Merrily Road, wondering how I'm going to reach her. It's not like I can just go ring the doorbell. I could do something cornball like toss pebbles at her window, but I don't know which window is hers. Turns out I'm worrying for nothing. George Farrow is sitting outside the gateposts, lighting wooden matches and tossing them into the gutter.

I roll the bike to a stop. "Hey."

She's wearing the same clothes she had on last night. Same outfit I saw her in at the grocery store. She can't have one set of clothes, can she?

The matchbox in her hand has a picture of a black cat on it. She slides the box closed. "I thought you'd chicken out."

I consider saying something trite like "ditto," but I just shrug. "You made me promise."

George shakes the matchbox. It's almost empty. "And you always keep a promise?"

"Hardly ever."

"Then why bother making them?"

This feels like a test, and I fucking hate tests. Am I supposed to care if I fail? "Do you always keep your promises?"

"Promises are cheap," she says, chewing a fingernail. "Declaring something is a promise already implies the lie, don't you think?"

"Never thought about it that way."

She gets to her feet and scans the yard, the house beyond. Lights in the first-floor windows, but no one lingering on the veranda. "Leave the bicycle here," she says.

Up close, the battered house looms over us like it has a score to settle. Grim, imposing, rotten. The backyard is a wide stretch of lawn that ends at the tree line, dark woods beyond that. There's a few outbuildings and a chicken coop off to one side. I can hear a few muted clucks from behind the mesh of chicken wire. There's even a greenhouse, the glass dull and fogged, grafted onto the back of the house like an afterthought.

I follow her through the dry grass to a garden shed. The wood door bangs open, and she's swallowed by the darkness inside.

"Close the door behind you," she says.

Another match is struck, which she uses to light the wick of a lantern. Shovels and rakes lean against the walls, and cobwebs stretch over the ceiling. There's a workbench cluttered with jars of penny nails and coffee tins of galvanized screws. It's hot inside the shed, and the smell of old paint is giving me a headache. There isn't enough room to keep a safe distance from the girl counting snail shells into an old jar. I don't expect her to attack me or anything, but there's a weird twitch to the way she moves. Pent up energy that makes her clumsy. She rubs her nose a lot like she has a cold.

"Is that it?" I ask, nodding to the jar.

"I don't know if it will work. All four witch bottles should be the same." She slides the box of matches across the bench to me. "Light that candle."

It's tall, like the ones you see in church, but this candle is black wax. I watch as she adds more ingredients in precise amounts: five pennies, seven rusty nails, and three fishhooks. A thorny stem clipped from a rosebush. Her lips are moving as she does this, like she's muttering something under her breath.

"What does that stuff do?"

The lantern light bounces off her eyes, but I can't tell what color they are.

"The sharp things will catch any bad energy thrown our way," she says, "skewering it before it reaches the house."

I nod like this makes complete sense. I watch her take another jar and tip its contents into the witch bottle. Dark, crumbly stuff like sand.

"What is that, dirt?"

"Yes." When she looks up this time, I can see that her eyes are brown. Plain old brown. "Taken from a grave."

"You're kidding me."

"It's the most important part."

I'm about to ask whose grave it's from when I realize how stupid the question is. My gut starts flip-flopping again.

She nods at my side of the bench. "Hand me that little skull."

The crumpled bits of tissue on my left turn out to be the tiny bones of a snake. The paper skull weighs absolutely nothing. I could crush it to dust in my fist. I place it gingerly into her waiting palm and notice her hand is clammy. Using a pair of chopsticks, she lowers the skull into the jar and nestles it gently into the dirt.

"Now the salt," she says. She pulls the spout on a carton and pours sea salt over the skull, burying it.

"What does that do?"

"Neutralizes bad magic."

She separates a few strands of greasy hair, plucking it out and adding it to the jar. Then she turns to me, thrusting the jar against my chest. "Now the last part. Spit."

Everything about this feels wrong, but it's kind of thrilling too. The air inside the shed is hot and stifling. I'm shivering.

She thumps the jar against my sternum again. "Do it."

Now this feels dangerous, like signing a contract with the Devil. The moment I spit into the jar, flames will erupt at my feet and Georgia Farrow will transform into something with horns and a spiked tail.

I do what she asks, but some of it misses and hits her knuckles. She doesn't seem to care. Something inside my chest clenches tight as I watch her spit into the jar and then push the cork lid in, sealing it forever. We're locked inside that glass, and this thrills me and repulses me at the same time. I feel myself getting hard, which makes it even more confusing.

I must be staring at her because her eyes turn sharp. "What?"

I force my greedy eyes elsewhere, pretend to be impatient. "Are we done?"

She hands me the spade. "Now we finish the job."

George pushes open the shed door and then stops cold. I hear a sharp intake of breath. The sisters are here.

They're surrounding the shed like it's an ambush. Neither of them look friendly. The older sister is taller than I am and her face is hard, menacing. Like she's ready to kill. Her hair is sandy, not dark like George, but it's got that same flat sheen to it like it's rarely washed. Her clothes have that same outdated look, hanging off her frame like something way past its expiration date.

Her voice is sharp and accusatory. "Did he hurt you?"

"No," George says. She has a hand up to keep them back. "It's not like that."

"Why were you hiding in the shed?" asks the smaller one.

The younger sister is twelve, maybe thirteen, and without the hostility of her older sibling. But the fear in her eyes is real. Her hair is dark like George's, but I can't see any resemblance among these three. Nothing that would hint at siblings, anyway.

"Why is he here?" demands the older sister. There's something in her hand, but I can't see what it is.

George slides in front of me. "Put the knife away, Claudia. He's here to help."

"Help?" says Claudia. "By slitting our throats in our sleep? You know the rules. Father will kill him. And then he'll kill us."

The younger sister speaks up. "Father won't kill him."

George and Claudia both turn to her. "Are you sure?"

"He doesn't die that way," says the younger one.

It's like I've dropped into a family squabble spoken in a foreign language. A weird stand-off plays out between the sisters. I need to find a way out of this gong show.

"I'm out of here." My hands go up in surrender. I move toward the gates where my bike is hidden. "Sorry."

George turns on me. "You can't go. We're not done."

"Yes we are." Coming back here was a stupid idea. I want out of this freak show, but her hand clamps over my wrist.

"We have to finish the job. You're part of it now."

Claudia moves closer, within striking distance with that knife in her hand. "What are you talking about? What job?"

The little sister already knows. "Our house isn't safe," she says.

George fetches the receptacle of snake bone and salt. "Mark is helping me with the jars. One broke, so he came back to fix it."

Claudia shakes, anger bubbling up. "You left us exposed? Are you kidding me?"

George blows the hair from her face and marches toward the tree line. She waves at me to follow. "We're going to fix it now. Don't panic."

We trudge through the brambles until we find the footpath. George leads the way with me following and Claudia on my heels. I expect a knife to my back any second now. The little sister ambles along at her own pace. There are no introductions, no niceties. The path is too narrow to walk alongside George, so I scurry up close behind and ask if her sisters are violent.

She waves the idea away. "Claudia is," she says. "But Tilly wouldn't hurt a fly. She's psychic."

"Psychic? Get outta here."

I expect her to laugh, but she just keeps marching ahead. "She knew you'd come to the house with some kind of overture."

"Overture?" I try not to sound ignorant but miss by a mile.

"The book."

I look over my shoulder, past Claudia who's breathing down my neck, to Tilly. Her eyes lock onto mine like she knows I'm talking about her. I straighten up and trudge on. Crazy images pop into my head of a fire burning in the woods and the slash of a knife, blood dribbling onto the flames as the sacrificial victim bleeds out. The sisters dance around the bonfire in some terrifying Pagan ritual, the harvest guaranteed for another season. This isn't paranoia. These girls would slit my throat if they knew what I'd done.

George holds the lantern high until its glow reveals the hole we dug last night. Shards of broken glass wink back at us in the lamplight.

"This is it."

Claudia takes the lantern, Tilly by her side. George drops to her knees and scoops the hole bigger. I follow her lead and claw at the dark soil until there's a tidy pocket in the earth. She cuts her finger on a shard of broken glass, spilling blood onto the soil. The new bottle is twisted into the ground, and we drag the dirt over it like it's a grave. With the hole backfilled, we pat the loose dirt with our palms. I don't know where the pinwheel came from, but it's there in her hand as she stabs it into the loose soil as a place marker.

"There," George says, sucking on her cut finger. "The house is safe."

"Are you sure?" Claudia doesn't look convinced. She nods at me. "Isn't it tainted because of him?"

The two of them turn to the youngest sister.

Tilly drops to one knee and flattens her palm on the ground like she can feel something. "It's working."

The night is sticky, the air still. Bullfrogs in the creek call to one another in the darkness. I don't know how to escape this coven in the woods without looking chicken-shit. The older one still has that damn knife, and now she's waving it toward the path. "You can go now."

I don't need to be told twice, but George disagrees. "He's not going anywhere." Ignoring Claudia's scowl, George turns to me. "Let's go up to the house."

Claudia turns red. "Are you crazy? That's too risky."

I'm in agreement with her, shaking my head at George. "I have to go."

"Please?" Tilly asks. "We never have guests."

George tugs my sleeve, and I follow her back through the trees to the lights of the house. I should have run when I had the chance, but here I am following this girl again, and I don't even know why.

We cross the open yard to the back of the house. Claudia is still protesting, but in a whisper to keep her voice down. I'm expecting to feel the blade in my back any second now.

I stop in my tracks. "This is a bad idea. I have to go."

George takes her finger out of her mouth. It's still bleeding. "Are you scared?"

Scared isn't the word for it. Ashamed? Sickened, maybe. I can't go into this house. I have no right to.

"Don't be a baby," Tilly scolds.

The screen door squeals as we pass through into a dim hallway. At the far end, I can see a kitchen and a shadow moving across its floor. The house smells like stale cooking—fried onions, maybe fish. Underneath that is another smell, a sour tang of mildew. George turns a corner and creeps up a narrow set of stairs. These must have been the servant's stairs a long time ago. I watch George's thick-soled shoes creep up each step before me. Her dingy socks fall limply around her ankles like the elastic has given up the ghost. There's a scar on the back of her right calf shaped like a crescent.

Our little parade hits the second floor. Dark wood paneling and dusty wall sconces, fractured cracks all along the plaster ceiling—old grandeur, dried up and withered like shed snake skin. There's even a small chandelier suspended over the landing, but the bulbs are dark and the crystal stringy with cobwebs. Doors on both sides of a long hallway.

How many people live in this house? Maybe there are more Farrows than I know about. Violent uncles and deranged cousins lurking behind these closed doors. Maybe it's the ambush I've been expecting, the punishment I know is coming to me, and here I am walking right into it.

George opens a door and ushers me into a dim bedroom. Claudia and Tilly remain out in in the hallway.

"You're going to get us all in trouble, George," Claudia warns.

"Then we'll have to be quiet," Tilly adds. "Mother will murder us if she finds out."

"She'll only kill me because it's my idea. Now go away." George closes the door on her sisters, turns the lock.

The room is twice the size of mine, with a high ceiling and a small alcove for the dormer window. There's a narrow bed with a green bedspread, and two dressers side by side. A battered desk cluttered with books and newspaper. There are more books on the floor, pushed up against the baseboard, but it's too dark to scan the titles. There's a stool next to the window and a line of candles along the sill, all lilting in puddles of cold wax.

I stand like an oaf in the middle of the rug, hands shoved into my pockets. "This is your room?"

George leans against the door, watching me from behind the fall of stringy hair. "Do you have brothers or sisters?"

"No."

"We get on each other's nerves," she says with a sigh, like she's exhausted. "Some days I'd kill for someone else to talk to."

I nod like I know what she's talking about. It's hard to get my bearings in this place. It's like the house isn't moored to the foundations; it's just floating around so you never know which way is north.

"Your parents. They're kinda strict?"

She rubs her nose. "Over-protective."

"How much trouble will you be in if they catch us?"

The rug at our feet is old and worn raw in spots. She sits down on it and folds her legs. "Hard to say. None of us has ever snuck a boy in before."

"What about girls? Like friends and stuff?"

"I told you, we don't have any friends."

I settle onto the rug across from her. "Why is that?"

"Too dangerous. People in town hate us. And we hate them back. So it's just the three of us."

I don't know how to respond to that, so I survey the room again. Something about her bedroom is bothering me, but it takes a moment to realize what it is. There are no posters on the walls. No rock bands or movie stars, no pictures cut out from magazines and taped over the bed.

"Is that why you don't go to school?"

"School just brainwashes what the government wants you to think. We learn the truth here."

Brainwashing. The word stands out even among all this oddness. It sounds like a memorized line, like dogma.

"So you're homeschooled?"

"Father teaches art, literature, and history," she says. "Mother teaches math and science. Law, too."

I've never known anyone who was homeschooled. I thought it was illegal to keep kids out of school.

"Doesn't sound too bad," I say. "High school is the worst."

"I wouldn't know." Her voice lowers to a whisper. "My parents are not great teachers. I sometimes think they just make stuff up."

I stretch out on the floor to take a closer look at the books lined up against the baseboard. There's a few titles I recognize like *Treasure Island* and *Jane Eyre*. *Frankenstein* and *The Time Machine*. There's a dusty hardback on the fall of the Roman empire and another about the Salem witch trials. Some spines don't even have titles, just Roman numerals. The newest book I find is a tattered paperback of *Watership Down*.

"Have you read all these?"

She nods. "Some, a number of times."

There's no horror here, nothing similar to the book she tried to steal. Unless you count the *Frankenstein* book, but that's like a hundred years old. I look back at her. George sits quietly with her elbows on knees, watching me.

"What about the book I gave you? I thought you wanted to read that."

"I do."

"So why rip it up?"

"We're not allowed junk," she says. "Father won't allow it."

"Junk?"

She lets out a sigh. "No junk literature. No trash television or movies. And absolutely no junk food. It's something of a creed in our house."

Point taken. I guess that explains the Twinkies I saw her wolfing down. "Can't you sneak books in?"

"Not horror. Father hates seeing it in the house. Same with science fiction, too. He says it gives him hives." Her hands are restless. She cracks a knuckle. "He searches our rooms every Tuesday."

And here I thought my old man was strict. "You like horror?"

Her eyes light up. "The weirder, the better. Don't you?"

"Not really."

I pull the H. G. Wells book from her collection. "What about this? Isn't this sci-fi?"

"Classic literature, according to my father. Have you read it?"

I nod. "I like how the mutant people eat the rich elites above ground. I forget what they're called."

"The Morlocks," she says with pride. "And the Eloi."

"Yeah, them. Reminds me of school."

She cracks her knuckles again, popping finger after finger. Her eyes are unflinching, making me squirm like a specimen under a microscope. Needing to escape that glare, I cross to the desk, which is draped in a big sheet of paper. What I assume to be newspaper turns out to be a blueprint.

"What's this?"

She joins me at the desk. "Just something I'm working on."

"For school? Homeschool, whatever."

"It's a pet project," she says, finding one last knuckle to pop. "A new spell, actually."

The building in the blueprint looks familiar. "I know this place."

"It's nothing," she says dismissively.

A closer look at the small print reveals a name and address. The Palisades. "Why do you have a blueprint for the movie theater?"

"I like architecture." She tugs the blueprint out from my hands and rolls it into a tube. "Don't you?"

"Not really." So she's an egghead with a lot of weird interests. Big news. "Is that what you want to be? An architect?"

"I'm just interested in how buildings work," she says, snapping an elastic band around the tube. "What do you want to be?"

The question bugs me because I don't have an answer to it. Petty sarcasm fills in the blank. "Me, I'm gonna be an astronaut."

"You want to ride the space shuttle?"

"Yeah. I'll be the civilian onboard who pushes the wrong button. Kaboom."

She doesn't laugh at my sick joke, but there is a slight smirk. It fades quickly, and the mood decays into awkward silence. She's less than a foot away and I have nothing for my hands to do. I shove them into my pockets and scan the bare walls, the cobwebs trailing from the naked bulb overhead.

"Isn't it lonely, just the three of you?"

She leans back against the desk, folding her arms, studying me again. "Do you have a lot of friends?"

"I dunno. What's a lot?"

"Are you popular at school?"

I'm wondering how to answer that when a loud *thump* overhead interrupts us. I look up at the ceiling and there's an ugly scraping noise, like someone's dragging furniture across the room.

"Who lives upstairs?"

"No one. It's just an attic."

"Do your sisters go up there?"

"No," she says. "That's just the house. It's haunted."

NO SUCH THINGS AS GHOSTS

THERE'S NO SMIRK on her face, no wink that suggests she's joking about the house being haunted. Her eyes are bright and belligerent, daring me to dispute it.

"For real. Who's up there?" I'm picturing a deformed cousin chained up in the attic. A dark family secret hidden away from the world.

"I told you, there's no one." She looks up at the swirling stucco pattern on the ceiling. "We're never really alone here."

This feels like a test. Maybe a prank. There's a punchline waiting to drop. I grin at her like I'm in on the joke. "You expect me to believe there's a ghost up there?"

"You don't believe in ghosts?"

Fuck, no. There's no such thing. Especially here in this house. That I couldn't take.

"That's just your sisters goofing around up in the attic."

George pivots from the desk to reach the door. It swings open, and there are the two sisters lingering in the hallway. All three Farrow sisters share that intensely weird stare.

"Where's Mother and Father?" George asks them.

"Downstairs," answers Tilly.

George turns back to me. "No one goes into the attic unless they have to."

"Unless they're being punished," Tilly adds.

"Why not?"

"Because it's haunted," Claudia huffs, as if there could be any other explanation.

As if to underline the point, there's another muffled thump overhead. I'm already listing all the logical explanations for the noise: mice, raccoons, the wind.

Tilly clings to the doorjamb, her small hands wrapped around the dark wood. Her eyes flick up to the ceiling and back to me. "She's mad that there's a stranger in the house."

"Who's mad?"

"Our sister," Tilly replies. "She watches over us."

And there's the punchline—the oldest Farrow sister, the one who died. Except it's not very funny. I have to get the hell out of here.

"What was her name?"

Tilly looks away. George brushes lint from her skirt. I'm waiting for another thud from the attic, but there isn't one.

"Tilly's right," Claudia says, the only one to keep eye contact. "She doesn't want you here. You should go."

No argument here. I'm out of the room like a shot, eager to leave.

George pouts and Claudia leads the way. Tilly plays tour guide as we go back down the hallway.

"That's my room," the little sister says, pointing out each room. "And that's Claudia's room over there."

The last door in the hall is ajar. I can see a bed and, weirdly, a poster on the wall above it. "Who's room is that?"

Tilly stops.

Claudia closes the door quickly. "Why is this open? Tilly, were you playing in here?"

"No."

"She must really be mad," George says.

Claudia shoos us on. "Come on, before we get caught."

Back down the servant's stairs we go, to the rear entrance. I can hear a voice echoing down the hallway from the kitchen—a man's voice, but I can't make out what he's saying. A shadow falls across the hallway, and I hustle my butt out of the house.

I sprint across the yard, not waiting for George. Dragging my dumb bike out of the thistle bush, I look up at the house, expecting to see her waving goodbye, but she isn't there.

Under the highest gable is a round attic window and I swear to God, the moth-eaten curtain flutters.

The thrust of a flamethrower burns blue as it idles, heating a copper coil. Four men are tied to chairs, waiting to be judged. Kurt Russell dips the heated wire into a petri dish of blood to determine which of the prisoners is really an alien masquerading as a human. The wire hisses as it hits the blood, exonerating the first man. The tests play out one after another, until a grotesque life-form erupts from the last blood sample, exposing the monster amongst them.

This is the best scene from *The Thing* movie, a gore-fest favorite among the three of us. Seeing it now, it cuts a bit too close to the bone. How long before I'm exposed as the traitor hiding among the normals?

We're in Eric's basement, captivated in the VHS glow of John Carpenter's masterpiece. Jiffy Pop is scattered over the rancid carpet, the coffee table littered with beers Kevin pilfered from his older brother's stash. The three of us have watched this scene countless times, but now I'm squirming. I used to empathize with Russell's character, cheering him on as he exposed the impostor among them, but this time I'm feeling more like one of those poor suckers tied to the chairs, waiting to be exposed and then fried in the purifying blast of the flamethrower.

"Torch his ass!" Kevin bellows at the TV screen.

Eric hoots along, bouncing in his seat. "Look at his head split open. Ha!"

I woke this morning wanting everything to be normal. I was even nice to Liz at the breakfast table when she asked Dad how she looked. He just grunted, so I told her she looked nice. She looked like she was going to cry. On my lunch break, I had phoned Eric to say we needed a movie night—something classic, like we always used to do. I thought he was gonna cry too.

Tracking lines scroll down the screen and blur the image, the video tape worn out from so many viewings. It was second-hand when Eric got it, scooping it from the used tape bin at the video store. This is what I want after the bizarro events of last night—normal, everyday stuff. My idiot friends, stolen beer, shitty popcorn, and John Carpenter's bloodbath of science fiction paranoia. A security blanket.

I tell myself I'm never going back to that creepy house with those weirdo girls. I got a peek into their world, and my curiosity's been satisfied. That's enough. So why do I keep thinking about them when I should be hollering at Kurt Russell to torch the monster to smithereens?

How insane are the Farrow sisters? George believes in spells and witch bottles. The youngest one thinks she's psychic. And all three believe their house is haunted by the ghost of their dead sister. Three girls locked up in that big creepy house with no outside friends—what kind of monsters do they have for parents? Norma Bates and Freddy Krueger, 'til death do they part? Who wouldn't grow up nuts?

Still, they're not the freaks that everyone assumes they are. They're strange; that much is true. George is different. I keep seeing her hands claw the dirt as she dug up the old bottle. Or the two of us spitting into the jar and sealing it up forever. It felt wrong and dangerous, but it was also electric. Like being scared and horny at the same time. Even with the ghost knocking stuff around in the attic, wanting me to leave. My ears get hot thinking about it, but the guys are too engrossed in the movie to notice.

I watch my friends shove popcorn into their gobs and shout at the TV. Eric's in his glory. When the movie ends, he'll suggest another flick from his collection. Or worse, he'll break out the Dungeons and Dragons. Kevin will want to wrestle or go find something to smash. Movies get him worked up, buzzing with an energy he needs to burn off. We'll end up doing something stupid that I'll regret, something that ends in broken glass or blood. And we'll convince ourselves that we're having a great time, that this is what life is all about. Do those two sense the lie we tell ourselves or is it just me? Am I the only alien in the room pretending to be human?

Kevin would fry my ass in a heartbeat if I was a shape-shifter from another planet. Hell, he'd jizz his shorts just to get his hands on a flamethrower.

I tilt my beer back, but it's empty. Kevin could only steal one for each of us, so I go up to the kitchen to raid the fridge. Eric's mom is there, waiting for the kettle to boil. I haven't seen her in a while.

"Hello, Mark. How's movie night?"

"Good," I say, reaching for the fridge handle. "Okay if I get a soda?"

Mrs. Chapman tells me to help myself, like she always does. Eric's mom has always been really kind to me. Three years ago, during the worst summer ever, she kind of took me in. I didn't want to be at home, so I spent a lot of time here. Mrs. Chapman said I was always welcome, never making a fuss if I wanted to stay for dinner or sleep over.

Mrs. Chapman gets a glass for me, sets it on the counter. "Eric said you're working the ice cream stand this summer. That sounds fun."

"It's okay. Kinda boring, actually. The ice cream isn't great."

"Maybe that's a good thing. I don't think I could trust myself being around all that stuff." She pats her belly, making that joke all women do. "It's a job, and that's what's important. It's already August and Eric still hasn't found a summer job."

"He mows the neighbor's lawn," I say in his defense.

"That's not the same thing. He needs a proper job."

I don't mention my other job at Mr. Dutton's RV yard. That would make Eric look even lazier. I hate when adults use one kid to shame another. "It's not hard or anything. I spend most of my time reading."

"That's beside the point. It shows responsibility." The kettle whistles, and she takes it off the stove. "How's your dad?"

I tell her he's fine, but I honestly don't know. He could be in the middle of a mental breakdown, but I wouldn't know. He'd never show it, and I wouldn't be interested enough to care.

"And Liz? How is she?"

Same answer. Everything's fine.

She dips the teabag up and down. "I'm glad she's settling in. I'm sure it's a big adjustment for everyone. I was worried you might have a rough go of it."

"What do you mean?"

"Well, change can be hard. I'm sure Liz finds it a challenge, too."

I shrug at this, having never thought about her side of the situation. I don't want to think about how shitty I am to her right now. "I guess."

Eric's mom lowers her voice like we're about to gossip. "The age difference between them is no small thing, you know. And that can be a challenge all on its own. I mean, Liz isn't that much older than Christine is."

Eric's older sister, the one whose name is ranked on the *Galaga* game at the arcade, started college last fall. "Christine didn't come home for the summer?"

"She didn't want to give up her apartment just to find another in September. So she got a job in town." Mrs. Chapman dangles the teabag on its string and drops it into the sink. Then she squares me with a look. "Just between you and me, Mark, I thought it was too soon. Your dad and Liz, I mean. It's only been, what, two years?"

"Three. Three and two months."

"My God, has it been that long already?"

I turn toward the basement stairs. "I should get back."

"I'm keeping you from your movie." Crossing to the living room with her cup, she pats my shoulder. "Listen, you're welcome here anytime, okay? Even if Eric's not here, you just come in and make yourself at home."

I thank her and head back downstairs. Eric's mom is sincere and I like that about her, but I don't know if I'd come here if I needed to get away. Not like before, anyway.

Another movie is cued up, but it's paused, the TV screen frozen on the blurry Vestron logo. Eric and Kevin are hunched over something on the coffee table. I assume they're rolling a joint, but I'm wrong.

"Check this out," Eric says, waving me closer. "You're not gonna believe it."

I join the huddle to see the knife Kevin's holding. Kevin has a lot of knives, but this one is different. It's more of a dagger, almost a foot long with a black leather scabbard. It's sleek and wicked-looking, with a silver crossguard and an eagle embossed on the handle. But it's the symbol clutched in the eagle's claws that screams out—a swastika inside a ring of laurels.

"Are you kidding me?" I stammer. "A Nazi knife?"

"It's a dagger, dumbass," Eric corrects me. "Waffen SS."

Kevin beams as he unsheathes the blade. "An officer's dagger. Check out the shine on that. No rust anywhere."

"Where'd you get it?"

"Friend of my old man's," says Kevin. "He hangs out with a biker gang."

This doesn't come as a surprise. Kevin's dad has a lot of sketchy friends. A lot of them have little dots tattooed on their hands, indicating their prison terms.

"Why do you have this?"

"Because it's fucking cool," Kevin sneers like the answer couldn't be more obvious. "It's worth a lot of money, too."

"So what, he just gave it to you?"

"Not exactly. Dude lost it around the campfire in the backyard. He was showing it off, then got drunk, dropped it in the dark. I found it in the grass the next morning."

Eric's holding the dagger with a reverence that makes me shudder. He tests his thumb against the blade. Disappointed, he says, "Kinda dull."

"Course the blade's dull, dummy," Kevin says. "It hasn't been sharpened since World War Two."

The two of them debate if the dagger's seen battle. Was it during the Blitz or farther east, in the siege of Stalingrad? Second World War stuff looms large in our idle conversations. Kombat Kevin considers himself an expert on these matters.

I pick up the scabbard for a closer look, turning it to the light. There's a small etching on the silver clasp. Tiny letters revealing the maker's mark. I point it out to the other two. "Says here: Made in Taiwan."

Eric's face sags, and Kevin tells me to go fuck myself. I just grin, pleased as punch to burst his balloon.

EVERYTHING IS A TEST

"DON'T YOU HAVE anything better to do?"

Stacy looks at me suspiciously, wondering why I'm hanging around on my night off. It's a hot night and the ticket booth at the Palisades is like an oven. She stands outside, smoking a cigarette and fanning her face with a magazine.

"I was gonna steal a car and go joyriding, but it's too hot," I say.

A lame joke, but it's better than admitting that I really don't have anything better to do. Eric's busy with his parents and Kevin's still miffed at me for shitting all over his Nazi toy. Antsy and restless, I got on the bike and rode downtown. A girl named Natalie is working the Dairy Scoop tonight. Despite the hot night, there are zero customers at the ice cream hut. The movie theater is dead, too. Stacy fans her face with a copy of the *Watchtower*. Every two weeks, the Jehovah's Witness people stop by the theater to save Stacy's soul. She often responds with a few choice quotes from *The Exorcist*.

"Don't you have a girlfriend or something?"

"No," I say. Too quick, too defensive.

"What happened to what's-her-name? Jenny?"

I shrug. "That was last year."

Jenny Kroger, my first and only real girlfriend. We started going out last fall, just after school started. It was over by Halloween. Jenny was cool one on one, but when she was with her friends, she became someone else. Everything was a test with her. *If you loved me*, she would say, *you'd spend less time with your friends. If you cared, you'd ask me over for dinner*. One Friday night, her best friend Marnie called and started saying all this crazy shit about how she had this secret crush on me and wanted to get together, but not tell Jenny about it. Our little secret, she whispered. Guess who was listening in on the other line to see if I'd take the bait? Jenny, of course. Another test. We broke up the next day, less than a week before the big Halloween dance.

I look at Stacy, trying to remember a name. "You still seeing that guy with the hockey hair? Tom?"

"Todd." She flicks her ash, watches the street. "I dunno."

"You don't know if you're going out with him?"

"We break up, we get back together." Stacy lets out a slow sigh. "It's exhausting."

Todd the Clod. What she sees in that goon, I'll never know. "Why don't you just dump him for good?"

"Why? You wanna ask me out?"

My throat constricts. Is she joking? I can't tell until she laughs and swats the back of my head.

"You wish, you little perv," she says, flinging the cigarette butt into the sewer grate. "Go do something with your life."

I ride up and down Main Street again, cutting through air as sticky and humid as a fog. I told myself I was never going back to the Farrow house, that I need to leave those girls alone. But even I don't believe my own bullshit.

The Farrow house rises behind the brick gateposts, one light in the bay window. I lean over the handlebars, scanning for any movement, but there's no one on the veranda, no fluttering curtain in a window. I can't knock on the door, and I don't know their number, or even if they have a phone. I expect George to step out of the shadows as if she knew I was coming, and I'm miffed when she doesn't appear. Sometimes I shock myself with my own stupid notions.

I remember the tin cans strung up on the fishing line—George's early warning system, so I stow the bike in the hawthorn and sneak out to the footpath on the far side of the property. It's dark back here, forcing me to take it slow until I find the tripwire. I jiggle the line just enough to rattle the cans. I don't want to alert the whole family, so it's just a light clink and a soft clank. I'm praying Mr. Farrow doesn't come out with a shotgun.

The crickets chirp around me and the frogs groan down in the creek, but that's all. I squat here long enough to regret this stupid idea until the screen door finally opens. Georgia Farrow scans the tree line and then clomps down the rickety steps to the grass. She gestures with a wave and then crosses the yard to a rusty swing set near the fence. How does she know it's me? Can she see in the dark?

I push through the underbrush to meet her. George sways on the swing, making the chain squeak. I shove my hands in my pockets and just stand there.

"How did you know it was me?"

"Who else would it be?"

Maybe the psychic sister predicted my return. Do I really want to know?

Her feet trail through the clover as she swings. "Why did you come back?"

"I don't know." I use that phrase all the time, for everything. *I don't know*. It sounds so stupid, like there's a vacuum of air between my ears, incapable of any thought. It's a lie like so many others I've told. I know exactly why I've come back here. "I was bored."

"I see. And I'm supposed to entertain you?"

Her hands grip the chain and her head hangs so that her hair hides her face. It's like her armor, that flat fall of greasy hair. Does she ever bathe? When she finally looks up, I can't read her expression. Disdain or complete indifference?

"You're weird."

She nods slowly. "Ah. You came to taunt me."

"No." I decide to just be honest for once. "I've never met anyone like you."

She swings back and forth saying nothing.

I take the swing next to her, testing it first because the chain looks ready to snap. And we sit there swaying so the chains don't squeal too loudly, neither of us say anything. I'm scrambling for something witty. There's a weird pressure to be funny or clever right now, but I'm choking.

"How's your ear?" I blurt out.

"What?"

"I said how's your ear?" Louder this time, tapping my ear like she's deaf.

Then she laughs at my gullibility. That fades, and we're back to square one.

"Where are your sisters?"

George glances over at the house. "Murdering each other."

"Do you guys fight a lot?"

"Constantly."

"What about?"

"Anything," she says with a shrug. "A wrong word, a borrowed book. We tear into each other until Mother wails, begging God to strike us all dead so she can have some quiet."

I try to picture George's mother, but I can't. Is she like her daughters, odd and weirdly dressed? Or is she like everybody else's mom? "What's her name?"

"Griselda."

Her expression is stony, then she laughs at me. "It's Audrey. You should see your face."

"Very funny."

She doesn't look so severe when she smiles. I wonder if that stern expression is like her hair, another plate of armor. The smile is the chink in her armor where the tip of a blade can slip through. My ears feel hot for no reason.

"What's your mother's name?" she asks.

I try to think of a funny witch name to bounce the joke back to her, but my brain goes flat. "Nancy."

"Nancy's a nice name. What's she like?"

I watch her toe the weeds to resume her momentum. I lie and say she's like everybody else's mom.

Her hand comes up to hook her hair behind her ear. I didn't know she had freckles until now. "Who were those boys you were with?" she asks. "The ones with the firecrackers. You said they're idiots."

"Sometimes," I say. "They're just my friends."

"What are they like? Tell me about them?"

"Why?"

She doesn't answer. It's hard to imagine what it must be like to not have friends. So I try to explain the two friends I've had since the seventh grade. "Eric's okay. He means well, but it's like he wants things to stay the same—just watching movies and going to the arcade. He hates when we talk about girls and stuff."

"You talk about girls?"

"Just stuff. Like who's pretty or who's dating who. You know, just stuff."

Her eyes narrow. "You have favorites?"

"Doesn't everybody?"

"I honestly don't know. It doesn't sound nice. What about the people who aren't considered favorites?"

"Never thought about it. I'm sure they have favorites of their own." I push off too hard, making the chain squeal. "Don't you have one? Like a movie star or something?"

Her brow knits, taking the question seriously. "Vincent Price."

Why am I not surprised? George flits past me on each pass until we sync together. Her hair flips out of the way on the forward swing.

She looks at me. "Who's the other friend?"

"Kevin." How do I explain him? "Kevin's all right. He's just a bit, I dunno, destructive."

George sways for a moment, considering this. "Sounds like a dangerous friend."

She's weirdly on the money there, but admitting it feels wrong. Like a betrayal. "Do you really not have any friends?"

"No."

"Isn't that kinda lonely?"

She toes the dirt with her shoe. "No."

My hands turn clammy from the chain. I wipe them down my jeans, stalling before I say what's on my mind. "We used to be in the same class. A long time ago, when you were still in school."

Her swing stops, but there's no flash of recognition in her expression. "I don't think so."

"Sixth grade. Mrs. Scorzi's class. Don't you remember?"

"No," she says, but her tone sounds forced.

"Didn't you have friends back then?"

"Everyone hated me."

I have a fuzzy memory of a girl on her own, sidelined from the chaos of the other kids. The other girls talked about her like she was an animal, something inhuman. Did I torment her like everyone else? Something tells me I piled on with the rest of them, eager to be part of the group. Was there any other choice? If you didn't go along, you'd get pushed out of the tribe just like the loser kid. Is it weird that I can't remember? My memory sometimes whitewashes all the bad shit I've done, like it never happened—censoring my own history so I don't have to consider my past behavior.

"Is that why your folks pulled you out of school?"

"It wasn't safe for us there. We were in danger."

That makes me straighten up. "Danger? From who?"

George squares me with a strange look. "From you. All of you. You people killed our sister. My parents pulled us out of school before you got us."

My tongue feels too thick to speak. "I thought your sister died in a car accident?"

"She was run off the road. They just made it look like an accident."

I scrutinize her face. There's a ferocity in her eyes that tells me this isn't just conspiracy theory stuff. "You're saying she was murdered?"

"Yes. They murdered my sister. Your people." She kicks off from one foot and sways under the grinding squeal of rusting metal. "And I hope they all die painful deaths because of it."

I'm still trying to understand this bombshell when she pops to her feet and steps away from the swing. Her expression alters, becomes frighteningly sober. "Sometimes I dream about the whole town going up in flames. About burning everything to the ground and everyone in it. And I'm holding the match that starts it."

Everything this girl says is like a grenade meant to knock me off balance. It's not necessarily unpleasant.

When she strides toward the greenhouse on the other side of the yard, she waves at me to follow. "Come. I want to show you something."

POISON

"I CAN'T TELL when you're joking."

The latch on the glass door clicks under her hand. "I'm no good at telling jokes," she says. "I never get the punchline right."

The greenhouse squats behind the main house like an ugly stepchild. The glass walls are clouded with condensation and grime, obscuring the interior from the outside. The air is stifling and whatever once thrived in here is now dead or dying. Flower petals dot the plank floor, squishing under our shoes as we move past rows of spindly vegetation.

"You really want to burn the whole town?"

George stops and nudges her foot at something under the bench, a red jerrycan with yellow lettering that reads *Gasoline*. Three more are lined up beside it.

"This is for my grand finale," she tells me, continuing down the rows of potted plants. "A spell to end all spells."

Despite what she said about punchlines, this feels like a wind-up. I lift the jerrycan and test its weight. Empty. Joke's on me, I guess. But now I've lost sight of her. Tendrils of dead vegetation snag my shoulder, snapping twigs and leaves to the floor.

"It's like a tomb in here," I call out. I always do that—relate everything to something from a movie. Maybe all that junk really has rotted my brains like my old man said it would.

George emerges from behind a potted palm. "Not so loud."

I catch up to her, mindful of how the wooden planks creak underfoot. "Who's the gardener?"

"My mother used to grow orchids in here," she says. "Along with other exotic things like hibiscus and nopal. We even had a fig tree that we would harvest."

I scan the rows of dried up foliage. "What happened to it?"

"She stopped gardening. She stopped doing a lot of things."

I'm waiting for a shoe to drop, but there isn't one. It's like pulling teeth to get a straight answer from this girl. "Why'd she stop?"

"Her heart wasn't in it anymore." She traces a finger through the dusty earth leaking from the cracked terra-cotta. "Have you ever seen black nightshade?"

It sounds familiar, but I thought it was just something out of a comic book. "Isn't that poisonous?"

A single plant thrives at the end of the bench like an oasis among the brown vegetation. George lifts the pot with its purple buds and holds it up to my face. "It can be lethal. Even a small dose can cause hallucinations and convulsions. Insanity." She strokes a leaf the way you would a pet. "I've been trying to grow nightshade forever, but this is the only one that's survived. Her name is Harriet."

I'm not sure I want the answer, but I ask anyway. "You're growing poison?"

"For my enemies. Why else would I want it?"

"How very medieval of you."

She thrusts the purple flower buds at my face again. "Are you scared I'm going to poison you?"

Honesty is the best policy, so I just go with that. "No. I just think you're crazy."

"Of course, you do. That's just lazy thinking, Mark."

God help me, there's a tiny zap of electricity when she says my name. Did it show? "Lazy how?"

"It's what boys always say about girls they don't like. She's nuts, she's crazy. Please."

My instinct is to deny it, but she's not wrong. Hell, how many times have I used those exact words? Or heard my dad dismiss my mom with it?

"You're not really growing this for poison. You want it 'cause it's cool. It's shocking."

"I wanted to grow enough to poison the town's water supply," she says. "But the amount required was more than I could grow. It was a stupid idea."

Another punchline without a set-up? I watch her set Harriet the nightshade plant back on the shelf. She rotates the pot a half-turn to face the glass. I nod at the other potted flowers. "What else you got here?"

Her eyes light up as she points out a row of dying plants, telling me about motherwort and stinging nettles. How one is good for healing wounds and another induces miscarriage. Half of it sounds made-up, but who cares? She's animated, eager to show off her knowledge. She brushes her hair behind her ear as she talks, exposing her face more, her armor drawing down bit by bit.

The greenhouse is gloomy and the air sticky. Her ears wiggle slightly when she speaks and her pronunciation goes wonky at times, like English is not her first language. We're alone in this sticky hothouse, and no one knows we're here.

I imagine kissing George. I think about the two of us rolling over the bench as we kiss. It makes me lightheaded, scared. My fingers itch thinking about touching her. I picture the nightshade plant crushed under our faces as we roll over it, poisoning us. The seizures hit and we convulse on the floor as the toxin destroys our nervous systems. Someone finds us three days later, twisted into a human pretzel and decomposing quickly in the fetid heat of the hothouse.

I need some air.

"What's wrong?"

"Just dizzy." I grip the bench to stay upright. Was it the nightshade? Did it touch my face?

"Do you need some water?"

I tell her I'm fine, but she takes my wrist and tugs. "Come with me. But don't make a sound."

We tiptoe into the house, George leading the way through one dark room after another until she motions for me to stay put. Her finger crosses her lips before she disappears.

The light is dim, but I can make out a cold fireplace with a thick mantel and paintings crowding the walls like a gallery. Portraits of stern-faced men with their shoulders set back, chests puffed out. Forgotten muckety-mucks of some bygone era who thought these portraits bought immortality. Or glory. They're covered in dust now, neglected.

"Sorry, fellas," I whisper to them. "You're just worm food now."

George slips back into the room with a glass of water. I thank her, but she keeps staring at me with that weird intensity.

I scan the portraits of the stuffy men looking down on us. "Who are these people?"

"Family," she says, surveying the paintings. "Long dead."

I squint at the puritan glares and pursed lips in oil. "I don't see any family resemblance."

She points to an ancestor with a hangdog face. "That one has my father's eyes."

"Is your family rich?"

George takes the glass from me and guzzles the rest. "They used to be. The fortune was lost a long time ago."

"Somebody gambled it away?"

She almost laughs. "I don't really know. My parents fight over money a lot. Mother wants to sell the house and move away. Father refuses because his family's been here for generations."

I watch the tiny slash of smile drain from her face. "Moving away doesn't sound so bad. Fresh start and all that."

"I'd kill to get out of this town." She looks into the empty glass before setting it down. "The loneliness here, it's like we're cursed."

I smell a story behind this. "Cursed? Sounds very Gothic."

"Pick a closet. Each one's stuffed with skeletons. The family gossip is that some sin was committed a long time ago, and it cursed every generation since."

This sounds weirdly Puritanical coming from her. Maybe the apple doesn't roll far after all. "What sin?"

"Depends on who's sharing the gossip. Sometimes it's murder, other times it's a scandalous pregnancy. Thematically, it runs the gamut. Revenge or fratricide. Incest. Witchcraft."

"Choose Your Own Adventure," I suggest.

"I suppose." She waves the idea away. "The sins of the fathers, blah-blah-blah."

"Like the House of Usher."

Her mouth twists into a smirk at this. I puff up at being clever enough to make her smile. But her story reminds me of another family, a juicy piece of local folklore. "It's like the Blaylocks, across town. They thought they were cursed, too."

"The Blaylocks?"

"You know the story? Family of whackos, all very religious. Something bad happened to them, and they thought they were cursed. Then the dad flips his nut and kills his whole family."

George's eyes light up, eager for details. "How?"

"Twelve gauge, point blank. Two kids, the mom, and then himself."

Her eyebrows scrunch together. "Why have I never heard this before?"

"The town tried to keep it quiet," I say. "Looks bad on our little Mayberry. But everyone knows. That's why the house is still on the market. No one wants to buy that haunted place."

"Is it really haunted?"

I shrug. "Dunno. It's a shithole. Kids go there to party and smash stuff."

Her eyes go the kind of wide where white is visible all around the iris. "You've been there?"

"Yeah. It's creepy as hell."

"I would kill to see it. Would you show me?"

This is an odd request, but everything is odd when it comes to George Farrow. "It's way across town. We can bike out there some night and break in."

Her face droops. "Oh. Can't we walk?"

"It would take a while. It's way over on Townsend Road." I watch her face fall even more. "You don't want to go?"

"I don't have a bicycle," she says. "And I can't be away that long. Not without getting caught, anyway."

Another reason to get the Galaxie on the road. I'm left scratching my head. "You don't have a bike?"

"No. Not after what happened to Liesl. Mother took them away. She said they would run us over the same way they did to her."

"Liesl?"

"My sister." She takes a framed photograph down from the mantel and shows it to me.

Four Farrow sisters. I recognize all but the tallest one. Her laugh is flash-frozen in the snapshot, big and toothy. Liesl Farrow—the ghost who rattles around the attic when a stranger is in the house. I study her face, but I don't remember her. The picture is striking not because it includes the lost sister, but because of the expressions of the other three Farrow siblings: Claudia, Georgia, and Tilly. They all look happy.

It's a slow day at the RV Emporium, the afternoon ticking by like drying paint. I call Eric. Mr. Dutton hates when I use the office phone. He doesn't want the business line tied up because some dumb teenager is hogging it. I lie and tell him it's important.

When Eric comes on the line, he sounds like he just woke up. It's almost three in the afternoon. "Hey, you still got Christine's bike?"

A yawn rolls out on the other end of the line. "Who?"

"Your sister, dummy. Is her bike still hanging in the garage?"

"Probably," Eric mumbles. "Why?"

I had a lie prepared before I dialed. "Liz wants a bike, but she doesn't want to spend a lot on a new one."

"Ooh, Step-Mommy wants a bike, huh? Does she wear those sexy bike shorts?"

Here we go. This joke is getting stale. "Can I buy it off you?"

The line goes quiet. I can almost hear the gears grinding in Eric's head. "Fifty bucks," is his answer.

"Fuck you, fifty bucks. The thing's sat there for years. I'll give you twenty."

He counters. "Twenty-five."

"You're a dick. Fine. I'll come by after work."

I bang the phone onto its cradle, which prompts a sour look from Mr. Dutton. He snaps a kerchief from his back pocket and lifts the handset.

"Mark, I shouldn't have to remind you that this is a business phone." He wipes down the mouthpiece as if it's been contaminated. "And I'll not have vulgarities poisoning it. Understand?"

I like Mr. Dutton a lot, but he has some really strange ideas about business. *People spend the same way they fornicate*, he once told me. *Some close their eyes and wince through it. Others dive in and whoop it up. Either works, 'cause in the end, they both get screwed.*

Faking interest in these nuggets of wisdom, I tell him he should write a book on the subject. This makes him puff up his chest, which glosses over whatever dumb thing I've done in his employ.

I head to Eric's house after work. Kevin's there. The two of them are in the backyard, firing and reloading Eric's old BB gun. Target practice consists of a troop of green plastic soldiers strategically placed on a sand hill. The BB rifle makes a muffled *pop* and a plastic army man goes flying. Eric is a decent marksmen, nailing most of the targets.

Kevin, not so much. For all his gung-ho war bullshit and camouflage, he's a crap shot with the gun. There's a tiny puff of sand, but no soldier goes flying. Kevin cranks the lever on the rifle impatiently and fires again. Another puff.

"The sight's off on this piece of shit." He thrusts the gun back to Eric. "The barrel must be bent."

"You just can't aim for shit," Eric says. For this, he gets a punch to the shoulder, almost knocking him off the ratty lawn chair.

I come up behind them and reach for the gun. "I'm surprised this thing still works."

The stock tucks into my shoulder and I tease the sight over a target, a plastic army man with a flamethrower. I do everything right—aim, hold my breath, squeeze the trigger. But I miss by a mile.

"He's worse than you," Eric says to Kevin. For this he gets another knuckle-duster to the shoulder.

I hand the rifle back. "Let's see the bike."

It's tucked away at the back of the musty garage, hanging from a stud. It's an old ten-speed with a bright yellow frame and a white basket with plastic daisies. The chain is slack, the front tire flat.

"The color matches your eyes," Kevin says.

I ignore him, look at Eric. "Needs more work than I thought."

"Dude, you're not weaseling me down on the price. It's still twenty-five."

I fork over a ten and a lot of crumpled singles. We pump up the front tire. There's a leak, but it's enough to walk it home.

Kevin looks on, bored. "What's wrong with your bike?"

"It's not for him," Eric pipes up for me. "It's for his step-mommy."

"No shit? How is luscious Liz? She gonna gwive her stepson a big kiss for her supwise?"

I keep pumping the tire. The two of them love talking about Liz and her Daisy Dukes and aerobics outfits. I tune it out, but there's this perverse urge to tell them about George, just to witness their reaction. They'd be shocked, then repulsed if I confessed about wanting to kiss her. They'd jam fingers down their throats in a pantomime of barfing. They'd wonder how anyone in their right mind could lust after such a repulsive creature. I suddenly want to just blurt it out in an act of self-destruction. It's like looking over the side of a tall building and feeling an alien urge to jump.

The conversation skids over to the possibility of shooting fireworks in the park tonight. Kevin has gotten hold of a new cache and he's eager to blow shit up.

"Where'd you get them?" Eric asks. "You can't find any after the beginning of July."

"My cousin." Kevin unzips his backpack to reveal a horde of long tubes of red paper. "They drive over the border and stock up."

Eric's lip quivers. "Dude. Roman candles?"

"Two dozen." Kevin's beaming a big shit-eating grin. "Let's hit the park and have a huge Roman candle war."

Roman candle wars are stupid and extremely dangerous. Which is what makes it fun. You light up a candle and fire it at your friends as they return fire. It hurts if you get hit. The incendiary tip burns right through clothes and leave nasty flesh wounds.

"That's a dumb idea," I say.

Kevin's face darkens. "Come on. We haven't done that in years. It'll be a blast."

"There's a reason for that. Shit happens playing that game."

"The hell you talking about? Nothing's happened."

"Are you kidding me?" I look at Eric, but he's clammed up completely, staying out of it. "Remember last time?"

Kevin's voice lowers. "You're delusional. Nothing happened last time, Mark. Nothing."

I'm not in the mood for this. Kevin's like a pit bull sometimes; he just won't let it go. I roll the yellow bike out of the garage to the road. "Count me out. I got stuff to do."

Just before I'm out of earshot, I hear Kevin asking Eric why I've become such a loser these days.

MURDER HOUSE

RIDING ACROSS TOWN while guiding a second bicycle at arm's length proves tricky, but I manage it without crashing or seeing anyone I know. I patched the inner tube on Christine's old bike and tightened the chain. The yellow frame has been masked under a layer of flat black spray paint that's still tacky in some places. The basket I cut away, tossed it out. By the time I roll onto Merrily Road, the sunset is turning the clouds pink.

George is sitting on the front steps with a book propped on her knees. Her head lifts at the sound of the bike tires as I pull up before the gates. Her ugly nun shoes clomp on the paving stones.

"Were you waiting for me?" I ask.

Her eyes drop to the bikes. "Why do you have two bicycles?"

I glide the spay-painted one in front of her. "Happy birthday."

Suspicion narrows her eyes. "It's not my birthday."

"Whatever. Give it a spin."

"Why?"

"So we can go for a ride. Give it a try."

She hesitates, as if expecting a trap, before taking it from me. Delight replaces suspicion as she climbs on and pushes off. The handlebars shake until she gains momentum and glides away. The bike turns a wide arc, and she rides back unsteadily, braking too hard and almost tumbling over the handlebars. Her face flits hard between joy and embarrassment.

"I'm a little rusty," she says, dismounting. "Whose bicycle is this?"

"It's yours now."

She recoils like it's poison. The bicycle falls to the grass. "I can't accept this."

"Sure you can."

"Why are you giving this to me?"

"I thought we could go for a ride, see that murder house I told you about."

Her smile is reluctant. "For real?"

"Yeah. Let's go."

The smile wilts. She looks back at the house. "Wait here."

"Where you going?"

"Just wait."

She runs back inside. A window on the second floor pops with light. I'm wondering if this was a mistake when the door opens, but it's not George who comes out. A man emerges and marches down the front steps. I scramble to hide behind the gatepost.

Her father is a lean shadow taking long strides across the yard, but it's too dark to make out any details. He's wearing a tie, his shirtsleeves rolled up. He strides across the gravel to the station wagon and climbs in. The door is left open, keeping the dome light on, but he doesn't turn the ignition. It looks like he's mid-conversation, all hand gestures and head shaking, but there's no one else in the car. He's there long enough for me to consider bailing on my dumb plan. I could stash the bike in the bushes, hoping George will find it later. Then the car door closes and Mr. Farrow marches back into the house, still talking to himself. He does not sound friendly.

George returns a minute later, coming around the side of the house.

"Are you in trouble?"

She picks up the bicycle. "No. I just needed to tell my sisters that I'm going out. They can cover for me."

Looking up at the house, I see two figures in a window on the second floor, Claudia and Tilly like neglected orphans pressed up against the glass, watching us.

"Maybe I should have brought bikes for them, too."

"Don't be dumb," George says. "They hate you."

We pedal away.

We take it slow while George gets comfortable on the bicycle. There's a joke to be made about remembering how to ride one, but it's too lame to attempt, so we just coast along without speaking. We cut across town and she only looks at me when I indicate the next turn. The streets are mostly deserted. I keep an eye out for the red Charger that tried to me run off the road, but I don't see it prowling the streets. I hope it crashed into a ditch while the driver was doing donuts.

We ride past the arena to a street of drab bungalows and there it is, the Blaylock house. A bland split-level ranch with a crumbling carport and a yard choked with weeds. There's a big bay window, and underneath that is a rose bush dipping with blooms. The only thing strange about it is the plywood covering up the windows.

George is underwhelmed. "It doesn't look haunted."

"Who said it was?"

She frowns, dismounts. "How do we get in?"

"Around back. We'll hide the bikes there."

"Will they get stolen?"

"No, but the cops cruise by here. If they see bikes out front, they'll stop and chase us out."

We push the bikes through the tall grass to the back of the house. The plywood patch on the kitchen window is loose and falls away with a push. This is how everyone gets in and out.

"Let me go first," I say, peering into the darkness. "Someone might be inside."

She doesn't hesitate, vaulting through the window before me. Inside, her eyes are thirsty, taking in the catastrophe that used to be a kitchen. The cupboards have been pulled down and kicked apart; the refrigerator lies face up on the floor like a white coffin. The smell is noxious, like ammonia or worse.

There are two flashlights in my backpack. I hand one to her. "What do you think?"

"It's creepy," she says. "I love it."

The stairs are appropriately squeaky as we explore the second floor. Garbage crunches under our shoes as we move from one bedroom to the next. A beer bottle gets kicked, rolls along the floor. The walls are marred with curse words and cartoon dicks drawn in spray paint.

George chases a cockroach with her flashlight. "The family that lived here—what were they like?"

"Dunno. The story depends on who's telling it." I train my flashlight over the crusty floor. "The story I heard was that the Blaylocks were religious whackos. Real holier-than-thou types, right? Until their eldest daughter got knocked up by some local greaseball. The shame kills them. The dad loses his job, hits the bottle. Christmas Eve, he goes crazy and loads his shotgun—blood splatter in every bedroom."

"Did the police catch him?"

"He phoned it in. Said God told him to do it. Then he blew his brains out."

George stomps a cockroach in the corner. "When was this?"

"Back in the sixties."

"It sounds like the Amityville murders," she says.

I shrug. All I remember from that movie is the flies swarming against the window. "I've also heard that the mom did it—laced the Christmas turkey with rat poison."

"Both of those stories sound made up," she says, moving to the door at the end of the hallway. "That's the thing with ghost stories. They reveal more about the teller than the truth."

I stop and look at her, but she doesn't see any irony in that.

We move on to the master bedroom. It's big, with French doors that open onto a walkout balcony. The putrid mattress on the floor flares up in the throw of our flashlights, a big dark stain in the center of it.

"Is that blood?"

"Could be anything."

Her face puckers into something sour. "Do people have sex on that?"

"Romantic." I'm trying to play it cool, but hearing her say that sends another zap down to my fingertips. "Let's keep the tour moving."

Downstairs, we step over the debris in the dining room to the broken glass salting the living room floor. Every wall drips with graffiti—more crude dicks and boobs, along with the inevitable headbanger tags like *Hail Satan* and *666*. A few band names, a lot of bad spelling.

But what draws the eye is the huge pentagram on the grimy hardwood floor—ten feet in diameter with melted candles at the endpoints. George is hypnotized by it. The trash and sludge that encrusts every floor is absent here, the floorboards inside the pentagram scrubbed clean. It looks like someone was just here.

"What do you make of this?" I ask.

She circles all the way around the pentagram as if reluctant to step inside. She scratches at the paint, flaking it away with a fingernail. "Looks amateurish."

"So it's not, like, real devil worship stuff?"

George steps over the barrier and sits down in the center of the five-pointed star. "Just kid stuff."

I join her, dropping the knapsack beside me. "Do you want to check out the basement?"

"What's the point? There's no ghosts here."

That surprises me. "How do you know?"

She flattens a palm against the floor and holds it there like she's testing the temperature. "I don't feel anything. No old ghosts or echoes of a tragedy. Just wood and plaster."

"Nothing at all?"

She brushes the grit from her hand. "You look disappointed."

"Not really. The story's always more interesting than the truth, isn't it?" Unzipping the knapsack, I pull out the two beers I pinched before leaving the house. I crack them both, pass one to her.

George doesn't touch it. "Is this a picnic?"

"Why not?" I shrug for the millionth time tonight. "I should have brought chips."

She takes a sip and winces at the taste. If this was anyone else, I'd mock them for that. There's no need to pretend that I like the taste of beer any more than she does. There's no pressure to be cool or anything, in fact. George is so far outside my group of friends that she might as well be from Mars. In a way, she's free. And that makes it easier. I don't know why, it just does.

"This is still fun." She nods at the room around us. "Even if it isn't haunted."

I sip my beer. Nod. My brain is abruptly empty.

"I understand the appeal," she says. "It's forbidden and dangerous. The ghost story makes it fun, but it's just an ugly house that no one wants." Her hands are restless, cracking knuckle after knuckle.

"We can go if you're bored."

She folds her hands together to quiet them. "I'm not bored. I just fidget a lot."

The house is quiet. Outside, I can hear the hum of a passing car. A dog barks far away.

Her teeth clamp over her bottom lip. Out of nowhere, she asks, "Do you ever feel like you're waiting?"

"For what?"

"For something to happen. For life to start."

All the time. That's what I want to say, but I don't. I default to my standard response. "I dunno."

Her hands start fussing again, but she's popped every knuckle. "I feel like life is out there, waiting for me to find it. Everything's on hold until then, while I'm stuck in this awful place."

"You really don't like it here, do you?"

"Does anyone?" She finds one last knuckle to crack. It's painfully loud. "I can't wait to get out of this vile town."

"And go where?"

George purses her lips and tilts her head, like she's weighing her options. She leans close to whisper, "University. Some place that isn't populated by half-wits."

That sounds far away and hard to imagine. I haven't given much thought to what happens after high school. "So that's when life starts? University?"

"It has to." She takes another sip, drags her wrist across her mouth. "There's gotta be someplace to find people who think like you do. To find friends?" Her voice cracks on that last syllable, and she curls up like a hermit crab into its shell.

I'm scrambling for something to say, anything that might assure her that she'll find what she's looking for. But all I come up with are empty phrases like "it's okay" or "don't worry." Too pathetic to say aloud.

Silence infects the room again. I can still hear that dog out there, barking its head off.

George stirs, straightens her back. "Sorry."

"Don't be." Out of nowhere, I'm feeling bold. I tip my beer can against hers. "Universities are full of brainy people, right? You'll fit right in."

The beer still tastes like swill, and the smell in this room is getting stronger, a sour tang that seeps into our clothes, our hair. Without realizing it, I study her face, drinking up every detail like I want to burn it into my memory.

"What?"

Busted. I flinch. "I didn't say anything."

"But you were about to," she says. "What was it?"

Somewhere deep down, there is something slithering to the surface and scratching to get out. A truth that wants to erupt from my ribs like the chest-burster in Alien. I panic, push it back down. It would ruin this moment—blood and guts everywhere.

"How are you gonna go to university without a high school diploma?"

She frowns at me. "That's not what you were going to say."

"I thought Tilly was the one who's psychic?"

"I have my moments. Tell me."

She's fishing, but I'm not taking the bait. That would be suicide. Cornered, I change the subject.

"I saw your dad," I say. "Back at the house. He was talking to himself."

"He does that sometimes," she says, but doesn't elaborate any further.

"Is he violent?"

"He yells a lot. He'll rant for hours about how the government is corrupt and how the whole world is controlled by some secret cabal of elites. How everyone is out to get us and we can't rely on anyone but ourselves."

"Sounds a bit paranoid."

Her face sours at this. "Is it, though? Everyone hates us. You and your friends attacked us for no reason. Is it really paranoia?"

The reminder of that stunt shuts me up. She's not wrong.

"It's like in the Lovecraft stories," she says, scratching at the painted pentagram again. "We live on this thin crust of order and civility, so smug in our fancy cars and pretty homes. But underneath all that? Chaos. Something waits to drag us down into the darkness."

This philosophical turn catches me off guard, and I have no response to it. Instead, I'm thinking about her father. How dangerous is he? Is George safe living in that house?

Her nose wrinkles. "It really smells in here."

"We can leave."

Out the kitchen window we go, the plywood pulled back into place. We collect the bikes and turn to the road. I tell her I'll ride home with her.

"I don't want to go home just yet," she says.

"Okay. You want to go down to the creek or something?"

Her mouth tilts, like a smirk gone all wrong. "Can I see your house?"

I tell her there's nothing special about it. Just a plain old house.

"I don't care. I want to see where you live."

A SWORD THAT EATS SOULS

I'VE NEVER REALLY contemplated my own home before. Looking at it now with George beside me, I see it for what it is, a drab little house with faded paint and a shabby yard, unremarkable from any of the other houses on our street. I never should have brought her here.

"It's not much to look at," I tell her.

George props her elbows on the handlebars and says, "I pictured something different."

"Like what? A mansion?"

"No," she says. "More *Brady Bunch*, I guess."

The house becomes sadder the more we gawk at it. The windows are milky with pollen, and the flowerbed under the window is just arid dirt.

"Let's keep riding," I say, turning the bike back to the open street.

"I want to see your room."

She can't be serious. "That's not a good idea."

"Why? Because your parents are home?"

The curtain in the picture window lights up blue, then silver. Dad and Liz are watching TV. There's no way in hell we can just waltz past them without triggering an interrogation. How would I explain bringing home a Farrow girl? More than that, I just don't want George to see the inside of my house, the cheap blandness of it. Maybe I can divert her curiosity.

"You want to see something cool?"

"Always," she says.

The garage door click-clacks as I ease it up slowly, trying to be quiet. I hit the light switch and make a sweep with my hand.

"Check it out," I say proudly.

George scans the whole of the garage, from the old fridge to the oil-stained workbench. Her eyes light up as she crosses to a shelf. "Ooh."

Bypassing the car, she finds a peach basket with half a dozen road flares. "Do these work? I love flares."

I can't figure this girl out. I point at the Galaxie. It's candy apple red, for Christ's sake. "Not that. The car."

"Oh," she says, unimpressed. "It's kind of old, isn't it?"

"It's a classic." I don't mean to gloat, but I can't help it. "It's a 1967 Galaxie 500. And it's mine."

"Really?" Her interest piques. She bends down to inspect the interior. "It's big."

"Hop in."

She slides into the driver's side. I hop into the passenger seat and watch her wiggle the big steering wheel.

"This is really yours?"

"Pretty cool, huh?"

The keys rest in the ignition. She wraps her fingers around it. "Can we go for a ride?"

"No. The engine needs work."

There's no mistaking the disappointment in her voice. "Too bad."

"I'm fixing it up," I say, too eager, too rushed. It comes out like an apology. "I can't wait to get this on the road."

"It's so aggressive, all this chrome and blood color." She punches the radio buttons, flips the vent lever, tests the transmission on the column. "When you get it running, will you take me for a ride?"

It's hard to imagine cruising Main Street with one of the Farrow sisters in the passenger side. But I answer without hesitation. "Of course."

Satisfied with the answer, she climbs out of the car, closes the door, and then bends low to look at me. "Show me your room now."

Here I thought I had dodged this bullet. "There's nothing to see, George. It's just a room."

"Well, that's hardly fair. I snuck you into my room." Her fingers drum along the metal frame. Then she looks at me. "Don't you have a back door?"

Fair is fair.

The screen door at the side of the house squeals like a mouse dying in a trap. My dad purposely refuses to oil it so he can hear me coming home. I need a plan here.

"Listen, when we go in, go straight down the hall, but don't make any noise. My room's the last door on the left."

"Where are you going?"

"I have to put in an appearance, just to tell my dad I'm home. Ready?"

The screen door sings out and we hustle inside. George makes a beeline down the hallway as I turn for the living room. Dad and Liz are deep in the sofa, wine glasses in hand. On the TV screen, the Carringtons of *Dynasty* plot against one another.

"Hey, I'm home." I poke my head in and wave, hoping this is enough to satisfy them.

Dad turns his head without taking his eyes off the TV. "How was work today?"

"The same. G'night."

Liz sits up. "Did you eat? There's leftovers in the fridge."

"I ate at the chip stand."

Satisfied, they settle back down, and I try not to dash to my room. I close the bedroom door and find George ransacking the bookshelf.

"Everything okay?" she asks.

"We're fine."

She plucks a paperback from the shelf, looks at the cover. *Conan of Cimmeria.* "Is this any good?"

"If you like fantasy."

She slides the book back. "Not really my thing."

My shelves are littered with those books. I went through a whole Conan phase when I was younger, collecting every book I could find. I doubt she'd be interested in the barbarian with the mighty thews. I slide another one from the shelf for her. "You might like these."

She studies the cover, skims the back copy. "*Elric*? What's it about?"

"This guy's an exiled prince, but he's an albino and he's weak. He uses magic to keep himself alive until he finds this demon sword. The sword gives him strength, but it also eats the souls of anyone he kills. He's reluctant to use it, but he has to just to survive."

"Why doesn't he get rid of it?"

"He tries, but it keeps coming back to him. They're bound to each other, until the sword eats him."

Her pupils dilate into black marbles. "Can I borrow it?"

I pull three more books from the shelf. "Take 'em all."

Pleased, she scans the room again while I quickly scoop my dirty clothes into the hamper. She's drawn to the catastrophe of the desk and picks through the rubble of my obsessions. She tests the blade of a pearl-handled jackknife and blows the dust from a model Spitfire. She finds my sketchbook and turns the pages. My ears burn as she leafs through drawings of ax-wielding barbarians, vampire queens, and zombies clawing out of their graves.

"You drew these?"

"They're just doodles." I have to fight the urge to snatch it away from her. The damage is already done.

"You didn't tell me you're an artist."

"I'm not." I reach for the sketchbook, but she elbows me away, keeps turning the pages. "Honestly, it's just junk. Please don't look at it."

Too late. She's found the back pages where I've sketched naked women. She doesn't react with disgust, her face indifferent as she turns page after page of lurid drawings. My face is on fire.

"That's a lot of naked ladies, Mark."

"It's not what it looks like." My denial only confirms my guilt, but George doesn't say anything. She lays the sketchbook aside and moves on. I make a note to burn it later.

"What's that?" she asks, eyes tilting to the ceiling, at the plastic stars and moon clotted in dust. Another embarrassment.

Why did I agree to this? "Just kid stuff. I keep meaning to scrape them off."

"Is it supposed to be the constellation? It's all wrong. Ursa Major doesn't look like that."

"It's not anything. They're supposed to glow in the dark. It's stupid."

She looks confused. "Then why put them up?"

Now the embarrassing part. "My mom put them up a long time ago."

George crosses the floor and hits the light switch. The room winks into darkness.

"What are you doing?"

"I want to see how it works."

There's a faint light streaming in through the window, enough for me to watch her gaze up at the ceiling. Nothing glows.

"See? Told you."

She sits down on the bed, her head still craned upward. "Maybe it just takes a while."

"They've never worked."

I sit down next to her. George keeps straining her eyes at the plastic stars, as if willing them to glow. I check the clock and wonder how much time we have. I listen to her breathing in the dark.

The alien claws at my ribcage again, screeching to come out. I push it down, but something else slips out instead. "What was your sister like?"

"Tilly?" she says. "Or Claudia?"

"The other one."

Her attention drops away from the plastic stars. "She was kind. And very protective."

"Protective?"

"Of all three of us. Liesl was the oldest, and she knew how to handle my parents when they lost their temper."

I hear a tiny pop. I can't see her hands, but I know she's cracking her knuckles again.

"She would sort of shield us from the worst of it, you know? Deflect the attention to herself, so we could run and hide."

"It's that bad?" I ask.

"It's like a bomb going off, strafing everyone with shrapnel. Liesl would take the brunt of it. But she's not around to do that anymore."

"How old was she? When she died, I mean."

"Seventeen." George stops twisting her fingers and flops back flat on the bed. "I'll be seventeen next year."

I don't know why I brought this up because now I don't know how to respond. And what I do say is stupid. "I'm sorry."

"I miss her. All the time."

The watery light from the window turns her silver. It's too dark to see if there are tears, but something changes in the air, like the barometer dropping real fast. Can grief do that—change the air pressure in a room?

I ease back and lie next to her, our feet safely on the floor. The pressure in the air keeps tightening around us. My hand brushes against hers in the dark. Her skin is cold. My chest is thumping hard. I hold my breath and fold my fingers around hers.

She squeezes tight, clamping on so hard it hurts.

I don't know how long it lasts, holding hands in the dark, but eventually her grip eases. I turn to look at her, but it's still too dark. I feel drunk and scared and brave all at the same time. She's right there. All I have to do is lean in, but I'm shaking because I'm such a chickenshit.

"Look." Her voice is a whisper against my face.

Little dots of pale light on the ceiling, the plastic stars are glowing in the dark.

"I don't believe it."

"They work," she says.

There isn't enough blood going to my brain to understand what's going on. "That's never happened before."

It doesn't last long, but suddenly and without warning, everything seems right with the world. It's a snapshot I want to capture and preserve like a wasp trapped in amber. That's the weird part about happiness or joy; you're doomed to realize it only after the moment has passed. And it passes quickly.

George flinches, sits up fast. "I should go."

"Now?" I force myself up, trying to clear the fog from my head.

She stands, straightens her skirt. "I think she's mad."

"Who's mad?"

"Liesl," she says, pointing up to the glow-in-the-dark stars. "I told you she's protective."

I jump up from the bed like a kid caught doing something bad. The idea of her dead sister haunting my room makes my flesh crawl. I ease the door open, and we slip down the hall and into the kitchen. The living room is dark, the television dead. Out the back door, we're in the clear.

"Mark?"

Busted. My knees go limp at the sound of a female voice. Thank God it's not Dad. Liz sits on a patio chair with her feet up, a cigarette in one hand. She sports a guilty expression until she spies the girl beside me. Surprise overtakes her face.

"Oh. Hello," she stammers, flicking the cigarette away.

Dad hates smoking. He's already gone to bed, and Liz is sneaking one before she turns in—while I'm sneaking a girl out of the house. A house full of sneaky people.

"I didn't know you had a friend over." Liz pulls her loose kimono tighter. Frazzled, but trying not to let it show, she slides the pack of cigarettes into her robe pocket.

"Yeah, sorry. Forgot to mention it." I maintain eye contact for a moment before conspicuously dropping my gaze to the ashtray on the patio table. "Where's Dad?"

"He's gone to bed," she says. The stalemate clicks into a deadlock. She extends a hand to George. "Hello. I'm Liz."

George has snapped into her defensive pose, eyes on the floor, hair shielding her face in a flat fall. But she knows the protocol and awkwardly shakes Liz's hand. "Georgia," she says.

"Nice to meet you." Liz smirks at me. "It's a bit late, isn't it?"

"We lost track of time." I take George by the arm and tug her to the driveway. "I'm gonna see George home. Be back soon."

We sprint for the bikes and burn rubber down the street. When I glance at her, George is laughing. There's a mad sense of glee on her face every time we pass under a streetlamp. By the time we get to Merrily Road, we're both out of breath.

"Are you in trouble?"

I shake my head. "I don't think so."

She blots a wrist over her brow. "I had fun tonight."

My face aches from grinning so hard. I ask if she'll be in trouble coming home late, but she waves the idea away. Her sisters will cover for her.

She slides off the bike. "Your mom seems nice. She's kinda young though."

I shrug, aim the bike back the way we came. "She's not my mom."

"Oh," George says. Her brow creases. "Where's your mom?"

I'm already coasting away, weaving around the potholes. One last wave, without looking back.

KNOCK DOWN THE NEST

I CAN'T SAY if I dreamed about George last night because I never remember my dreams, but I woke up thinking about her. What it was like lying next to her in the dark, her breath on my face. I'm already hard and I don't want to fight it, so I just keep thinking about George. Until a sharp sound breaks the spell. The shelf on the wall snaps on one end. The books slide off one by one, flopping to the floor.

I blink at it in disbelief for a long time. I must have put too much weight on it, causing a screw to pop from the drywall. Unless something else caused it to fall. George did say that her sister was overprotective. I guess she doesn't like me thinking about George that way.

No. It was definitely just a faulty screw in the wall. Because the idea that the ghost knows where I live is just too terrifying to contemplate.

In the kitchen, Liz stirs sugar into her coffee and offers me an awkward greeting as I pour a bowl of cereal. I'm praying she doesn't mention anything about last night, but there's a smirk on her face.

"How did you sleep?"

"Where's Dad?"

"Early start this morning. He was gone before I got up."

The cereal crunching is loud in my ears, blocking out the prattle of the morning radio. I assumed Liz and I had an understanding, but maybe I'm wrong.

"So," Liz says, laying her coffee spoon down. "Do you want to tell me about your little friend?"

"Nothing happened." I'm hoping this is enough to end the conversation.

She nods slowly. "But you still snuck a girl in without telling us."

"Did you tell Dad?"

"I didn't get a chance to."

She wraps her hands around the mug to warm them. She isn't angry or disappointed. Just curious. Nosy.

"He doesn't need to know," I say.

"Don't put me in that position, Mark. I don't want to keep secrets from your dad."

"Nothing happened," I say, trying not to sound desperate. "If that's what you're asking."

"That's none of my business," she says. "I get it, you know. I remember being your age."

I don't know what this means. She used to sneak boys into her room? Or I'm off the hook?

"Is she your girlfriend?"

"Just a friend."

Liz sets the cup down again. "I have to admit, I was surprised. She's one of the Farrow girls, isn't she?"

My spoon clatters against the bowl. How does she know who George is? I don't want to discuss this, so I clam up.

"Is that why you were asking about the Farrows the other day?" Liz keeps at it with the questions. She's enjoying this. "How did you meet her?"

"Just around. They walk to the store sometimes."

"I see." The smirk returns to her face. "Are you two dating?"

"No."

"Right. You're just sneaking her into your bedroom to play checkers?"

"It's not like that." I feel sick and push the bowl away. "It's complicated. But you can't tell anyone, okay?"

"You want me to lie to your dad and your friends about her?"

"You don't understand. No one can know we're friends. My life would be over." I wipe my hands down my face. I don't know how to explain this. "Like I said, it's complicated."

"I'm sure it feels that way. It always does." Liz gets up, takes her mug to the sink. "Is it complicated for her too?"

"What do you mean?"

"Does she want to keep this secret, too?"

"Well, yeah. Why wouldn't she?"

She dumps her coffee down the sink, rinses the cup. "Maybe you should ask her."

I grumble something about being late for work, even though I'm not, and leave the room. I'm so stupid. It doesn't occur to me until now to threaten her with telling Dad that she's still smoking. I could march back into the kitchen to bargain it out, but I can't be bothered.

"Todd's history," Stacy says. Her jaw keeps flexing like she's grinding her teeth.

"Weren't you already broken up?"

"For reals this time. It's over."

Stacy's outside the ticket booth having a smoke. Tonight's movie is *American Ninja 2*, and only six people have bought tickets. Not a single person has stopped by the ice cream hut and I'm bored out of my mind. Tonight's dead wasp tally is six, all in the black cherry. Everything is normal and as it should be.

Stacy's talkative and restless—her third cigarette inside of an hour. She's wearing a lot of make-up and her hair is teased up higher than normal. I don't know if that's due to the break-up. Must be.

"So what happened?" I say. "With Todd the Clod."

She holds the cigarette at arm's length and flicks the ash away. "He was cheating. With Tiffany Ducharme, no less. Can you believe that skank?"

Stacy's love life confuses me. There's always a lot of drama with her breaking up with Todd, then getting back together. It's hard to keep track.

"How was he cheating on you if you're broken up?"

She looks at me like I'm stupid and clicks her teeth. "He's been sneaking around with Tiffany since Easter. All that time when we were going out. What a bitch."

Somehow Tiffany is to blame for all of this, not Todd. I've seen it before. The other girl gets tarred and feathered while the boyfriend gets off with a scolding. I'm a little disappointed. Stacy's smarter than this, but I can't say that to her face.

"Never trust anyone named Tiffany," I tell her. This is the best condolence I can come up with.

She stabs at the air with her smoke, underscoring her point. "You know what really pisses me off about it? How I'm the one who looks stupid. I'm the clueless dummy while those two were sneaking around behind my back. So not fair."

Saying sorry won't help. "He doesn't deserve you."

"I get what I deserve," she says, looking at the sky. "It's all karma, you know?"

"Don't say that."

"You're sweet." The smile is tepid, but it washes the anger from her eyes. "Do you have a girlfriend?"

I stammer, confused. But then Stacy laughs and shoves me away. "You should see your face!" She flicks her cigarette butt at me and nods at something across the street. "Looks like you got customers."

Two figures on bicycles, circling the ice cream hut like they're laying siege to it. These are not customers.

Kevin leans over the handlebars, impatient for me to cross the street. "Where the hell you been?"

"Nowhere." I duck back to my station, passing under the wasp nest. "What's going on?"

"We called you last night." His tone is hostile. It's always hostile, but there's an edge to it now. "Liz said you weren't home."

I scoop another wasp out of the bin, flick it out the window. "Just went for a ride."

Eric pipes in. "Liz was surprised. She thought you were with us."

"Am I supposed to care what she thinks?"

Kevin leans over the grubby counter. "Where do you go at night, man? You got some girl stashed away?"

I wipe down the countertop, avoiding eye contact, trying real hard to look like I'm doing nothing and not reacting. "I wish I had a girl stashed away. I wouldn't have to hang out with you homos."

"So what? You got some new friends or something?" Eric isn't hostile like Kevin, he just looks hurt. Betrayed, maybe.

"I don't have other friends." This statement is no longer true, but it seems to satisfy them.

Kevin circles the hut again, gliding past the open window over and over. "What time you finish here?"

I tell him. Eric wants to know what we're doing tonight. Kevin shuts him down before he suggests watching movies in his basement again. Options are tossed up and shot down like clay pigeons. Egging cars from the overpass? Bang. Jumping the fence at the public pool for a midnight swim? Bang. Going to the graveyard to get high? Maybe. A whole lot of nothing is planned for tonight.

Kevin rolls out of sight again, then his voice hollers out. "Dude, why don't you knock this thing down?"

I step outside. He's squinting up at the wasp nest bulging under the eave.

"Are you blind?" he asks. "How did you not see this?"

Eric rolls up. "That's huge. No wonder there's so many wasps here."

"That's gonna be ugly when it comes down," Kevin says. He's off the bike, already gathering stones to chuck at it. "Bet I can knock it down in three hits."

"Leave it alone."

He looks at me like I'm soft in the head. Eric freezes, unsure of what to do. When Kevin gives him a nod, he gathers up a handful of stones.

"You want to work under that nasty thing?" Kevin says with disbelief. "Come on. Let's have some fun."

It's after dark. The wasps are inside the nest, bedded down for the night. They won't know what hit them if Kevin and Eric rain missiles at it.

"Just leave it," I say.

Kevin spits. "You want to get stung? What's the matter with you?"

"If you knock it down now, the wasps are gonna scramble out. They'll be all over the hut in the morning."

"Who the fuck cares?"

"I do. I gotta work here."

The disappointment on their faces is severe. This is exactly what they've been looking for to alleviate the boredom. Something destructive with a risk of getting hurt, of laughing at whoever gets stung. The stones fall to the pavement. I'm called a pussy.

The night drags on. With nothing to do, the two of them linger at the hut, scaring off any potential customers. Kevin claims to have weed on him. When I close the hut, we ride out to the bridge and spit off the side into the river below. The pot Kevin got from his brother is as harsh as mustard gas, but it doesn't get any of us high.

EMPIRE CITY

THE FARROW SISTERS are having a picnic in the dark. The three of them lie flat on a gingham blanket in the backyard, staring up at the night sky. There's a bowl of popcorn centered between them, which they all reach into. Tilly holds an antique spyglass to her eye, the brass kind that collapses. I look up, but all I see is a watery moon blurred through the gauze of clouds.

"What are we looking at?"

"The Perseids," Tilly says.

Like this is supposed to make sense to me. I almost regret coming tonight. Almost. It's been two days and all I've done is kill all the hours until I can make it back here. My plan was to go around back and jiggle the tin cans to let George know I'm here, only to find this twilight picnic. None of them are surprised to see me. Maybe Tilly predicted that I would show up.

I finally cave and ask the obvious. "What's a Perseid?"

"It's a meteor shower, stupid," Claudia says. She's annoyed that I'm here and makes no attempt to hide it. "Comes every year. Three weeks after the summer solstice."

"Oh, that Perseid," I say. "Hard to keep track of them all."

George scooches over to make room, pats the spot next to her. "Come look. Tilly, hand me the glass."

"I'm not done with it."

"Hand it over so Mark can see."

Claudia groans. "What's the point? He's not going to see anything."

Lying back, all I see is the night sky, vast and endless. A few stars cut through the haze and the moon pulses against each passing cloud. "How do you know it's tonight?"

"We don't know exactly which night," Tilly says. "We have to watch for it."

"I've never seen a meteor shower."

"Big surprise," says the oldest sister.

"Some years it's clear and bright," George says. "Other times, you can barely see it."

When she smiles at me, I have to remind myself how strange this is, lying on the lawn with the Farrow sisters, watching for falling stars. Tilly doesn't seem to mind my being here, and Claudia tolerates me for George's sake. It's like I've been accepted into a secret club. Lying next to George, I'm acutely aware of her body next to mine. It's as if her skin is giving off an electrical charge that tingles the hair on my arm. It's hard not to let my hand spider-walk across the blanket to hers. It's like being hot and cold at the same time.

"Is it supposed to be visible this time?" I turn to look at George, but her face is squared at the sky above us.

"There's no way to know until it happens."

I turn back to the void. The sheer vastness of it makes me feel insignificant and tiny. A wasp drowning in ice cream. "So what's the big deal about these Percy stars?"

"The Perseids are special," George tells me. "It's like a rip between our world and the next."

Here we go. I've gotten used to playing catch up with these girls. "Like a rip in time and space? Or reality?"

Claudia's tone is scolding. "Between the living and the dead."

"It's like Halloween," Tilly adds. "Or the night before Christmas. When the veil between the two is thinnest."

I lean up on one elbow and study the Farrow sisters lying on their backs, faces to the stars. "What happens then? The dead come back?"

"The dead don't come back. They're always here," George says. "But there's a better chance of contact when the Perseids cut the veil."

I lie back down, an inch closer to George. My arm touches hers. "Do you know how crazy you sound?"

They laugh at me and keep watching the sky. Being around them is like being told a punchline without the joke. Little makes sense. The popcorn runs out, then the chatter dies away. After a while, they get up and fold the picnic blanket. No shooting stars tonight.

George looks at me. "Let's go somewhere."

"Where?"

"Anywhere." She kicks at a pebble in the grass. "Did you bring your bike? We can just go for a ride."

Claudia collapses the brass spyglass. "I don't think that's a good idea."

"We won't be gone long," George tells her.

"You're going to get in trouble, George."

"Only if you snitch to Mother."

"I don't mean here," Claudia says. She looks toward the street, to the town beyond their gateposts. "Out there. You know what they're like. They'll hurt you."

"Whatever," George says, taking my hand and tugging me away.

We stick to the side streets, gliding under the dipping trees, and dull street lamps. The houses are quiet like dogs curled up and gone to sleep. We don't say much, coasting aimlessly, and avoiding the potholes. Eventually we run out of streets and come to the main road. We stop and watch a big tractor trailer rumble past us.

"Is this what you normally do with girls?" George asks. When her hair falls over her face, she tucks it away behind her ear. The armor comes down a little more each time. "Ride around town?"

"No."

She looks suspicious. "So, what do you do then? Do you take them to the movies? Or to Lover's Lane?"

"I don't really go out with girls that much."

She doesn't believe me, but it's true. Besides Jenny, my one and only girlfriend, the dates I've had have been dullsville. The last time I went out with a girl was back in the spring. Leah Hamilton sat next to me in history class. We joked around a lot and cheated off each other's tests. The Spring Fling was coming up, and Leah actually asked me out. Shocked, I said yes. Kevin and Eric razzed me about it for a week. I knew Leah had broken up with her longtime boyfriend the week before, but I didn't think anything of it. Big mistake. The boyfriend was at the dance that night, eyeballing Leah the whole time. "Stairway to Heaven" was the last song at every school dance, and by the time that dumb song played, Leah was back with her old boyfriend, leaving me stranded on the far side of the gym like a stupid wallflower. It was humiliating. In history class the following Monday, Leah wouldn't even look at me. I gave up after that.

I consider telling George the story, but it's too lame, too embarrassing. Looking back at the town, I'm stuck for somewhere we can go. Most places are out of the question: the movies, the pizza place, the arcade—all too busy. For a moment, I imagine walking into the movie theater with George and seeing people gawk.

"Do you like lemon meringue pie?" I ask.

George raises one eyebrow. "Who doesn't?"

"I know a place."

The Big Wheel is on the other side of the river, a half-mile outside of town on the main road, a truck stop with a huge parking lot to accommodate the big rigs. And it's open all night. I figure it's safe enough. We stash the bikes, go inside, and slip into a booth at the back. There's a few long-haul truckers at the counter, men with ballcaps and big belt buckles. A woman sits alone at a table, reading a book. No one local. We're safe here.

George studies the place, taking in every detail from the tacky souvenirs behind the counter to the old license plates on the wall. The bored expression on the waitress's face.

"I've always wondered what this place is like," she says. "It looks lonely from the outside."

"I guess it is." I look over at the truck drivers chatting with the waitress behind the counter. Lonely long-haul drivers who probably live on the other side of the country. "Everyone here is from someplace else."

We order pie and coffee. When it arrives, George tucks into the lemon meringue and her shoulders go slack. There is a tiny moan of pleasure with each bite that is so primal it makes me squirm. She agrees it's delicious and devours it quickly. This makes me weirdly happy.

"Do you bring other girls here?" she asks, dabbing a finger to collect the flakes of crust on her plate.

"No. Me and Eric and Kevin come here sometimes. The video games in the back aren't bad." I stir more sugar into the coffee. "Sometimes I come here alone."

She watches the men at the counter. "I'd come here alone too. Just to watch people and wonder who they are, where they're from."

"Like the guys at the counter?"

"Not them. The woman by herself."

The woman in the corner, reading her book. She's almost invisible.

"Maybe she works here," I suggest.

"That's boring," George says. "I bet she's on the run. Like the woman in *Psycho*."

This surprises me. "You like Hitchcock?"

"Yeah. But that movie made me mad."

Another surprise. "I thought it was cool. Especially the dead mom in the basement, all dried up like a mummy. Why did it make you mad?"

"Because Janet Leigh dies." George's plate is spotless. She takes mine, dabs at the crumbs. "She goes to all that trouble to steal money from work and drive across the country to meet her lover. Lots of risk, but she does it. She escapes, ready to make a new life far away where no one knows her. And then that little twerp takes it all away from her. That's what made me mad."

Watching her clean the plate, I think back to the girl in the grocery store wolfing down Twinkies like she was starving. George Farrow is a sugar junkie.

"I never thought about it that way," I say. "I thought the shower scene was cool."

The smirk makes her eyes squint. "You like watching naked women get stabbed?"

"Doesn't everybody?"

Both plates are clean. The coffee is gone. I dig the change out of my pocket and find six quarters. Bonanza.

"Do you like video games?"

We head to the back where four arcade consoles line the hallway to the bathrooms, and I plug two quarters into *Empire City*. I hand her one of the plastic pistols and say that all you have to do is shoot the gangsters before they shoot you. George picks it up quickly, blasting away Depression-era hoodlums with accuracy. One gangster holds a woman hostage and when George learns that you lose points killing the hostage, she squeals with delight and guns her down.

The quarters go fast, and we return to our booth. She wants more pie, so we pool all our change and find we have enough for one more slice. The coffee is bottomless.

George takes her time with the second helping, testing the meringue separately from the lemon filling. She wags her fork at me. "Individually, it's passable. But together, that's where the magic happens."

"Do you really believe in magic?" The question just comes out of nowhere.

"Of course," she says. "Belief is the crucial part. If you don't believe, then you're just making a fool of yourself."

"So the witch bottles, you believe they actually keep you safe?"

"They catch all the hatred directed at us and trap it in the bottle." She licks the lemon from her fork and inspects the tines. Then her eyes drop to mine. "Did your parents divorce?"

"No."

"Where's your mother?"

The lemon turns bitter. Everything was going so well.

"She died."

George doesn't react. She must have guessed it. "How?"

"She was sick for a while." I put the fork down and push the plate away.

"You don't like talking about it?"

"Talking about it doesn't change anything," I say. "She got sick, she died. That's all."

"Talking about it brings it all back. And that's painful." She taps the fork against her front teeth, watching me. "Do you do that with everything painful? Block it out?"

My first instinct is denial, but I catch myself first. "I guess I do. Does that mean I'm turning psycho?"

"Definitely," George says. "When did she die?"

"Three years ago."

"You didn't keep her mummified corpse in the basement, did you?"

I smile back at her. "No. But I did a bunch of stupid stuff back then. I went a little crazy, actually."

My throat constricts. I'm a hair away from vomiting the truth up all over the table. All over her. But that would destroy everything, so I swallow it back down again. It's vile-tasting, and it stings.

She picks at the pie crust with her fork, slowing down like she's lost her appetite.

"Sometimes," she says, "I wish my parents were dead."

"Don't wish that. I mean it."

"You haven't met my parents."

I look down into my cup, then back to her. "What would they do if they found out about me?"

"That would be fatal."

"Your dad would kill me?"

"No," she says. "Mother would murder you. And then she'd make me help dump your corpse in the swamp behind the house."

A ruckus pulls our attention toward the entrance. Customers pile into the truck stop and flop into a booth. Older kids, home from college. A few people I recognize and a bunch that I don't. They swarm the place, hungry for something greasy after a night of drinking. Three girls rush past us toward the bathrooms at the back.

I watch George finish the pie, humming contentedly with each bite. "You got a real sweet tooth, huh?"

She stops dabbing at the pie crumbs. "Is it gross?"

"No. I do, too."

"We're not allowed junk food at home. Mother says sugar is the mind killer."

The reference makes me smile. "I thought fear was the mind killer?"

"According to my mother, it's a poison laced into food to make the populace stupid."

The booth of rowdy people gets louder and more rambunctious, impatient for their food. Won't be long before one of them turns their attention our way. "We should go."

She agrees. "I'm just going to use the bathroom."

The lone waitress hustles to keep up with her new customers, unfazed by their dumb antics and lewd banter. I keep my head down, waiting for George to return so we can leave. But the inevitable happens, and I hear someone call my name.

"Mark Prewitt."

Travis Johnston spots me on his way to the bathroom—a gangly stretch of a guy who wanted to play basketball but never made it to college. We worked together last summer at the RV Emporium. I don't know where he works now.

"Hey, Travis."

He slides into the bench across from me. "What are you doing here?"

"Just came for some pie."

He looks down at the two plates. "Who with? Your psycho friends?"

Travis knows Kevin through Kevin's older brothers. He told me once that Kevin was trouble and said I should stay away from him. I ignored his warning.

"Just a friend," I say. "No one you'd know."

I keep one eye trained on the hallway, now dreading George's return. But I can't just blow Travis off. He's not a bad guy. "What have you been up to?"

"Working up at the stockyard, out by the Bends. You still working at the RV yard?"

I nod. My T-shirt is damp, clinging to my skin. "So far."

He laughs. "How is Mr. Dutton? Crazier than ever?"

The chitchat pings back and forth like this, rambling over nothing. I keep sweating, and Travis keeps jawing, and George still hasn't come back from the bathroom. More people swagger into the truck stop now. The lone waitress does not look happy. The woman reading in the corner has vanished.

"Take it easy, Mark." Travis unfolds his long legs from under the table and wanders to the restrooms. The relief is short-lived because George is still AWOL. I know girls take their time in the bathroom, but this is crazy and the diner's becoming dangerously crowded. Travis was a close call, but I don't want to push our luck.

I cross to the back, past the video games, where the bathrooms are. The hallway is empty. I bang on the door and holler a boy's name at the girl's bathroom.

The door swings open, and a girl who is not George Farrow comes out, big teased hair and a look of disgust on her face at finding me there.

"Is there a girl in there?"

She clicks her teeth. "What do you think, pervo? It's the girls washroom."

She walks away. I'm telling myself not to panic. Did George leave without telling me, or is she trapped in there?

To hell with it.

The bathroom is painfully bright, all fluorescent light against white tiles. George is a column of black against it, hovering over the far sink and dabbing her face with paper towel. When she looks up, I see dots of red on the coarse brown paper.

"Jesus Christ. What happened?"

She dabs her face again, trying to staunch the trickle of blood from her nose.

"Did someone hit you?"

She takes another towel without answering me, and rinses it under the cold water. Her face is red with anger and humiliation. I reach for her arm, but she pulls away.

"Don't touch me."

"Who hit you?"

She glances into the mirror and then looks away. "It doesn't matter."

My hands are vibrating and all I want to do is go out there and stab a fork into their stupid faces. But they're older, and they outnumber us. Revenge is never like it is in the movies. You can't punch up. Life just doesn't work that way.

George looks at the paper towel in her hand, deep red seeping through brown paper. "I want to leave now."

Back out to the hallway, we march straight for the exit. I glare at the raucous group at the tables, hoping to catch a guilty look from whoever attacked George, but the only one who looks up is Travis. He waves goodbye, oblivious.

We hit the gravel of the parking lot and get the bikes. There are two cars parked out front that weren't there when we arrived. One of them is a red Dodge Charger—the shark that prowls the town streets.

"Hold the bike," I say, tilting the handlebars to her.

"What are you doing?"

"Being petty." The jackknife in my pocket has a hook tool on it. Kneeling beside the Charger's front tire, I unscrew the cap from the air nozzle and use the hook tool to twist the valve out of the stem. Air hits my face in a loud hiss. I chuck the valve into the weeds, get my bike, and we ride away.

BRANDENBURG BULLDOGS

THE SUN IS punishing and there's no shade on the bleachers. Dad yells at the players on the field, barking that the play is to third. Liz plays first base on her softball team, the Brandenburg Bulldogs. She motions for Bill to pipe down as the next batter taps the dust from her cleats. My Sundays have been hijacked since Liz joined the league because Dad insists we go to each game. We need to cheer her on, he says, and show Liz some moral support. It'll be fun, he says. The first game he dragged me to, I said I couldn't recall him ever doing anything like that for Mom. He lost his shit on me, barking until his face turned red. I haven't mentioned it again, so off we go to the baseball field every Sunday like all the normal families.

It wouldn't be so bad if I actually liked the game. It's blasphemy, I know, but baseball is as exciting as watching grass turn brown in August. The whole thing just breaks down into a tedious contest between pitcher and hitter, while every other player holds their nuts and adjusts their ballcaps. That's why the TV commentators prattle endlessly about statistics, just to fill up all that dead space.

Liz is a pretty good player. She's got an eye for where the ball goes, and she's deadly at snatching a straight right out of the air. She chews gum and even spits onto the grass like a pro. Her batting average is better than most of the other women on her team. Two Sundays ago, she almost took the pitcher's head off.

There's a runner on second, and when the bat cracks, everything becomes a whirlwind. I'm dozing under the hot sun, so I miss the call. All I see is the catcher yelling at the umpire, which brings Liz rushing in to cool off her teammate before things get ugly. Most guys will loudmouth about women not being as competitive as dudes, but a few weeks into ladies baseball has completely disproved that assumption. The catcher is furious, and when she yanks the mask off, her outrage visible in her bared teeth. I have a flashback to George, teeth clenched in that same way, seething in anger.

Last night, we rode home from the truck stop in silence, George pushing ahead the whole time. She wouldn't look at me, so I lagged behind and let her lead the way. At her driveway, she let the bike crash to the pavement and stormed off. When I caught up to her, she turned on me with bared teeth, raving about wanting to kill the bitch who hit her. She didn't know the girl's name, but it didn't matter. They all deserve to die, and if there was any justice in the world, she would be the one to strike the match and burn them all in their beds.

She wanted to know why I took her to that place. Had I planned for that to happen? Did I enjoy seeing her humiliated? She jabbed my sternum and said that Claudia was right—leaving with me could only lead to disaster.

I was dumbstruck. It was like a switch had been flipped and she'd become this other person, this volcano. Everything I said only made it worse. She told me to take the bike back, that she never wanted to see it or me again.

My first thought was to just leave the damn bike where she'd dropped it, but I rolled it into the bushes near the gate. My hands were shaking on the ride home. Her anger had drained everything out of me. To be honest, it scared me. I know George is different, but for the first time I thought there was something wrong with her. Like, really wrong and wrong all the way through. I went to bed convinced that would be the last I'd ever see of George Farrow. That was two days ago.

A roar erupts from the bleachers around me. The game is over. Dad elbows me in the ribs until I join in the applause. The Bulldogs lost, seven to three. Car trunks are popped open, hibachis and lawn chairs hauled out. A team barbecue sprawls in the dry grass of the picnic area. Dad tells me to stick around for a while, in a tone that implies I don't really have a choice. He tosses me a ginger ale from the cooler.

Paper plates of burgers and potato salad are balanced on knees, and there's the constant ice tinkle of beer being fetched out of coolers. Liz leans back in a yellow lawn chair, grinning happily even though they lost. Her face is flushed, her eyes bright. She looks even younger now, which only underscores the age discrepancy between them. When Dad fishes another beer out of the cooler, Liz reminds him to go easy. They still have to drive home, she says. He dismisses that with a wave, saying it's just a short drive. When she pushes back, they bicker over it in discrete snipes. Liz lets it go before it becomes a thing.

"I don't know why you ladies always fret over nothing," Dad says, unwilling to let it go. Two of the other husbands nod like this is something profound. "It's three blocks on a Sunday," he adds. "In August, no less."

Liz picks at her plate, avoids looking at him.

Dad keeps talking. "I'll never understand this need to turn petty shit into Greek drama. Jesus."

He looks my way when he says this and then winks. Now I'm implicated in this, like the other dudes nodding along.

Liz gets up and goes to talk to one of her teammates.

The barbecue drags on, eating up the whole afternoon. I'm brainstorming excuses to leave when the sky grows overcast, threatening rain. Dad tells me to start loading the car. Ashes are dumped from hibachis, sending chalky clouds over the field. I haul the cooler to the car while Liz folds the lawn chairs, the flush from the game is long gone from her face.

"You played a good game," I say. "That one lady was so pissed when you snatched her line drive out of the air."

"I got lucky." Her smile looks forced.

"Dad says stupid stuff sometimes. He doesn't mean it."

"He just has to have the last word, doesn't he?" She drops the smile completely, nudges me with her elbow. "Hey, how's your little friend?"

Little friend. That's almost funny. Or insulting. I can't decide.

"Dunno. Haven't seen her in a few days."

"Oh. Did you have a fight or something?"

"No, nothing like that." I see Dad crossing the parking lot to the car. He's a bit wobbly. "You didn't tell Dad, did you? Or anyone?"

Liz frowns at this. "No. Not my secret to tell."

Dad leans on the fender, jingling his car keys. His way of signaling that it's time to go. Liz holds out a hand for the keys, and he hands them over without an argument.

Sunday nights are almost as boring as the days. Dad insists we have "family time," which usually means the three of us watching a movie together. We stop at Video Hut on the way home. It's Liz's turn to pick the movie, and we go home with something called *Peggy Sue Got Married*. It's about a woman who time-travels back to her high school days to rethink her life choices. Watching it, I'm wondering why anyone in their right mind would want to go back to high school, but Liz enjoys the movie. She laughs at the funny parts and tears up at the sad parts. Dad's asleep by the time the credits roll.

I retreat to my room and pull out the sketchbook. Nothing in particular, just doodling skulls or swords. My focus keeps rolling back to the fury on George's face. It was like a mask had been peeled away, revealing something she never meant to expose. I can remember a few times I've done the same thing—let something out that should have remained locked up. The shame of it felt bitter and salty.

I try to draw George's face, teasing it out with pencil strokes, but the sketch looks nothing like her. Just a girl with dark hair. I turn to a fresh page and try again. There's a moment where the eyes almost look right, but I overdo it and the result is the same. A generic face, not George.

I like her. It takes forever to admit that to myself, but I don't know if she feels the same way. I'm presuming she does, but that's not right. George is so lonely and friendless that anyone would do. I'm nothing special to her. I'm just the only friend she has.

A shiver fumbles my pencil stroke. The humidity has evaporated, the air rapidly turning cold. Which is weird because our house doesn't have air-conditioning. Dad insists it's too expensive. Something else has made the temperature drop. My skin prickles as the hair on my arm stands on end.

Now there's a smell, too. Strange, but not entirely unpleasant. Not rotting flesh or the brimstone stink of devils. It's that musty perfume oil that hippie chicks like. I can't remember the name of it. No one in this house wears that stuff.

On the ceiling above me, a single plastic moon glows among all the dead stars. That's how I know it's the sister. The dead one. She's angry at me again. So I rip out the sketch of George's face and pitch it into the wastebasket.

"Go away," I say to the cold air in my room.

The bravado is cheap because I go to bed with the light on and pull the blanket up to my nose. I'm fucking terrified.

In the morning, my left arm is throbbing from three raw scratch marks ripped red down the skin.

WEIRD FICTION

THERE ARE NO wasps in the cherry bin when I open the ice cream stand. No wasps anywhere, in fact. This is a sign—something bad has happened to George. Or will happen. I don't know which. I step outside to check on the wasp nest, thinking Kevin knocked it down, but the papery husk is still there, clinging to the gable end. Wasps walk its face, crawling in and out of the aperture. One lazily buzzes past my ear. I'm starting to think like George now, seeing omens in small things. I find this weirdly comforting.

Finding connections to George comes easily now, and in the strangest of places. Significant connections, like how we've both lost someone close to us, and smaller details like a common love for books or truck stop pie. How I feel like a freak and an impostor all the time, and how George is truly an outsider. Her belief in witch bottles and magic is no different than my old tapping rituals; both are means of protection from disaster. A weird attempt to control chaos.

I keep a running tally of all these points of connection in my head, and that leads to even wilder notions. Like maybe this is fate. Despite the odds, I wonder if George Farrow and I were meant to be together. What are the chances of me seeing her trying to shoplift a book at the grocery store? Was that fate? Even the stupid prank we pulled on the sisters becomes a gear in some divine engine. Their family car was meant to break down, so the Farrow girls had to walk into town in the first place. Fate, destiny, all that stuff.

The notion stretches too far and snaps when I consider the oldest sister. Doesn't that mean Liesl was meant to die? That can't be right. What happened to her was an accident. I'm just greedy for connections to George, and when I don't find them, I simply invent them. Like magic, it's just illusion.

I remember all that rage on her face. She doesn't want me hanging around anymore. I replay that moment over and over not just because it hurts, but because everything else just feels numb.

There is only one customer tonight—Grinning Greg, the weirdo who runs the photo booth down the next block. He buys two scoops of Tiger Tail in a cone. His eyes never stop darting around and he licks his lips a lot. Lapping at his ice cream, he asks a lot of questions about school and my job and if I like photography. He says he can teach me how to use a camera and develop film. When he says he has his own darkroom at home, my Spidey-senses tingle. Maybe this is what the wasp omen was warning me about—Greg the creepy child toucher. I'd like to tell him to get lost, but he's harmless. Maybe he isn't a diddler, just lonely. He rotates the cone around his extended tongue to keep it from dripping onto his hand. It's a vile sight. I tell him I'm closing up shop, so he wanders across the street to badger Stacy with his boring questions. I watch him, worried he'll pull something on her, but he moves away quickly. Stacy has no problem telling creeps to fuck off. She's probably had to do it her whole life.

Cashing out doesn't take long with only one pathetic sale. I make a half-assed attempt at sweeping the floor and kill the lights, eager to get out of here. When I turn to close the big shutter, I find an object on the counter that wasn't there a moment ago—a small stack of paperbacks. My own.

I scan the street, but the whole strip is quieter than a ghost town. Stepping out the door, I find George waiting in the shadow on the other side of the hut. She's holding the bike, but it's too dark to see her face.

"Hey." This is all my brain comes up with, like she's just another acquaintance. The inside of my mouth is chalky. "Why are you hiding in the dark?"

"I wanted to return your books. But you weren't supposed to see me."

"Oh." I take a step closer, wanting to see her face. "Like a ninja?"

Her shoulders shift in a shrug. "Where have you been?"

"Nowhere."

She rubs her nose. "You hate me."

"Huh? Why would you say that?"

"It's been three days," she says. "Anyway, thanks for lending me the books."

Before she moves away, I unstick my tongue from the roof of my mouth. "So what did you think?"

"Not bad," she says. "I liked how doomed Elric was. How he betrays his own people and destroys the entire kingdom."

The tragic part is what appeals to her. Figures. I gather up the books, tilt the spines to the light. There is one too many here. I check the cover of the strange paperback. A hooded figure opening her robe to reveal a skeleton underneath, the author name in bold red type—Lovecraft.

"This one isn't mine," I say, holding it up for her to see. "Must have snuck in by accident."

"No. That's for you."

"Oh. I don't read a lot of horror."

George wheels the bike closer and peers through the glass at the ice cream. "It's not horror. It's weird fiction."

I scan the cover again. "There's a difference?"

"Read it and find out." She looks the place over. "So, this is where you work, huh?"

I set the books aside, make a sweeping wave over the plywood shack. "Fancy, isn't it?"

"Give me the tour?"

I lead her inside, reach for the wall switch. "Let me turn the lights back on."

"Leave it off," she says.

This is probably for the best. The inside of the shack is even shittier than the outside. A rectangle of street light angles across the glass counter, revealing an array of smudgy handprints. George slides open the Plexiglas hatch and looks over pails of ice cream.

"Do you eat a lot of this when you're working?"

"No. It's pretty crappy." I get a plastic spoon from the tray and hold it out to her. "See for yourself."

She tries them all, turning her nose up at the orange sherbet, but goes back to the black cherry for seconds.

"The wasps like that one," I say.

She listens, the spoon stuck in her mouth, as I explain the bug corpses that have to be picked out of the bin every day. Except today, of course. She dives in for more cherry, but the little spoon breaks off in her hand. I get a waffle cone and scoop it high for her.

She dips her knees in an archaic curtsy. "Thanks."

I ask what she's been up to. Nothing much, she says. Watching the night skies but the Perseid meteor shower has yet to appear. When I ask her what that's all about, George just licks her ice cream cone in the dark and doesn't say anything.

The greasy light from the streetlamp casts two shadows on the slimy floor. She tells me that vinegar is the best way to neutralize a wasp sting. I tell her about the rat problem at the movie theater across the street and how the staff aren't supposed to talk about it. She looks out the window to read the banner on the marquee—*SpaceCamp*.

"I haven't been to the movies in a long time."

I recall her talking about Hitchcock. "Don't you like movies?"

"I love them," she says. "But we're not allowed to go to the theater. My parents think movies today are trash. They're meant to dull our brains so we don't notice how terrible the world is."

This leaves me scratching my head. "So what, you just rent movies?"

"I wish," she says with a sigh. There's a mustache of ice cream on her upper lip. "We watch them on TV. But only old movies. Classics."

"Black-and-white flicks," I say. "Like on Saturday nights?"

"Do you watch it, too?" Out of nowhere, she beams at me. "I love Elwy Yost."

A shared interest. *Saturday Night at the Movies* is a program on the educational channel, hosted by a guy with the weirdest name ever. A double-feature of classic Hollywood flicks, with Elwy interviewing the filmmakers during the intermission.

"He's pretty cool," I say. "Do you think that's his real name?"

"It's so odd, it must be." Her ice cream cone drips in the humid air. It's now a race against time as she twirls it around, tracing divots in the black cherry. "I don't think he's seen a movie he doesn't like."

"He ran one a couple of weeks ago. *The Thing from Another Planet*. Did you see that?"

"I liked it. Except for the ending."

I'm trying to remember the climax to that picture. "The monster went up in flames, right? What's wrong with that?"

Ice cream drips down her sharp knuckles. I slide the napkin carton to her.

"The square-jawed hero wins the day with fire? A caveman's tool?" She rolls her eyes. "The alien was a superior life form. By rights, it should have slaughtered them all."

Point taken. "You should see the remake. You'd like it."

"Little chance of that," she says.

A car drives past, then the street goes quiet again. George bites into the waffle cone. It's stale, so there's no crunch to it.

Across the street, the bright lights of the Palisades snap off like a death sentence. Main Street goes dark, deepening the inkiness inside the Dairy Scoop.

"I like talking to you in the dark," she says. "It's more truthful."

She's not wrong. There's a weird intimacy when you can't see the other person. Just the sound of their voice and the vague sense that they're here in the dark with you. They could be right next to you or across the room.

"I like talking to you either way," I tell her.

"But it's easier in the dark."

The air inside the hut is stuffy, and it smells of rancid cream and old lumber. It reminds me of the confessional booth, tight and claustrophobic. So I fess up.

"I'm sorry you got hurt. I never would've taken you there if I knew that would happen."

"I know."

We watch Stacy lock the front door of the theater and walk to her car. I wonder if she'll wave goodbye or even look in this direction, but she doesn't.

Gathering up the books to shove in my backpack, I take a second look at the horror title she added. "You know, I read the other one by this guy. The one you ripped in half."

She perks up at this information. "Oh? What did you think?"

"I don't get it."

"Get what?"

"The appeal. I mean, there's creepy stuff, but it's all so vague. There's no big battles between good and evil. No heroes. The characters run away or they go insane."

"That is the appeal, Mark." She smiles at me like I'm simple, a dog with its tongue lolling out. "They don't confront the terror because there's no way to understand it. It's alien, it's chaos, and it's all around us, waiting to swallow us up."

"Usually there's a balance to these things. Good and evil. Know what I mean?"

"Not in these stories." She takes the book from me, inspects the cover. "It's like everything we know is a lie. Our reality, our world, is a thin shell over a void of chaos and monsters. Alien gods lie sleeping below the sea, watching us with indifference. They can't be bargained with; they don't care about our prayers. They're just biding their time until they can plunge this world back into darkness."

I've forgotten to blink. "That's appealing?"

"Yeah. Isn't it great?"

"You're weird." I drop the books into the bag, zip it up. "Most girls I know read romance."

"That's all Claudia reads," she says. "Makes me ill."

"Love stories?"

"All that happily-ever-after stuff? Please."

"You don't buy it?"

"Do you?" she replies, folding her arms like she's offended.

"So, what? Love is just a fairy tale?"

"It is," she concedes. "It's just not a very happy one."

A stray dog crosses the empty street. It stops and regards us for a moment and then moves on.

George stirs. "Do you want to come to my house and look for meteors?"

The darkness is too cloying and this awful fluttering in my stomach won't stop. Out of nowhere, I remember the lack of wasps in the ice cream earlier. Of course, it was an omen. The only trouble is, I don't know if it was telling me to go or warning me to stay away. It's kind of a moot point, really. Like I'm going to turn down the chance to look for stars with George Farrow.

MUTUALLY ASSURED DESTRUCTION

"MY AUNT THINKS the world is going to end."

She says this out of the blue as we coast along her street. It's dark, no cars. A cat darts across the road ahead of us.

"She thinks the nukes are gonna fly?"

George weaves her bike around a puddle. "She says it's inevitable. One side or the other will panic and launch World War Three."

Both sides have enough nukes to fry the planet ten times over. And they just keep stockpiling more and more in an insane arms race. All it takes is one itchy trigger finger and we are all collectively fucked.

"I don't like to think about it," I say.

Her brakes squeal a little. I should have fixed that before I gave it to her.

"Why not?"

"Because there's nothing we can do about it. Some idiot in a bunker is going to panic and launch the missiles."

"Then the darkness will swallow us all."

George cruises ahead of me until we glide to a stop before the gates.

"Who's this aunt?"

"My Aunt Carla," she says. "She wants us to come live with her. She has a bomb shelter."

"She thinks that's gonna save her?"

"Oh, she's convinced she'll survive. She's stockpiled water and canned goods. Even gas masks. I don't have the heart to tell her she's going to burn like the rest of us when the missiles fly."

We pass through the gates and I look up at that big house. It looks abandoned—a weak light in one window.

"Are your parents home?"

George leans her bicycle against the railing. "Mother suffers migraines. She keeps the house dark when that happens."

This time we go up the veranda steps to the front door. I ask if we shouldn't go the back way.

"Father's in the back room," she says, teasing the door open. "We have to go this way. Don't make a sound."

The foyer folds into gloom as George eases the door shut behind us. There's a grand stairway in the front hall and rooms leading off both sides. George tiptoes to a doorway on the left and peeks into the room. Then she makes for the stairs, tugging me after her.

All I get is a quick glimpse of a parlor with wood paneling and old furniture. There's a figure lying on the sofa, but I can't see her face. One hand draped dramatically over a cushion. Lots of rings.

"Georgia?"

Her voice is hoarse, the way a smoker's is. There's an accent, too, but I can't tell from where.

I flatten against the wall.

George sighs and steps back into the open doorway. "Yes?"

"Why are you sneaking past me?" Mrs. Farrow asks.

I'm straining my ears, but I still can't make out that accent. Not British, something else.

"I didn't want to disturb you," George says.

There's a muffled thud, like a cup landing on carpet. "Well, it's too late for that, isn't it?" the mother says. "Have you checked the traps?"

"Yes. Nothing yet."

"That's disappointing," the mother says. "Are you using the proper bait?"

"Yes, Mother."

I hear Mrs. Farrow let out a dramatic sigh. "Very well," she says. "Would you pour me some cold tea before you go up? There's a dear."

George disappears into the parlor, and I hear the clink of glass against china. She reappears in the hallway and says goodnight to her mother. If there's a response, I don't hear it, because George is shoving me up the stairs, shushing me the whole time, which is funny because her clunky nun shoes clomp against every step. On our right is a run of framed portraits going up the wall, more stern-faced ancestors looking down in disapproval at a girl sneaking a boy into the house.

I wait until we make the landing before speaking. "What traps is she talking about?"

"We have rats."

Of course, this house has rats. There are probably bats in the attic, too. Skeletons piled high in every closet, bodies buried in the basement.

The bedroom door makes a soft click behind us. George crosses the room, pushes up the window, and chocks it with a stick. One leg over the sill, she waves at me to follow. "This way."

The window opens onto the roof over a bay window below. There's enough room for the two of us to sit and dangle our feet over the side. I lean forward to see a straight drop into the rose bushes. Above us is the gaudy vastness of the night sky with its pinprick lights and watery moon.

"No falling stars."

"It's still early," she says, bumping her shoes against the clapboard.

The moon casts everything silver, including her face. I squint but don't see any bruise or discoloration. "So what's the big deal with these Perseid things?"

"I can't say."

"You don't know or you won't tell me?"

"It's a secret," she says. "You wouldn't understand."

My back gets up. "You think I'm stupid?"

"No. You don't believe the same things I do. That's all."

We lie back and watch the sky as the crickets buzz all around us. I don't realize until now how much I've missed this. Missed her. There's no pretense with George, no pressure to conform to the cutthroat social cues of my other friends. I've been starving for this for the last three days.

"I thought I wouldn't see you again."

She stirs. "Did that bother you?"

"Yeah. It did."

"Sorry I lost my temper," she says.

"You had every reason to."

Her hands fidget, a knuckle cracks. She turns to look at me. "If we passed on the street, would you pretend not to know me?"

Out of the blue like that, she catches me off guard. My shirt feels itchy. "I don't know. Maybe."

"Yes, you do. You wouldn't have a choice."

My guts are churning at this weird urgency to blurt out things I can't tell anyone else. She wouldn't blab them to other people, wouldn't use it as a weapon against me. It's thrilling and terrifying all at the same time.

"Sometimes I do things, and I don't know why. It's like I'm floating outside of my body, watching myself doing something stupid. But I can't stop it."

George sits up, looks down at our dangling feet. "I do that, too."

Moonlight washes everything silver. Her face and hands, the quivering leaves on the trees. I can smell the marsh from here.

"A while ago, I started really acting out," I tell her. "Stupid, destructive stuff. Burning things and smashing windows and stuff. I don't know why. I knew it was wrong, but I did it anyway."

George looks at me. She may or may not have inched closer, I can't tell. "When was this?"

"A few years ago."

"When your mom died?"

"After. How did you know?"

"It's not hard to figure out."

My chest hurts, it's pounding so hard. I can't calm down and that weird feeling takes over again, like I'm floating outside of my body and watching myself do something insane. It's terrifying. "I did some really stupid shit, George. Stuff I'm ashamed of."

George leans closer the softer my voice gets. "People act out," she says. "It's normal."

"That's just it," I argue. "I'm not normal. I try to be. I pretend to be normal like everyone else, but it's just an act. It's exhausting."

She doesn't say anything, and I have no idea what she's thinking right now. The hair hides her face again, the armor back in place. This is coming out all wrong.

"I'm not a good person," I blather on. "I don't even know why you're hanging out with me."

"You're a monster," she says. "Is that what you mean?"

"Yes. No. I don't know."

"Wait here." She clambers through the window. I hear the clatter of a drawer, and then she comes back. "Hold still."

I balk at the enormous scissors in her hand. Thick metal, the handle painted blue. "What are you doing?"

"Just hold still. And close your eyes."

I can already picture the blade slicing into my windpipe, choking on my own blood as it geysers from my jugular. But I close my eyes anyway. All I hear is the snip of the blades. When I open my eyes, she's pinching a lock of hair between her fingers.

"I'm taking this," she says.

"What for?"

"Protection."

I watch her coil the hair up and slip it into a pocket. "Another spell?"

"Yes. Along with a few things I stole from your room. Put together the right way, it'll become a pact of mutually assured destruction."

Her hand grazes mine, sparking a zap from finger to shoulder socket. "Destruction?"

Her expression is flat. Dead serious. "If you hurt me, I will hurt you back."

How long have I been thinking about kissing her? The whole night or just now when she makes this threat? My brain is already working overtime to second-guess myself out of this moment.

She'll kiss you back.

No, she'll recoil in horror.

She feels the same way.

No, you're imagining it. She doesn't feel the same way at all.

Open your eyes. She likes you.

I'm just a friend. Her only friend.

I lean in and dive straight off the cliff. She stiffens like wood, but doesn't pull away. Her eyes stay open. Then she pushes in. I taste her breath and I feel drunk. Her teeth bite down on my bottom lip, frying my brains. It's a clumsy, awkward kiss.

It is fucking glorious.

I open my eyes, but her face is too close, her eyes intense like she's trying to mind-meld. Out of breath, my heart clangs hard like a trapped bird.

"I liked that," she says.

"Me too."

There's a sudden ruckus at our backs. And then her sisters barge in and ruin everything.

Tilly looks at me curiously.

Claudia is outright hostile. "What is he doing here?"

George pulls away, acting like nothing happened. "We're watching the sky. That's all."

"Are you blind?" Claudia spits. She points up. "Look."

There's nothing to see at first, then a tiny spark streaks across the black before burning out. Followed by another and another.

"The Perseids," Tilly says. "They're here."

George is already on her feet. "We have to hurry."

I'm as confused as ever around these three. I follow George back through the window. "What's going on?"

Tilly's pushing me to the door. "You have to leave," she says. "We have a lot to do."

I plant my feet on the carpet. "Why? What's the big deal?"

Claudia stares me down. She's taller than I am. "Just leave, Mark. Before you ruin everything."

"Ruin what?" I turn to George. "What are you up to?"

Tilly catches the mischievous twist on George's face. She tugs her wrist. "Don't tell him."

George just keeps grinning at me. In the window behind her, another meteor flares and dies.

"We're having a seance," she says.

WHITE CANDLE, RED CANDLE

SEANCE. I LAUGH out loud. I can't help it. "You're shitting me. Right?"

They are not shitting me. Claudia's shoving me out the door, telling me to leave. Tilly says they need to act quickly.

"Mark stays," George says. This is a statement, not a request.

Claudia won't hear of it. "No. He'll ruin everything."

"He's part of it now."

"It won't work with him here, George," Tilly says. "Having a boy in the room will keep her away."

Claudia gloats. "See?"

George won't budge. It's a stand-off. "I disagree. Mark's presence will help bring her close."

"It will scare her off."

"She liked boys, remember?"

Tilly also agrees with this. I can't tell who's side she's on.

This isn't a game they're playing or a joke at my expense. The fact that they are serious about this makes my blood run cold. I stick my nose into it. "Hold on," I say. "Are you talking about Liesl?"

The Farrow sisters frown like I'm a simpleton. Not far off the mark, I suppose.

Tilly rolls her eyes. "Who else would we hold a seance for?"

My hands are up, calling a time-out. "You really want to contact your dead sister?"

Disgusted at the delay, Claudia marches out of the room. "We're wasting time. He's your responsibility, George. Keep him on a leash."

A consensus is reached and just like that, I'm in. I'm not sure if I want to be, but my curiosity is itching me. I follow them across the hallway into another room, only to stop cold in the doorway. I recognize this room from my first trip into this house.

The walls are tacked with band posters and pictures torn from magazines, like any regular bedroom. There's a record player under the window with a stack of albums leaned up against the baseboard. On the desk in the corner sits an open textbook, loose sheet music, and an old Polaroid camera. A blue ribbon hangs from a nail on the wall. I get the sense that nothing has been touched in this room for a long time. The bedroom of the dead sister has been preserved like the tombs of Egyptian kings. Sacred and forbidden. The four of us are grave robbers.

George is already lighting candles, while Claudia opens the curtains to expose the night sky and its falling stars. Tilly rolls up the small braided rug to clear space on the hardwood floor.

There's an odor in the room that's nagging at me, but I can't place it—heavy and musky. "What's that smell?"

"Patchouli oil," George says. "It was her favorite."

The hippie chick perfume. Like the posters and the records, it clashes with the Gothic gloom of this old house. Who was this girl? Was she the black sheep of the family? I watch the three of them push furniture out of the way and dim the lights. Christ, they are actually going through with this.

"Guys, this is crazy." I'm not trying to be disrespectful. I just think this is a bad idea. "A seance? Come on. Why would you want to contact your dead sister?"

"Because we love her," Tilly replies in that matter-of-fact way that only kids can pull off.

"And we miss her," Claudia adds. "We need to know if she's okay."

George checks the window as a fingernail of light scratches the sky. "Let's sit down. Claudia, hand me the sweater. Tilly, you sit on the north point of the circle."

They've done this before. Each sister settles into their prescribed place in a circle on the floor. George motions for me to sit next to her. Tilly sets two candles on the floor before us, one red, one white. Claudia opens a dresser drawer and sits down with a sweater in her hands. Hand-knit army green with a red Soviet star on the front. This further muddies the question of who Liesl Farrow was. Claudia tugs at a loose thread on the sweater, pulling at it like she means to unravel the whole thing. The loose wool spools over her knee in a heap.

My mouth is dry. "What's with the sweater?"

George ignores the question, turns to her sisters. "That's long enough, Claudia. Tilly, the scissors."

Out come the same metal shears George used to snip my hair. They're so huge they make George's hand look like a child's as she pops them open and cuts the line of wool.

"What's that for?" I ask.

Claudia untangles the loose thread. "Everyone's lifespan is dictated by the three Fates. Even the gods. This thread represents Liesl's, cut too short."

"Unfurl it," George says. "Make sure there's enough to go around."

The thread is passed around the circle, including me. Each sister loops it around her left wrist.

Tilly points at the thread in my hand. "You too, Mark. Like this."

I follow her lead, twisting it around my wrist. Now we are all linked by the thread of a dead girl's garment. George ties the end, closing the circle. A dozen questions itch the end of my tongue, but the solemn mood strangles my stupid questions for now. The twine links us without the need to hold hands. Which is for the best, since my palms stay clammy no matter how many times I wipe them on my jeans.

"Tilly," George says, "will you light the candles?"

A box of wooden matches is produced, the one with the black cat logo. Tilly strikes one and lights the white candle first, then the red.

"We're ready." George takes a deep breath before she goes on. "Everybody, clear your mind. Don't just think about Liesl, feel her. Our love for her is what will bring her close."

Tilly opens her eyes. "What about Mark? He didn't know her."

"Just think of her name, like you're calling her," George says. She squeezes my wrist to caution me. "But be careful with your feelings. We only want to call Liesl, not someone else. Okay?"

I nod like this is a given, and George closes her eyes. Is she afraid I'll accidentally summon my mom's spirit instead of Liesl's? I dislike George at this moment, but the seance is rolling on, so I just go with it. It's what I always do, anyway.

It's quiet for a long time. Long enough for me to start feeling stupid. And then George speaks.

"Tilly, is she here?"

The youngest sister focuses on the candles. "Something is here," she whispers. "Liesl? Are you with us?"

All three sisters hold their breath. Even the crickets in the yard have shut up. Tilly calls her sister's name again.

I feel George tense up. "Liesl? The white candle is for yes. The red is for no."

Fuck me. The white candle just bloomed taller than the other one. I swear to God, I just saw it. The open window—the breeze must have fluttered the flame. There is a tug on the string around my wrist.

George looks at me and whispers, "Don't fight it. Just go with it. Okay?"

I nod, but when I look at Tilly, I'm ashamed. There are tears in her eyes.

"Liesl," Tilly says. "Are you okay? Are you in pain?"

The red candle flares hot for a moment.

Claudia's lip is trembling. She swallows. "Are you trapped here? Are you afraid to move on?"

The red candle glows again.

"Are you watching over us?" George asks. When the white candle rises this time, I suddenly do not want to be part of this. But I can't just run for the door. What happens if I break the circle?

George continues with her questions. "Are we in danger?"

The white again. Yes.

"From who?"

"She can't answer that," Tilly says.

George frowns.

Claudia narrows her eyes at me. "Is it Mark?"

My turn to hold my breath, but nothing happens, as neither wick changes.

Disappointed, Claudia continues. "Are you mad there's a boy here?"

There's still no response.

George looks worried. "Have we lost her? That was too soon."

"No, she's still here," Tilly says. "I think she wants to talk about something else."

Claudia sits up straight. "Did someone murder you?"

"Claudia!" Tilly scolds.

The room goes real cold, real fast. None of the girls seem to notice it. Nothing happens for a moment, and then a response burns from the red candle. A shudder runs through all three sisters, a collective exhale of breath.

Claudia sighs at the ceiling. "Did you fall asleep behind the wheel?"

Red. No.

George's face tips into a frown. "Was it an accident?"

Both candles burn equally. The girls trade glances.

"That doesn't make sense," George says.

A frightened look falls over Tilly's face. "What if it's not Liesl?"

That sends a chill through all of us.

"Don't say that," George scolds. "It has to be her."

"Was someone involved in your death?" Claudia asks.

Nothing changes for a long time, then a slight flicker. I can't be sure, but I think the white candle fluttered.

"Was that a yes?"

Claudia says, "Maybe she doesn't want to talk about it."

Tilly's eyes go to the window. "I don't see any more falling stars. We're going to lose her."

"Already?" Claudia looks to George. "Can we ask about us?"

"I don't think we should."

The white candle rises hot.

"Okay," George says. "One question each. And then we say goodbye."

Her voice sounds brittle, as if the seance is wearing her down. I feel it too. It's like my energy is being sapped out of me.

Tilly nods at Claudia. "Oldest first."

Claudia bites her lip. "Will I ever be published?"

A glow from the white candle.

Then it's George's turn. "Will I go to university?"

Another yes. Tilly hesitates, like she can't decide what to ask. "Will Mother and Father ever get better?"

The flare of the red candle flattens the air in the room. George and Claudia share a quick glance, but neither says a word. I turn to the window, but I don't see any more falling stars. The sound of the crickets resumes from the yard.

"Say goodbye," George says. "We have to end the session properly."

Tilly sits up, looking worried. "What about Mark? He didn't get a turn."

"He doesn't get to ask a question," Claudia snaps.

"He's part of this." George tugs the thread on my wrist. "Go on. Ask a question."

"It's okay," I say. I just want this to be over. "I don't need a turn."

Tilly is adamant that the seance be fair. George urges me to be quick. Claudia becomes impatient, so I lob a question without really thinking about it.

"Will I ever get out of this town?"

The red candle doesn't just glow, it flares up twice its height. Wax spills down the side and drips onto the floor. No one says anything, and then the outside world resumes its normal racket of crickets and croaking bullfrogs.

The scream, when it comes, makes all of us jump. The wool thread snaps, breaking the circle. My balls shrivel up because the dead sister is really here, shrieking at us from beyond the grave.

Except it isn't Liesl. We were so wrapped up in the seance that no one heard the footsteps in the hallway or the door pushing open. All we heard was the mother shrieking at us to get out of Liesl's room.

TOWNIE-TRASH

WE'RE MARCHED DOWNSTAIRS and lined up against the wall like prisoners awaiting the firing squad. The Farrow sisters are mute and trembling before their outraged mother. She's a garish sight, flapping about in a teal mumu with a gold bird print. Her straw-colored hair tilts in a limp beehive, the eyelashes absurdly long, like caterpillars crawling over her face. She doesn't look that old, but everything about her seems cast from some other era, petrified and fraying at the edges.

Her voice is raw from berating the girls for violating the sanctity of their sister's room. How could they? What were they thinking? It's almost a verbatim recital of my own father's rants.

"Haven't we suffered enough?" she wails. "Where have we gone wrong with you three?"

The sisters hang their heads, eyes firmly on the floor. They don't dare look up at their mother now. Not a side-glance in my direction, not even from George. Her face is red with shame.

Then the mother's anger finds me, a finger jabbing in my direction. "And this! This bully-boy in my home." She leans close, all clenched teeth and caterpillar lashes. "Who are you? What's your name?"

My jaw locks tight. I should have made a run for it when I had the chance.

"Speak up!"

"Mark." It blurts out like a reflex through gritted teeth.

"Mark what?"

"Nobody."

The slap is sharp and stinging against my cheek. Then she goes off again, the long sleeves of her mumu flapping about. Spittle flicks from her chomping teeth. "And what are you doing in my house, Mark Nobody? Did you come sniffing after my girls?"

"No." I should have added a *ma'am*, but it's too late. The woman is crazy. I need to get the hell out of here.

She jabs my chest with a scarlet fingernail. "You had better not be. Because I will castrate you otherwise."

"Look, I'm sorry. I got to go."

Her rage evaporates, and she becomes weirdly calm. Her hand clamps over my shoulder. "If you're not here for them, why are you here? Did you come to spy on us, Mark Nobody? Come to scout our defenses and report back to those brutes in town? Did you come to smash a window?"

My eyes flip to the sisters for a lifeline, a rope to grab onto, but they all keep their heads down.

"Maybe you came to start a fire to smoke us out? For all the townies to laugh at. Is that it?"

"No. It's not like that."

"What were you doing in Liesl's room? Did you come here to steal something, some souvenir to flaunt to your cronies?"

I look away, unable to bear the ferocity of her eyes. Anything I say at this point will only deepen my grave, so I clam up, stare at the floor.

Her anger pivots back to her three daughters. "Why were you all sitting in a circle like that? Answer me."

No one speaks.

Like any good interrogator, George's mother zeroes in on the weakest link in the chain. She grips Tilly's arm and shakes her. The girl's face is wet with tears.

"We just wanted to talk to her," Tilly sobs. "That's all."

"A seance?" Mrs. Farrow reels back, hands covering her mouth in horror. "Please tell me none of you are that stupid."

Tilly tries to respond, but her sobs render her speech unintelligible.

"Tell me!"

Tilly dissolves into a racking, trembling mess.

Her mother is oblivious as she whiplashes between all three girls. "Whose idea was this?" She levels a deadly eye on her middle child. "This reeks of you, Georgia. Was it your idea?"

The muscle in George's jaw flexes. I watch her marshal everything she's got to keep herself upright, eyes down, fists tight. She says nothing.

The mother's rage rolls downhill back to me, those mollusk eyes flaring hot. "Then it was you, wasn't it? This whole seance idea. You put my daughters up to this, didn't you?"

"What? No."

Another whoosh of the sleeves as she pounces on her daughters. "Well? Was it him? Look at me."

I watch Claudia nod. Tilly follows suit. George keeps her head down, saying nothing, and her silence pushes me over the cliff as the scapegoat. I'm furious, but the terror on the sister's faces throws cold water on my rage. It's the smarter move to blame me. I don't have to live under this roof. They do.

"Why?" Mrs. Farrow comes back around to me. Her bony fist shakes before my face. All those rings could do a lot of damage. "Why torment us like this? It's not enough you people took my Liesl away, but now you want to salt the wound, too. What is wrong with you people? You're all monsters."

She waits for an answer, but I don't have one. Then the gavel comes down in judgment as she recoils in disgust. She summons a name from the darkness. Nathan. The father.

A voice tumbles in from the shadowed hallway—male, menacing. "I heard."

He's taller than I am, but wiry like coiled rope, shirtsleeves rolled to his biceps, his tie askew. Dirty hands and a buzz cut. He looks like a NASA engineer who stopped for happy hour on the way home. And the way he's glaring at me means that this isn't just a beating I'm in for; this man wants to kill me.

"Do something," his wife demands, pressing a hand to her brow.

"Come with me," he says, gripping my elbow and walking me out the front door.

George looks terrified. All three of the sisters do, but it's George who speaks up. "Father…"

"Not a word, Georgia!"

Down the front steps to the flagstones we go. There's no porch light and the weeping willows blot out the street lamps. His face is cold, like chiseled marble. The gateposts aren't that far away. If he takes a swing, I'll bolt for the street.

"Who sent you?"

"No one." It's an honest answer.

"Was it Pastor Beecham? Or those cowards on the town council?"

"No one sent me. Honest."

He folds his veiny arms, studying me. My whole body is vibrating in anticipation of a punch. I'm crap at fighting.

"What's your name?" His hand comes up, index finger raised in warning. "If you say 'Nobody,' I will smash that look off your dumb face."

"Mark Prewitt."

"Where do you live, Mark Prewitt?"

What does that have to do with anything? "Across town," I say. "On Prospect Street."

"What number?"

Oh shit. He wants to know who to confront about this. The thought of him talking to my dad scares me more than a beating, but I cough it up all the same. "Thirty-two."

Satisfied for the moment, Mr. Farrow looks past the gates to the street. "What were you doing in my house?"

"Nothing. Just hanging out."

"With my daughters?"

"Just George. We're friends."

His gaze rotates back to me and it's pure murder. "You expect me to believe that my Georgia is friends with townie-trash like you?"

"It's true—"

I'm flat on my back so fast I'm not even sure what happened, some Chuck Norris combination of a hard shove and a sweep to my legs. Wham. I'm more shocked than hurt. Humiliated, I glance at the house but can't tell if George is watching.

He calls me a liar. I get up and walk away. He orders me to come back. I don't run until I'm past the gatepost and out of sight of the house.

CRAZY TRAIN

I CONNECT THE dots, seeing the chain of events that explains just how disturbed the Farrows of Merrily Road are. It all traces back to the dead daughter. The family was always strange, eccentric weirdos from a different social class who considered themselves better than us townies. Then tragedy strikes and an already unconventional family is plunged into a tailspin of grief from which they never recover. The parents become paranoid and hostile to the outside world, believing their eldest daughter was murdered. They pull the remaining children from school and draw up the gates, fill the moat with crocodiles. Isolated, they just get worse, believing the people in town are plotting to kill them, that the government is out to get them. Secluded from the outside world, the Farrow sisters become strange. George practices witchcraft and

Tilly believes she's psychic. All three of them believe the spirit of their dead sister watches over them like some kind of guardian angel.

What is a ghost, anyway? A restless spirit out for revenge or a soul trapped here because the grieving won't let go? Is it just a guilty conscience? I don't like ghost stories. It's always the need for vengeance that drives the ghost, and that's the part that scares me. The skeletal hand reaching up from under the bed or the ghastly face in the bathroom mirror, pulling the guilty into the darkness behind the shower curtain.

In the morning, I'll convince myself the seance was bullshit—a trick of the light or a breeze fluttering the candle. But lying here in the dark, I'm not so sure. Did the dead sister really return as the meteors were falling outside the window? Is she watching over the family or is she hungry for revenge?

I've been nursing a sting of betrayal since the sisters let me take the blame for the seance. George, especially. But I know why they did it. What must it be like living under that roof with those parents? Being crazy is one thing, but those two seem dangerous. I can see why George is desperate to get out of that nuthouse.

Did I imagine the kiss? No, I can still smell her unwashed hair and feel the skull-jarring clunk when our teeth bumped together. Cold shivers and hot hands, the lightheaded feeling of being drunk. Am I really falling for the girl everyone hates? What would people think if they knew? They would reach for the nearest rock to stone me to death.

How do I even know if I'm falling for her? I don't think I felt anything for Jenny Kroger when we went out. Don't people in love walk around in a goofy daze? TV gets everything wrong. There's one thing I'm sure of; if I'm falling for Georgia Farrow, I am screwed. The weight of that secret is thrilling and terrifying at the same time, like holding onto a grenade all day. Everything is fine as long as I don't relax my grip.

In the morning, I find another book pushed from the shelf. The Lovecraft book that George lent me. The book smells weird, a thick musky scent. I drop it when I recognize the smell of patchouli. I scrub my hands in the bathroom sink because I don't want to think about ghosts anymore.

My shift at the RV Emporium is a disaster. I bash my thumb with a hammer and crack a window on a Winnebago. I'm so distracted and out to lunch that Silvio, the mechanic, asks me if I'm high. Worst of all, Mr. Dutton lets me practice parking a trailer, but I screw it up so bad he loses his patience, orders me out of the pickup, and parks the rig himself. Quitting time can't come soon enough.

How much trouble is George in? I imagine her with a black eye or locked in a closet like a prisoner. Maybe her father lost his mind and killed her, burying the body out in the woods next to one of her own witch bottles.

On the way home, I bike across town to Merrily Road and coast slowly past the brick gateposts. I'm hoping to catch a glimpse of her in the window or, better yet, on the front veranda. I don't even need to talk to her—a wave will do. Something so I know she's okay.

A figure rises from the wicker chair on the porch, but it's not George. Mrs. Farrow slips her sunglasses down her nose, trying to see who's skulking at her gates.

I keep rolling.

"Stuffed poblanos," Dad announces.

He's in the kitchen with his shirtsleeves rolled up, a dishtowel flung over one shoulder, slaving over a hot stove. I must have walked into the wrong house.

"What's the occasion?" Liz asks, dropping her bag by the door. We get home at the same time, both puzzled at the clatter of pots and pans as we walk through the door.

"Nothing special," Dad says. "I got home early, thought: what the hell?"

I have no idea what stuffed poblanos are, but the smell from the oven is surprisingly good. I'm still trying to square the image of my old man making dinner. He cooked for Liz a few times when they were dating, showcasing a skill I never knew he had. Before that, he never set foot in the kitchen. Mom even fixed his coffee for him. That's how bad he was when it came to anything he labeled "women's work." I have no idea who this stranger is setting the table and peeking into the oven to check on this exotic-sounding dish. If he puts on an apron, my head is going to explode.

What's he up to? Is this because Liz is younger and he has to try harder? Does that mean Mom wasn't worth the effort? Or she didn't demand it?

Last winter, Dad had made a huge screw-up by calling Liz by Mom's name. It was an accident. He was under the sink, replacing the old faucet, cursing up a storm like he does with every repair job. He thrusts out a hand and says, "Nancy, hand me a rag, will ya?" Liz froze. I looked up from my homework. When no rag appeared, Dad poked his head out from under the sink and realized his gaff. He went pale, apologized. Liz waved it away, saying it was no big deal. But later that day, the two of them went into the bedroom and closed the door. I couldn't hear what they were saying, but the tone was clear enough. She was hurt, and he was apologizing. He's never made that mistake again.

Maybe Mom was a doormat. Maybe Dad was just an asshole back then. I don't know.

The poblanos turn out to be beef and rice stuffed into a hollowed-out pepper and baked until the whole thing is steaming. Liz and I are both impressed. The old man grins proudly and proceeds to bore us with the details of how he made it. A bottle of red is uncorked, and Dad even splashes a little into a glass for me. Too tart for my liking. The dinner is going so well I'm about to ask if he'll share a beer with me, but then the phone rings and everything goes to hell.

Dad loathes phone calls during dinner, usually forbidding anyone from answering it. This time, he just frowns when Liz gets up. She holds the phone out to him. "It's for you."

"At this hour? Better not be work."

All the laughter drains out of Liz's face. A quick glance in my direction follows. "It's Mr. Farrow."

My guts drop through the chair and splatter across the linoleum. Confused, Dad takes the phone and stretches the cord all the way across the kitchen and into the hallway. He doesn't say much. "Yes. I see. I understand. Won't happen again." *Click.*

Liz pretends to eat, but I can see she's rattled. My heart is jack-rabbiting. I can't believe that asshole called to rat me out.

Dad sits down and reaches for his wine, takes a long slow a sip. He's a master at the dramatic pause before an outburst. All I can do is hold my breath.

"What the hell were you thinking?" The disappointment on his face is biblical. "The Farrow girls?"

It's worse than I imagine. According to Mr. Farrow, I broke into their house to get my hands on his daughters. The middle one, specifically. The word "rape" isn't said aloud, but it's implied. Mr. Farrow also informed Bill Prewitt that his son is into some dangerous occult practices. Was he aware, Mr. Farrow wanted to know, that his son is a Satan worshiper? The call ended with Mr. Farrow warning my dad that if he caught me in the house again, he wouldn't have any choice but to defend his family from a degenerate.

My response, as usual, is the wrong one. "You know he's crazy, right?"

The plates jump as Dad's fist hits the table. Liz tells him to go easy, but the look he gives her is murderous and silencing. His son, his rules.

"Why," he wants to know, "would you go anywhere near those people?" He waits, like there's an answer to this question. Liz keeps her eyes on her plate. "Do you have rocks in your head? What are people going to think if my son is palling around with the Farrows?"

"I hadn't thought of that." This is a stone-cold lie. It's all I think about. "They're not bad people. At least, the sisters aren't."

Dad looks at Liz and shakes his head. "Can you believe this? How the hell do you even know them?"

I shrug. He hates when I do that. "I dunno. I just got to know George."

"George? Who the hell is George?"

"Georgia. The middle one."

Dad fumes. "So you snuck in there to get your mitts on George? Is she queer?"
He's asking if I'm queer. "No!"

Silence rises around the table, swallowing all of us. Liz tries to dial down the temperature. "What's she like?"

"Liz," he snaps, shutting her up. He reaches for the wine bottle, fills his glass. "Did you touch that girl?"

"We're just friends."

"You're just friends?" The sneer in his voice could cut glass. "The kind of friend who plays with Ouija boards and raises demons?"

"We were just goofing around." I really need to keep my mouth shut instead of digging my own grave. "The seance was their idea, not mine."

"Seance?" Liz says. Her face turns three shades of pale. "Oh no. Not the dead sister?"

"Jesus Christ!" Dad explodes. "No wonder the man's upset. How stupid are you?"

Liz covers her mouth. "That poor girl. No wonder she looks so sad."

I glare at Liz with all the venom I can muster. She blusters, trying to walk it back, but the damage is done.

Dad glares at his new wife. The wine glass slowly settles on the table. "You knew? You knew and didn't tell me?"

"Bill…" Her voice trails off without saying anything more.

He gets up, taking the glass with him. "The two of you," he snarls. He's about to walk away, but then he turns on me, spilling wine on the floor. "You are grounded! Work, home. That's it."

I don't even bother protesting. Dad walks away. A moment later, I hear the TV come to life.

Liz looks like she's going to be sick. I tell her I'm sorry.

"I've only got myself to blame." She folds her napkin and drops it on the table. "I never should have kept it secret."

She takes her wine out to the back patio. I look down at the remains of dinner. One untouched poblano sags on the platter. My turn to do the dishes.

MAROONED

GROUNDED FOR THE week. How lame. First chance I get, I test the boundaries, but the old man comes down hard.

"Don't push your luck," he says. "Break curfew and I will sell that damn car of yours in a heartbeat. Better yet, I'll take it to the wreckers myself and watch them demolish it."

When I protest, he reminds me that the name on the pink slip is his. He can do anything he wants with it. He'd love nothing more than to get the car out of here so he could have his garage back. So I fall in line, coming straight home after work and making excuses to my friends about why I can't hang out. When they ask why I'm grounded, I make up a story about calling Liz a bitch and they eat it up without question. My nights are spent in the garage working on the Galaxie, partly to spite the old man. The ignition switch is a little wonky, but I got a replacement from the parts supplier at work. Swapped out the old one for the new, and now it starts up fine. The engine doesn't run for long before the faulty fuel pumps kills it. Seems like I'll never find a replacement for that damn part. I fix the dashboard lights, scrub the interior spotless. The car's looking prettier each night, but without a working fuel pump, it's just a giant paper weight.

So I'm stranded on a desert island waiting for a message in a bottle, but nothing washes ashore. I look for George when I'm at the ice cream hut, hoping she'll pedal up on Christine's old bike, but she never shows. The wasps have stopped buzzing around the bins completely, which worries me. The titles on the movie marquee change, but no *RoboCop* appears. Stacy even comes over to visit me, asking if anything's wrong. I'm tempted to tell her. She's a girl; she might have some advice. But I can't trust that she won't blab it all over town. Still, it's nice that she senses something is wrong.

George's book waits on my desk. I read it. It's weird. Not the kind of stuff I normally read. A geological expedition to Antarctica uncovers the ruins of a city built by prehistoric gods. The crew is slaughtered by the awakened monsters, and the few survivors are driven insane by the experience. The other stories in the book are equally strange and disturbing. There are no heroes, no titanic battles between good and evil. It's more like evil piled on top of more evil, poisoning everything. Not what you'd expect from an author named Lovecraft. Still, there's something almost thrilling about reading a book that George loves. A shared experience. It's a kind of magic in itself.

Two days into my punishment, I ride past the Farrow house on my way home. The windows are all dark like the place is empty and, for a moment, I panic, thinking the family has moved away. Turns out this isn't the case. The next night I see the Farrow family station wagon rolling down Main Street. Mrs. Farrow is behind the wheel, one hand out the window flicking a cigarette as she drives past the Dairy Scoop. I'm relieved they haven't moved away, but disappointed to see that the family car has been fixed. That means the sisters won't be walking to the grocery store anymore.

Dad doesn't notice that I'm getting home later each night. This is usually how punishment unravels around here. My old man's all adamant the first few days, but then it tapers off until it's forgotten about. On the third night, I push my luck further and ride to the creek behind the Farrow property—a sneak attack from behind. I wade through the creek to the wooded area where the witch bottles are buried. The bear trap is still there, the rusty iron jaws waiting to amputate a stray foot. I watch the house for a while, hoping to catch a glimpse of George in a window, but every curtain is drawn.

I miss her. That's all there is to it. I even miss her weird sisters. Out of every girl in town, I'm drawn to the one locked away like a prisoner in a tower. The irony isn't even funny. I suppose it's karma for the terrible thing I've done.

I need to know that George is okay and not chained up in the basement. What if they're all dead? What if that lunatic killed his own daughters and buried them out here in the woods? I could be kneeling over George's unmarked grave right now and not even know it.

Stop it.

The alarm system is still in place. I prod the fishing line, jangling the tin cans together, hoping George will hear it and come running. At the very least, she'll know I'm out here. Nothing happens, then more nothing. I wait until the back door flings open at last, but I hit the dirt when I see it's Mr. Farrow. Was that a shotgun in his hands? I don't wait to find out, running for the creek as fast as I can.

I race home, trying not to think about George being buried in the back forty or how late I am. I catch a break because Dad's car isn't in the driveway yet. Liz is in the kitchen when I barge in out of breath.

She rolls a conspicuous eye at the clock. "That's cutting it close. You're lucky your dad isn't home yet."

"Traffic was a bitch."

She doesn't find this funny. "I don't want to have to make excuses for you. Okay?"

"Fair enough."

Light flares up in the kitchen window, Dad's Buick pulling into the driveway. He likes to make a racket when he gets home from work, dropping his keys on the counter while letting rip an epic sigh that translates to: *You wouldn't believe the day I had.* It's a routine I don't even notice anymore.

Liz opens a beer and sets it down in front of him as he flops into a chair. "Tough day?"

"The usual shitshow," he says, patting her behind. "You?"

"Oh, it was very exciting," she says. "Darryl plowed the forklift into the shelves, knocking down a fortune in inventory. We lost the whole day just cleaning up the mess."

"How does that idiot still have a job?" He laughs, chugging down his beer. Then he looks at me, sweaty and red-faced across the table. "Did you go jogging?"

"Ten miles." I head for the hallway. "Later."

"Hold on, sport." He waves me back. "You working Sunday?"

"At the Scoop. Not 'til four."

"Good. Your grandmother called again. I told her you'd visit Sunday."

"Grandma Jean?" I deflate like a punctured tire. "Why didn't you ask me first? What if I had plans?"

"What plans? You're grounded. Besides, you've put it off long enough. Bring her some danishes or something. She'll like that."

I don't try to hide how much I hate him right now. "What, you're not coming with me?"

"She sure as shit doesn't want to see me." He laughs and looks at his new wife, but she just looks away. I guess Liz doesn't find it funny either.

STRAWBERRY-RHUBARB

THE LAST TWO nights of my penance are spent keeping an eye out for George and trying to think of an excuse to get out of visiting my grandmother. I fail at both, and when Sunday rolls around, I'm convinced I'll never see George again. I'll never get to tell her the truth.

Grandma Jean lives in the next town over, in an old farmhouse with a row of pine trees lining the driveway. I call her Grandma Jean to differentiate her from my dad's mom, which is stupid because I hardly see either of them. The ride to Grandma Jean's is two hours on the bike. Dad promised he'd drive me there.

"If the Galaxie was on the road, I could drive myself," I tell him over breakfast. "Maybe you could help me find a new fuel pump?"

"Nice try," he says, snapping the newspaper straight. "You want that car, you find the parts. And foot the bill for it, too."

The phone rings and our plans fall apart—an emergency at work. Dad has to go into the office. Relieved, I say something stupid about postponing the visit with Grandma Jean.

"Not a chance," he says. "You're going. Liz will drive you."

Liz looks up from her newspaper. She's still in her pajamas and is not happy about having her Sunday morning hijacked. "I can't do it," she says. "Grandma Jean hates me."

"She doesn't hate you," my dad counters.

"Then she disapproves of me in the strongest way possible." Liz turns her attention back to the paper. Discussion over. "No, thank you."

I tell them I'll just take the bike. Dad wields his patented look of disappointment and the two of them bicker over it until Liz folds the newspaper with a frustrated sigh and goes to get dressed.

For someone who is meticulous about her appearance, Liz's gray Tercel is a junkyard of old coffee cups and crumpled candy wrappers. She doesn't even apologize over its state, sweeping the mess off the passenger bucket so I can sit. Dad refuses to go anywhere in her vehicle. He only drives American, he says. The suspension in this little Toyota isn't hot, and we feel it thumping over the trestle bridge that Eric and Kevin and I leapt off of earlier this summer. No one's jumping off it now. The August water level in the creek is way too low.

"Sorry you had to drive me."

"That's okay," she says, shifting the gear stick. She's offered to teach me how to drive manual, but I haven't taken her up on it. "It's a nice day for it."

We don't say much on the drive. Old farmhouses pass by in the window, then fields of yellowing timothy and tall corn stalks. Horses flicking their tails in the sun. Everything is slower out here in the countryside.

The ashtray is full of cigarette butts. Liz pushed it closed when I got in, hoping I wouldn't notice. But I see her tapping her fingers on the steering wheel, getting antsy.

"Go ahead."

She does a poor job of pretending to be puzzled. "Pardon?"

"Go ahead and smoke," I tell her. "I won't tell."

She sighs in defeat, nods at the dashboard. "There's a pack in the glove box."

I hand them over and she lights up. She blows out a long plume of smoke.

"Don't ask for one, okay?"

"I don't smoke." I watch the remains of a dead skunk on the side of the road zip past the window. "It's not that big a secret, really."

Liz relaxes, one hand draped over the steering wheel, the other flicking ash out the window. "I quit last winter, but sometimes I fall off the wagon. I just don't want your dad to know."

"Okay."

A bug splats the windshield, leaving a greasy trail up the glass.

"How's your little friend?"

Little friend. I guess she thinks that's cute. "Her parents are keeping them all locked up."

Liz shakes her head. "That poor girl."

"Why do you keep saying that?"

This time Liz shrugs. "The teen stuff is hard enough as it is, but to have crazy parents as well? I see a lot of therapy in that girl's future."

"She's a witch."

The look she gives me is sharp. "That's not a nice thing to say."

"Not like that. She does spells and stuff. It's weird."

Her eyebrows arc up. "Like witchcraft?"

"Yeah, but not the dumb stuff you see in movies. It's like the real thing. Folk magic or whatever. She's really smart about that stuff."

She hangs a right onto a dirt road and the procession of pine trees comes into view. Road dust billows up behind us as the Tercel bumps along the driveway. Grandma's house is a narrow two-story of white clapboard and faded shutters. The roof needs fixing, but she can't afford the repairs. Dad offered to help pay for it, but Grandma Jean won't accept his charity. She's proud that way.

Liz leaves the car running.

"You coming in?"

"No thanks. I don't want to ruin your visit for you."

I thank her for the ride and watch the car roll away. Grandma Jean comes out onto the porch, her arms wide and waiting for a hug. She's four-foot-nothing, and she smells like laundry dried on the line. Her eyes crinkle into thin lines as she smiles.

"Look at you," she says, clinging to my arm. She chucks a thumb at the driveway. "Your dad didn't want to come in?"

"Uh, no. He had to go into work," I say. "Liz dropped me off."

Her mouth puckers, a scattering of lines creasing her lips. "She did? And here I thought she wasn't old enough to drive. Come in, come in."

She ushers me inside. The table is laid out like Christmas dinner, all polished silverware and lace doilies. It reminds me of a child's tea set. There's the usual banter about how much taller I am since last time she saw me and how much I look like my dad, but I still have my mom's eyes. Neither of those things are true, but I just smile and ask her how she's been. Grandma Jean enjoys talking about her arthritis and how poorly she sleeps. Her aches and pains and how lonely she is out here since Grandpa Gene died. I know, Jean and Gene. How weird is that? Answering the phone must have been real confusing when Grandpa was alive.

A bell chimes from the kitchen and Grandma Jean gets up slowly. Lunch is ready. I ask how I can help, but she pooh-poohs the idea and totters off.

She returns with a heavy platter and pulls away the shroud of tinfoil. Grandma Jean has made a whole glazed ham just for me. Pineapple rings steam over the browned skin, centered with maraschino cherries on toothpicks. There's enough meat here to feed a baseball team. My plate is overloaded with thick slabs of it, complete with slices of singed pineapple and cherries. I tell her she shouldn't have made something so extravagant, but she waves the notion away. She knows it's my favorite. This also isn't true. It was my mom's fave, not mine, but I chow down happily. It's delicious, I'll give her that. I'm polite and polish off a second helping. By the time my plate is scraped clean, I feel light-headed and queasy.

Grandma Jean claps, like I've accomplished something remarkable by stuffing my face.

"I made pie," she says, squinting at me. "Your favorite, strawberry-rhubarb. I just took it out of the oven."

It's probably sitting on the windowsill to cool, just like in the cartoons. I need to lie down, but I make a show of being excited about desert. "Great."

She asks how my school year was and where I'm working this summer. She's tickled to hear I'm working two jobs, especially the ice cream hut. She's horrified to learn about the wasps drowning in the ice cream bins. Wasps are pure evil, she tells me. She asks if I have a girlfriend.

"No," I say.

It's the truth, but she finds this hard to believe. Her eyes go all squinty again as she smiles. "A good-looking boy like you? There must be someone special?"

My face betrays me, and she pokes my shoulder. "There is a girl," I confess. "But she's not my girlfriend or anything."

Grandma Jean's brow knits into a hundred folds. "Oh? Why not?"

Some evil part of me wants to tell her exactly who George Farrow is, just to see her reaction. Grandma Jean was born and raised here. She'd know all about the Farrows. But then I picture her dropping dead from a heart attack, so I just shrug it away. "It's complicated."

"Complicated?" She covers her mouth when she laughs. "Everything is such a drama at your age."

She fusses over me, brushing the hair out of my eyes and asking when I'm getting a haircut. Patting my hand constantly as if I need reassuring at all times.

"And how's your father?"

"He's okay." It's the best I can manage, because I don't really know. He could be facing bankruptcy or a cancer scare and I wouldn't know. He's always so buttoned down. Not that I give a shit, of course.

"He must be quite pleased with his little Kewpie doll. She's pretty, that one. But then all girls are pretty when they're young." She stirs her tea, then pats my hand again. "It must be hard for you, having a stranger in the house like that. Has she started redecorating yet? Painting rooms and buying new furniture?"

The look of our drab house hasn't changed at all since Liz moved in. It could probably use some freshening up. "No. I don't think she's into that stuff."

Her hands are shaky and the teacup rattles against the saucer as she sets it down. "She's biding her time, then. Smart girl. The ruthless ones always are. But it won't be long before she starts taking pictures down from the wall and scrubbing the place free of your mother's memory."

My stomach is bloated and uncomfortable. All that meat is making me drowsy. "She's not a bad person, Grandma. Honest."

"Of course. She just moves fast, doesn't she?"

I don't want to start an argument with my grandmother, but that isn't fair. "She makes him happy. What else matters?"

"Oh, I have no doubt about that," she says with a shudder, making it sound dirty. "I'm sure she's eager to get her own family started. She's Italian, isn't she?"

Damned if I know. She has dark hair.

"Well, those people love to breed. Won't be long, I suppose."

Ding. Another kitchen timer goes off.

"That pie must be cooled by now." Grandma Jean scoots into the kitchen while I die of shame. It amazes me how this little old lady can be sweet one moment and then toss out a nasty remark like it's nothing.

She brings out the pie, and I try not to turn green at the prospect of stuffing more food into my gullet. I don't really have a choice, what with Grandma Jean making a show of putting a slice in front of me and waiting for my reaction. It's delicious. The woman's a ninja when it comes to baking.

"Where's my head," she pipes up. "I forgot the ice cream."

"This is fine. Honest."

"Are you sure? Pie is always better with ice cream."

I fabricate a lie about eating too much ice cream at the hut, and she settles back down. She's content to watch me eat, her gaze all dreamy and weird with nostalgia. And then she says what I've been dreading since I arrived.

"Your mother used to love strawberry-rhubarb."

The tears erupt and she presses a napkin to her mouth like she can't breathe. Between sobs she says she still can't believe that Nancy is gone and what a beautiful daughter she was. How bright and full of life she had been. She clutches my wrist and says it's not fair that I have to grow up without a mom. How she won't be there to see me graduate or get married.

Fuck.

It's always like this.

Grandma Jean takes a deep breath and lets it out slowly. The grief exhausts her. She pats my hand again as if I'm the one who needs bolstering. "I'm going to get the photo albums. Won't that be fun?"

She hobbles out of the room, and I look at the old mantel clock above the fireplace. It's only been an hour and I've still got the rest of the afternoon to grind out. Killing time with an old woman and the ghost between us.

The pie sits before me on its china plate, one small bite marring its perfectly triangular shape. If I wolf it all down, I might puke it back up, derailing the dreaded trip down memory lane.

LOVECRAFT

THE REST OF the day is lousy, and the day after that. I grunt when Liz asks if I want more potato salad, and I snap at Dad when he tells me to mow the lawn. I keep thinking about exactly what I don't want to think about, and it's all Grandma Jean's fault. This is why I avoid seeing her, all the damn waterworks.

Everything changes when Liz collects the mail from the battered box in the yard.

"There's a letter for you." She plucks a black envelope from the junk mail in her hand.

The spoon is halfway to my mouth. I never get mail, and it's not my birthday. "Who from?"

Liz flips the envelope to read the return address. "Hester Philippa Lovecraft?"

My stomach drops. It's from George. My chair squeaks against the floor as I leap up to snatch it from her hand. "Thanks."

Her brow wrinkles at me. "Is that a joke?"

"Sort of."

"Quite the racy name," she says, smirking. "Sounds like a love letter."

I feel heat flood my face.

Liz laughs, hiding her mouth behind a hand. "You've gone red."

I make a beeline for my room and bolt the door behind me. My hands are shaking. The letter has a smell to it. Her smell.

I tear it open to find a strange symbol drawn on one side of the page, the letter to me on the other. Her handwriting is weirdly old-fashioned, with long loops and dipping tails.

Dear Mark,

I don't know if you like mail as much as I do, but this is my last resort. I heard you the other night, rattling the tin cans in the woods, but I couldn't come out to meet you. My parents are keeping us under house arrest since the incident in Liesl's room. But I am happy you came to visit.

Are you all right? Tilly had a sense that you were in pain the other day. Did my father hurt you? He can be violent sometimes. Or was something else causing the pain?

I'm sorry for how you were treated, and sorrier still for letting you take the blame for the seance. It's hard to explain, but it would have been so much worse for us if our parents knew the truth. Still, I regret not standing up for you when I should have. That was unfair.

Are you happy? Are you sad? I wish I knew. I miss talking to you. Everything is so dull here I want to scream.

I will understand if you never want to see me again. Everyone hates us, so you might as well join them. But I will miss our talks. I hope life takes you where you want it to and you escape from here. I don't think this town is good for you.

Do you like correspondence? You don't strike me as a letter-writer, but if you want to write back, DO NOT send it by mail. Mother will intercept it, and there will be much drama about a mystery letter for me. Did I show you the loose brick in the gatepost? The one on the west side? There is a loose brick at the bottom that can be pulled out. Stuff the letter in there and put the brick back. It's the safest route I can think of.

Adieu,

George Farrow

P.S. I have been running your cards, but the throw keeps showing disaster. The symbol on the back of this letter is for your protection. Scribe it on the back of your bedroom door. It should shield you from any malevolent force seeking to hurt you. Including me. That's a joke. I would like to visit your room again someday.

I read the letter a second time. My ear starts to ring with this high-pitched tone. I study the diagram on the other side of the page. Two crossed spears inside a circle with a few squiggly lines at the compass points. I scrutinize each line for some hidden meaning or coded message, but there isn't one. It's all there in plain English. My fingers leave smudgy prints on the paper.

I burn two hours trying to compose a response, but I'm terrible at writing. My English grades are proof of that. I scratch it out, start again, scratch that out as well. I can't decide if I should admit missing her too or just play it cool. Playing it cool never works for me. The pad of paper dwindles down before I chuck all the nonsense and try to speak as plainly as she has. I tell her I understand what happened and don't blame her. I ask if she's all right, if she and her sisters are in danger. I ask what she means when she said her father is a violent man, adding that he phoned here to talk to my dad. Then I explain how I got grounded, which is why I haven't been back to rattle the cans. I tell her the last few days have been boring as hell and that I miss talking to her too.

I almost scratch out that last remark because it's way too revealing, but I fold the letter into an envelope and seal it up before I can change my mind. When the sun sinks below the treetops, I'm halfway across town with the letter stuffed in my back pocket. The house is dark as I skulk up to the gatepost and search for the loose brick. It's near the base, a red slab that shimmies out of its slot. The letter goes in and the brick slides back into place just like that. I watch the house for a while, but there's no movement, no lights in the windows. I pedal away, wondering if the Farrows are all vampires. I've never seen any of them in the daylight.

When I get home, I rummage the junk drawer in the kitchen for a black marker and draw George's protective symbol on the back of my bedroom door. The result isn't bad, and when I'm satisfied with it, I hang my robe on the peg to hide it.

I read the letter two more times before going to bed. My eye keeps going back to one line. *I miss talking to you.* I think about George as a vampire. She kind of looks like one, except for the freckles. Freckles make it hard to take a creature of the night seriously. Then I remember that I had invited George into my room, breaking one of those bizarre rules you see in horror movies. That one always seemed kinda stupid to me, like etiquette would stop a monster from busting through the window to rip your veins open. I picture George crawling through my bedroom window and my ears burn. I get up and slide the window sash all the way up and prop it up with a stick because the window won't stay up on its own. There's no screen and I'll probably get mosquitoes in here, but to hell with it. Let her come.

Please.

STACY

THE FIRE IS huge, the flames lashing fifteen feet into the night air. A dozen hay bales, doused with lighter fluid and lit up. It's a tradition around here, the bonfire party before the start of school. Summer is dying a slow death and everyone is dreading the forced march back to Brandenburg High and its wretched class system. The bonfire is one last kick against the end of freedom in a secret, almost Pagan ritual. The location changes every year because the cops will eventually find it, but it's good for a few hours of reckless abandon as everyone kicks against our collective chains.

That's the romantic view of it, anyway. In reality, it's just a bunch of kids burning stuff and getting hosed on whatever they could steal from their parent's liquor cabinets. It's a lot of howling and chest-thumping and these god-awful rebel yells are so phony that they make my skin crawl.

I had completely forgotten about it until Kevin called. "It's the bonfire," he said over the phone. "You have to come. I don't care if you're grounded or dying of syphilis, get on your bike and come to Eric's. We'll ride from there."

I haven't seen either of them for almost a week, but I can't hide under the excuse of being grounded anymore. Not for the bonfire. "Where is it this time?"

"Essex farm. Out on highway two."

Smart choice. The Essex farm is outside of town, far from any neighbors. The bonfire won't be spotted for a long time, which means more time to party before the cops find out.

Kombat Kevin is weirdly standoffish when we meet at Eric's house. He's in full camouflage gear, army boots, and a sheathed hunting knife. Not a good sign. We've both brought beers, but all Eric could steal was a bottle of peach schnapps, and he's roundly mocked for it. We ride out to the Essex farm to find the place crawling with kids, some I haven't seen since June and others I don't even recognize. Everyone's gathered around the fire, hoisting beers up or leaping over the flames in sad daredevil attempts to impress others.

There's a tension in the air, like something big is about to happen, and everyone's waiting for the spark that will set it off. Some meathead will throw a punch, or one of the queen bees will have a titanic fight with her best friend. Maybe a drunk idiot will set himself on fire. If you listen, you can almost hear the ticking of the time-bomb.

"What set it off last year?" Eric asks as we wade into the throng.

"Tracy Staunton?" I say. "When she pushed her best friend into the fire."

Kevin corrects me. "That was the year before. Last time Jason Burrows drove his dad's car into a ditch. Remember?"

Eric looks at me. "Speaking of cars, how's the Galaxie?"

He offers up the bottle of schnapps, but I wave it away. "Stuck in dry dock."

"All that talk about us cruising in style this summer," adds Kevin, "and here we are, three days from school. Thanks for nothing, man."

I consider chucking my beer at his head. "What do you want? I can't find the right parts."

"Yeah, yeah. Last time it was the brake lines. Before that, the ignition." He spits onto the straw-covered earth. "You ain't ever getting that shitbox on the road."

"I will too." I sound like a little kid.

"No, you won't. You wanna know why? Because you're a waffler, Mark." Kevin tosses his beer bottle at the bonfire, narrowly missing someone's head. "You talk a lot, but you got no follow-through."

Eric offers his two-cents. "Car parts are expensive, man. What do you want from him?"

"You say shit you don't mean," Kevin continues. "And you make a lot of promises, but you never show up, never follow through."

That stings, but he's not wrong. I've been avoiding the pair of them for weeks now. As usual, Eric plays the peacemaker by diverting the conversation. "Look who showed up."

Kevin grins. "Your girlfriend's here, Marko."

Panic spikes until I see who Eric is pointing at. Stacy Gibbons looks a little drunk. Her boyfriend, Todd the Clod, looks even more sloshed. They're arguing, but I can't hear what they're saying. She shoves him, and he stomps off in a huff. Stacy's girlfriends huddle around her like a presidential security detail. This might be the spark that sets the party off.

Eric shakes his head. "What does she see in that goon?"

Kevin agrees. "I thought they split?"

All I offer is a shrug. "Stacy's a glutton for punishment."

Eric stabs me in the ribs with his bony elbow. "Now's your chance. Go act all concerned about her and she'll be all over you."

He honestly thinks he's being helpful here, daring me to go hit on Stacy. Eric Chapman has never had a girlfriend in his entire short life. I doubt he ever will.

The party drags on, but nothing happens. One guy tries to leap over the flames, but he flops right into it, rolling out with his hair on fire. His friends laugh at him and pour beer on his head, then they clap him on the back like he's some kind of hero. I hate parties like this. There's this weird pressure to act out and laugh harder than usual, as if to prove to everyone that you are having the MOST AWESOME TIME EVER. It's like a contest to see who can outperform who. People whoop that fake rebel yell while others have defaulted to simply hollering the word "party!" like it's a credo or a command. Kevin disappears first, and then I lose Eric somewhere. I watch the bonfire for a while. No one talks to me, a minor blessing.

I wonder if George found my letter yet. Did she write back? Would she leave her reply in the same spot, behind the loose brick in the gatepost? Is it too early to ditch this stupid party and go find out?

"Mark!"

Stacy pushes through the crowd with a lopsided grin on her face. Draping her arm around my shoulders, she leans clumsily into me. Her eyes are bloodshot. I ask if she's okay.

"Never better." She ruffles my hair like I'm her little brother. "You?"

"I think I'm gonna split."

"What? No, no, no." She gives my shoulder a sharp tug to shake me out of such a stupid idea. "The party's just getting started."

She leans too far and we stumble sideways until we hit a hay bale and plop down. There's a cigarette in her hand and she's chewing gum like always, until the gum falls out of her mouth and bounces off her knee.

"Whoops."

"I saw you and Todd earlier. Did you dump him?"

"Always. He's such a jealous dick." She takes a sip from a plastic cup and looks out at the crowd before the fire. "Where's your girlfriend?"

How drunk is she? "I don't have one."

"Oh, come on," she scolds. "Who's that girl that came to see you at work? The one on the bike?"

My backbone goes rigid. I scramble for a lie that doesn't sound ridiculous. "Just a girl from school."

"Ooh, is it a secret?" Stacy grins, her teeth tinted red.

"She's just a friend."

"Okay, be that way." She slips her arm through mine and we sit linked at the elbows. "I'm sure you'll be nice to her, whoever she is. You're a decent guy. I need to find a decent guy. No more thugs."

We watch another dude leap over the fire with equally disastrous results. I feel exposed like this, arm in arm with Stacy. I keep an eye peeled for the Clod.

"I hate the end of summer," she says, her voice fuzzy and wistful. "I meant to make a clean start. Draw a line in the sand, you know?"

It takes a moment to sort out. "You mean Todd?"

Stacy nods. "When school ended, I put my foot down. No more. Things were going to be different this summer. But he kept coming around. And now school starts and everything will go back to normal. Including him."

I'm sure it's the booze, but I've never seen Stacy this low. "It doesn't have to be that way. You can do better than that guy."

"I know that, up here," she says, tapping a finger against her temple. "But something happens when I'm around all my friends. It's like I become someone else. I'm such a schizo."

That makes me laugh, but there's some truth to what she's saying. "Maybe we're all schizos."

"I need a refill." She looks down at her cup, but it's empty. "Do you have anything?"

"I got one beer left. You wanna share it?"

Stacy pushes on my shoulder to get to her feet. "I'm gonna find more wine. Where'd Amy go?"

"Maybe you've had enough." Jesus. Could I sound any lamer?

"No such thing." She moves away unsteadily, then stops. "Oh, hey. Your movie showed up. Robot-Man?"

The lightbulb takes a moment to flick on. "*RoboCop?*"

She snaps her fingers. "That's it. We're running it in a couple days."

Yes!

I push through the crowd, looking for Kevin and Eric to drop the good news on them. When I find them, Kevin's stabbing a hay bale with his knife while Eric stares vacantly at the flames. All they want to talk about is Stacy. Why didn't you go for it, they want to know. She's wasted! She's into you! Are you gay? The interrogation about why I didn't jump Stacy's bones trumps my news about *RoboCop*. I don't understand these idiots.

"Maybe you just don't like girls," Eric suggests. "You know, deep down."

Kevin shakes his head. "Nah, he's just a pussy."

"Why do I bother with you two?" I dig into my backpack for my last beer, but it's not there. Somebody nicked it. "Did either of you even talk to a girl tonight?"

"There's no girls here," Kevin spits. "Just the same ugly faces."

"Like you're in a position to be choosy? Look around, man. There's girls everywhere. Some of them might even be desperate enough to talk to you."

He doesn't think this is funny, but Eric howls. He sounds like a deranged donkey when he laughs. Kevin keeps jabbing his knife into the hay bale. His eyes are glassy, refracting the light of the fire.

"What is it with you?" he says. "You been getting real uppity lately."

"Did you take my last beer?"

Kevin's an expert at the unnerving stare. He doesn't blink, doesn't look away. "You been acting like you're better than us or something. Like you got somewhere cooler to be. Where do you gotta be, Mark?"

"Dunno. Fucking your sister, maybe." This is an empty jab. Kevin only has brothers. The oldest one is in jail.

The crowd has thinned out, people slinking away or passing out in the field. The hooting and hollering has died down to a few pathetic yelps, the bonfire dwindled to a cozy campfire level.

Eric takes a slug of his vile schnapps. "You guys remember Michelle Kernsdotter?"

Kevin nods. "The Nordic fox? Who could forget her?"

Eric pulls out the oddest memories sometimes. Michelle Kernsdotter was a year older than us back in grade school. Tall and lanky with hair so blonde it was almost silver. For reasons none of us could ever fathom, she hung out with us. We were toast after that.

Eric plucks a straw from the bale, chews on it. "You remember how crazy we were about her? We kept arguing about who was gonna ask her out?"

"None of us did," Kevin says. His stare finally breaks away, wanders to the bonfire.

"Then boom," Eric says, "Trevor Mills swoops in, asks her out."

I shake my head at the memory. "Trevor. What a dick."

Kevin laughs first, then me. Eric brays like a donkey. "We almost stopped being friends over it," Eric adds.

We can always count on Eric to cut the tension. But then he keeps talking.

"Fucking chicks, man. We can't let them come between us." He raises his schnapps bottle for a toast like we're the three musketeers, but I got nothing to cheer with. The goodwill fizzles. The fire pops, firing up a plume of sparks.

"This party's getting boring," Kevin declares. He grabs his knapsack and yanks it open to show us what's inside. "Time to liven things up."

Roman candles. Maybe a dozen of them. Kevin's already got one out, lighter at the ready.

"For fuck's sake, Kev," I groan at him. "Put that shit away."

"Don't kill the fun, Dad," he scolds, unwrapping the wick of the firework. Eric reaches for one, telling me not to be such a narc.

I snatch the candle out of Kevin's hand. "I'm serious. Knock it off with that shit."

"When did you get so lame?" Kevin holds out his hand for the stick. "Give it back."

"Did you forget what happened last time?"

Eric wrinkles his brow. "What are you talking about?"

Kevin's fast. I don't even see it coming, a single motion. The candle is snatched from my hand and I'm sent tumbling over a hay bale. His face leers down at me with bared teeth. "Nothing happened, asshole. Nothing."

The wick is lit and Kevin aims it at a cluster of people on the far side of the bonfire. The candle pops and a red meteor screeches into the night, ricocheting off one kid before it spins across the field. The candle keeps popping, firing red arcs into the party. People scream, duck and cover.

I go numb, reliving a nightmare. I lose Eric and Kevin in the cloud of smoke and the stink of gunpowder.

A blinding light cuts through the fog and then someone screams the signal that ends every party.

"Cops!"

YOURS IN SHACKLES

A SECOND LETTER from George. This is what it says:

Every séance must be closed properly. Ours wasn't. I think something else slipped through. Something not friendly.

I wish this was just a dumb joke.

Three people got busted at the bonfire party. I wasn't one of them, but I lost Kevin and Eric when the cops swooped in. It was every dumbass for himself. One cop grabbed me by the collar with his beefy hand, but I shook him off and booked it the hell across the field to where we'd left the bikes. Kevin's and Eric's wheels were both gone. I took off and did not look back.

I check the mailbox every morning for another letter from George, but nothing arrives. Miffed, I ride across town hoping she left a letter for me behind the loose brick in the gatepost. Merrily Road is busy on Sunday afternoon—cars parked along the curb, more rumbling up and down the street. The after-church crowd. The smoke from barbecues rises from backyards, kids playing on front lawns. It's all very *Leave it to Beaver*. Do these church-types know that their neighbors are practicing witches?

A stranger waves to me from a passing minivan. I try my best to fit in, to look like I'm on my way to someone's after-church hoedown as I wheel up to the familiar gates. There are no extra cars parked in the Farrow's driveway, no trail of charcoal smoke from the backyard. When the coast is clear, I pry out the loose brick and reach inside. An envelope is there, gritty with red dust. I shove the brick back and book it the hell out of there.

There's a small park near the trestle bridge. It's not much of a picnic area, just a patch of grass that overlooks the river. No one ever picnics here. The bike flops to the grass while I tear open the envelope. The opening line about the seance baffles me, but I keep reading.

Mark,

Something has changed here. It's mostly a feeling, but it's oppressive and weighing on us all. Claudia fell down the stairs, claiming she was pushed. A fox got into the coop and killed Tilly's pigeon. Both of my parents are manic, seeing spies around every corner, doomsday in every newspaper headline. No one laughs. I don't want to be here anymore. We are still being punished for violating Liesl's room.

Do you feel it, this ghost or presence? You were part of the seance. It will find you too. The three of us tried to close the seance properly, but whatever slipped through is, I'm afraid, here to stay. Did you scribe the protective symbol on your door? Please do it soon. I don't like the thought of something hurting you.

I was very happy to find your letter in the gatepost. I'm grateful to feel happy about anything these days. Have you made any progress with the car? I wish I knew how to drive. Will you teach me? The thought of escaping thrills me. Have you ever heard of Charles Starkweather and Caril Ann Fugate? They tore across the country in a murder spree during the 1950s. If you ever want to go on a romantic crime-spree, please take me with you. I have never fired a gun before.

My father confiscated all my spell books and witch bottles. His temper is volcanic these days. Mother buried my Ouija board and burned almost every issue of Witchcraft Magazine *(I managed to hide a few). They're saying the seance was my fault now. Which, of course, it was. Yesterday, they threatened to drag us to church to exorcise us of this diabolical infatuation. We've never attended church before and the thought terrifies me. It would be hell (ha ha!). I picture myself bursting into flames, stepping across the threshold.*

We are no longer allowed to walk to the store. The car is fixed, so there's no need, but I miss those walks. Even with the taunts and jeers of those awful townies. I miss the freedom of it. Or the chance of running into you. I don't know how long our punishment will last, so I suppose I will just have to be patient until my parents' anger dries up and I can sneak out to visit you. Or sneak you in here. If you want to, I mean. I don't know.

Yours in shackles,
George Farrow

When I get to the end of the letter, the shaking in my hand has moved to my insides, churning everything up. The note about her father's temper worries me. The thought of George being hurt cuts a hole right through me.

The letter is folded carefully away in my pocket, and I get back on the bike. I'll save the second read until I get home and close the bedroom door against whatever evil spirit we let slip into this world.

The first three attempts at writing a reply end up crushed and tossed across the room. The fact that I can tell George absolutely anything is thrilling, but it's also a little terrifying. I softball it at first, writing that school starts in two days and how I'm dreading it. It's not the end of summer or the thought of homework that's making me anxious. School is a zoo with a ruthless class system that has to be navigated carefully. There's the upper crust Eloi, the middle-class clingers, and the lowly Morlocks. Some are born into a better social class. Others claw their way up. But everyone is standing on banana peels. One slip and everyone turns on you. The thought of going back makes me want to throw up.

I tell George she's not missing much, being home-schooled. The zoo is cutthroat, Darwinian. Still, I'd imagine it must get lonely for the three of them. I ask her how she plans to apply to university without a high school diploma. Maybe there's an equivalency test or something.

I ramble on about nothing, about the bonfire and how *RoboCop* is finally coming to the Palisades. I think she'd like this movie. At the end of the letter, I hesitate before telling her that I miss her. A zap of electricity jolts clean through me as I scratch it out on paper. I almost throw up.

The zap lingers like low level static as I head back across town to hide the letter in the gatepost. Slotting the loose brick back into place, I see a car turning onto Merrily Road—the family station wagon. I barely have time to hide before the car rumbles through the gates and into the driveway. I watch the family climb out and march up the front steps. They are all dressed up, George, Tilly, and Claudia, but their heads are down, their feet dragging. The parents must have made good on their promise to drag them to church, but I can't imagine what church they would attend. I only get a glimpse of George before she disappears. Weird to see her hair pinned up like that, leaving her exposed and without armor. How she must hate that.

When it's safe to leave, I bike over to the RV Emporium to pick up my paycheck and say goodbye. Friday was my last day. Mr. Dutton wishes me luck at school and, with a wink, tells me to focus on my studies, not the girls. I tell him I'd like to come back next summer, if he needs me. Clapping a hand on my shoulder, he says we'll see if the business survives the off-season. Before riding off, I peek into the envelope to find a fifty-dollar bill alongside the check. I wasn't expecting a bonus.

Coasting down Main Street on my way home, I see Stacy outside the movie theater. She's on a ladder, reaching up to change the letters on the marquee. She waves. Then I spot the guy holding the ladder for her—Todd, her dimwitted boyfriend.

Jesus, doesn't anything ever change?

OUT OF BODY EXPERIENCE

WHEN THE SUN goes down over Brandenburg, the three of us hurtle toward the Palisades theater like lunatics, pumped to finally see a cyborg cop blast his way through the industrial hellscape of future Detroit. Kevin almost trashes his bike jumping over a trash can, which leaves Eric giggling like a madman. We're twelve all over again.

The day has been an excruciating slog getting to this moment. Dad insists we go to the Labor Day parade to watch beer-bellied dudes waddling behind a marching band. The Shriners brought the whole fiasco to a halt when their float died right in the middle of the street, bottlenecking the parade behind them. I saw a fallen fez get crushed flat under the wheels of the Local 212 float as the parade limped to the town square where trade unionists served up hot dogs and watermelon punch.

As soon as I could get away, I hustled over to Merrily Road, but there was no envelope waiting for me behind the loose brick in the gate. Was my letter intercepted by her nutso parents? I tried not to worry about it on the ride home. There is enough to stress about as it is with school starting tomorrow.

Right now, however, the giddiness of finally seeing *RoboCop* trumps any thoughts of school.

"Check it out," Kevin says, when we roll up to the movie house. "Looks like half the school turned out for this."

There's a mob outside the ticket booth tonight, all teenagers clinging to the last dregs of summer before our collective prison term begins. Headbangers and preps, football goons and girls in penny loafers. Even the town's small Goth contingent is here, draped in black like it's already Halloween.

"Guess they got nothing better to do the night before school," I say.

"Don't mention that word," Kevin groans. "I might blow my brains out before first bell."

I don't like school, but Kevin...he despises it. He's always struggled, and it's only gotten worse with each grade. Last year, he barely squeaked by. And that was only because our principal is reluctant to fail anyone.

Eric beams up at the movie marquee. "Not a bad way to end summer, if you ask me."

I laugh. "Yeah, watching a movie the rest of the world saw months ago."

I scan faces I haven't seen for two months. Everyone's back from summer cottages or trips to their cousins, resuming their status in the cutthroat hierarchy. Tribes slip back into place, cliques reassemble. Strays are folded into new tribes or cast out into the cold. School hasn't even started, but the social meatgrinder is already swallowing us up. The Eloi are distancing themselves from the Morlocks. It makes my skin crawl. Fit in. Be cool. Don't become a target.

Stacy's behind the glass, doling out tickets. She hasn't been this busy all summer. When it's our turn, I crack a joke about the Palisades having a full house for the first time.

"Can you believe this?" she says, scooping our cash from the slot in the glass. "I thought only you dorks were coming to see this."

Eric lets loose with a quote from the movie. He taped the commercial months ago, and we obsessed over it. Stacy ignores him. Everyone ignores Eric. Kevin's grinning and elbowing me in front of Stacy, which is such a dick move because he's too chickenshit to even talk to her.

"Did you get busted at the bonfire?" she asks.

"I booked it soon as the cops showed. Did you get away?"

"I don't know how. I was trashed."

"You're funny when you're trashed."

"You're the only one who thinks so." She slides the tickets across to me. "Shit. We didn't make out, did we?"

Eric and Kevin gape, speechless.

Stacy laughs at their gullibility and reddening faces. She waves us on. "Enjoy the movie, dorks."

And just like that, my social status rockets because Stacy cracked a joke. Kevin and Eric are harassing me with questions and making crude jokes. One of the cool girls waved her wand and momentarily transformed this Morlock into an Eloi. How messed up is that? This is just a taste of what tomorrow will bring and I, for one, am not ready for it.

It's almost show time, but everyone's playing it cool like they got all the time in the world. It's like a game of chicken to see who can loiter the longest and just stroll in at the last minute. Hell with that, I've been waiting forever to see this.

But something changes, like a bad smell wafting over everyone. Heads turn in one direction and my first thought is that a fight has broken out between two meatheads, but I'm wrong. Jesus, am I wrong.

The crowd splits to reveal a single figure, alone on the sidewalk, gasps and whispers all around me.

"The hell is she doing here?"

"I thought they kept those freaks chained up."

"What the hell is she staring at?"

She's standing at the curb, searching the faces bottlenecked at the theater doors. The crowd splits like the Red Sea and her gaze locks on me. Something cold leaks out of my backbone all the way to my fingertips.

It's like she's trying to keep her guts from spilling out. Her face is pinched by something I've never seen before. Fear or desperation? Eyes wet, lip swollen.

Kevin is a mosquito in my ear, Eric a gnat. Their voices drone in my ears. "Dude, she's staring right at you. What the hell?"

Every eyeball rotates to see what the strange girl is looking at. I can't breathe. I'm gonna throw up. Time slows down like in a car crash, and I'm floating above everything, looking down at it all. At me and George.

Eric won't shut up with the questions. "What does she want? Earth to Mark, hello."

Kevin cuts right to the bone. "Dude. Do you know her?"

I'm still floating above it all, like it's happening to someone else. I hear myself deny it, the words slow and robotic. "No. I don't know her."

When I die, this is what I will go to Hell for. This lie, this Judas moment of cowardice. I know this, even as I say it, but the words still come out the same way.

The jeers have already started, the taunts, but the cinema doors swing open and everyone's pushing inside. Kevin and Eric pull me along. I look back, but all I see are the faces of everyone pushing behind me.

We sit up front, the screen lit so high we have to crane our necks to see it. I don't remember how we got here. Kevin and Eric are twitchy and restless, elbowing one another with dumb jokes. Someone's throwing popcorn. I'm not even here. I'm still floating outside the theater like a ghost looking down at its own corpse on the ground.

Why was her lip swollen? How did she get hurt? What could have made George venture out alone into enemy territory like that?

The lights dim and the screen flashes hot with the coming attractions. A rat scampers over my foot. I get up and march for the door. Popcorn is hurled at me. Kevin and Eric hiss at me, asking where the hell I'm going. I break into a run.

The street is empty. She's gone. The only other person out here is Stacy.

"Where did she go?"

Stacy frowns. "Who?"

When she realizes who I'm looking for, revulsion sours her face. Her voice drips through the glass like an accusation. "You know that girl?"

The door props open and Eric sticks his head out, frantically waving me inside, saying I'm missing the movie.

I don't remember walking away. I don't remember much of anything after throwing George Farrow to the wolves.

SMOTHERED IN HUGS

"THEY LEFT ALREADY?"

"Twenty minutes ago," says Eric's mom. She holds the screen door open, wet hair wrapped in a towel. "I thought they were going to your house."

I scan the street but there's no sign of them. "The plan was to meet here first, then go together."

"I don't know what to tell you," Mrs. Chapman says. "Maybe you can catch up with them on the way."

Down the steps I go, hoisting my bike from the grass. "Sure. Thanks, Mrs. Chapman."

"Have a good first day of school, Mark."

I zip down Clark Street and cut through the shopping plaza to get to Grove Avenue. Everywhere I look there are other zombie kids dragging their sorry butts to school.

Why did they leave without me? Eric's house is closest to school. We were supposed to meet there. They must be pissed at me for taking off on them last night at the theater. Seeing George show up out the blue like that was surreal. It was like the end of *Invasion of the Body Snatchers* when Donald Sutherland betrays the survivors to the pod-people. And on top of that, I missed the movie altogether.

Kevin and Eric will get over it. That's what I tell myself, marching up the front steps of educational purgatory. Brandenburg Secondary is a relic from the 1940s that somehow hasn't collapsed in on itself. It smells of floor polish and asbestos. I nod hello to a few people only to be greeted with awkward half-smiles and shifty eyes. Others gawk and whisper to a friend. By the time I get to the second-floor lockers, my skin is itchy with gooseflesh.

Eric and Kevin are at the end of the hall, near the window. The bell has already rung, and the hall swarms as everyone runs for homeroom. Some of these people actually look happy to be here. When Kevin and Eric spot me, their expressions drop like someone just told them their dog got run over.

"Why didn't you guys wait for me this morning?"

Kevin's stance is all too familiar; a hard stare and all out belligerence. "Plans changed. Guess we kept it secret from you."

Alarm bells clang. This is bad, but I have no other option than to play stupid. "What does that mean?"

Eric won't look at me. Kevin's face twists into disgust. "What is wrong with you? You're fucking sick."

My guts drop and splatter across the polished floor. They know. They figured it out.

"Her?" Kevin goes on. "Of all the girls in town, you're banging that freakshow?"

"It's not like that." My brain overheats trying to explain it. It shuts down, goes flat.

Kevin's revulsion goes into overdrive. "Who are you, man?"

"I thought we were friends," Eric adds, still refusing to look me in the eye. "Why did you lie to us?"

"Nobody lied."

"You kept it secret. Same diff." Kevin shakes his head. The hallway is now empty except for us. "I don't get it, man. That chick isn't even human. Is she a good lay? Is that it?"

"It's not like that. We're just, I don't know, friends."

"Friends?" Eric stammers, mouth drooping in disbelief. "How? Why?"

Kevin's finger jabs my sternum. "This is why you been acting squirrelly all summer? Because of that freak? Lying that you're too busy to hang out, that you're grounded and shit. You betrayed us, man."

I roll my eyes, which is the wrong take in this moment. "Don't get all dramatic. It's no big deal."

"You hear that?" Kevin turns to Eric. "I guess best friends aren't a big deal to Marko here."

"Not cool," Eric says.

"You chose a girl over your friends." Kevin gets up close, nose to nose. A fist is coming next, anyone can see that. "Out of all the girls in town, you go after that one? You're fucking sick, dude."

Footsteps behind us—Mr. Stabler, the history teacher with a widow's peak so severe he looks like Dracula. "Bell's gone, boys. Get to homeroom. Now."

Kevin adds another jab before he steps away. "I don't even know who you are anymore."

I look to Eric, but he just shoulders his bag and follows Kevin down the hall. Mr. Stabler glares until I leave.

We're all in the same homeroom: Miss Treblinski's English class. She welcomes me with an appropriate amount of sarcasm for being late on the first day. Kevin and Eric collapse into desks at the back of the room. The only seat left is at the front of the class with the brown-nosers and losers. I take a seat. I guess it's where I belong now.

It's all downhill from here. My two best friends refuse to talk to me, other people avoid me like I'm dripping with VD. I see them huddle and titter to each other. Gossip moves fast, infecting the student body. Even the minor-niners, who are new to school, sense it and avoid me for fear of contamination.

At lunch, Eric and Kevin vanish. I sit alone on the back stairs near the smoking area. It's all seniors here, lighting up and waving their smokes around as they talk. Stacy's among them, locked in with all her regular school clique and, of course, her boyfriend, Todd the Clod. She had predicted this would happen, clicking back into place in the pecking order. I try to catch her eye to wave a hello, but she doesn't look this way. I can't unsee the look of horror on Stacy's face when she saw me looking for George. I guess she feels betrayed too.

When the first day of school finally grinds to its shitty end, I ride back to the Farrow house. I don't know what else to do. Wading through the creek and sidestepping the bear trap, only to find the path blocked. The string of tin cans have been doubled, completely sealing off the back forty from intruders. Like me.

I can't stop replaying the look on George's face. The pain stitched there when I denied knowing her. Her face is there as my head hits the pillow, and I know it will be there when I open my eyes in the morning. One thing I've learned from all the sci-fi and fantasy I've read is that Hell is always personalized. It's never demons boiling souls in a cauldron or stretching victims over a torture rack. True Hell is tailored to each plaintive spirit. This will be mine, forever replaying the hurt on her face.

Just as I'm drifting off, a sudden noise lifts my head from the pillow. A riffle of paper followed by a thud. Another paperback pushed from the shelf by an unseen force. The ghost is back, angry at me for not telling George the truth.

Does it matter? My life is over.

I'm a ghost. No one talks to me.

At school, people twist about to avoid brushing my shoulder, their eyes looking right through me. I wonder if this is what it's like for Liesl as a ghost. Screaming at her family as they pass through her, deaf to her cries for help. That would be her version of Hell.

Even Eric avoids me. He's alone in the chemistry room when I spot him. I ask him how the movie was, but Eric looks away and hustles it out of the room. "Sorry," is all he has to say.

It's hard being a ghost. It's not like Casper or something, tweaking noses and pulling hair. But you can get used to anything. Two days into the new school year, I find a few silver linings to being untouchable. Gone is the pressure that comes with talking to people, to be funny or be cool. It's a relief. Being invisible lets me observe those around me and hear their little dramas. Darryl Lamb wants to punch out Bo McKinley because he flirted with his girlfriend. Trisha Jackson is spreading nasty rumors behind her friend's back. The friend in question is clueless to the source of the gossip, believing her boyfriend's ex is doing the trash talking. Minor incidents are blown up into earth-shattering crises. Vendettas are planned against one person, only to be redirected to another kid the next day. It's laughable, really. All these kids pretending to be adults, aping the soap opera bullshit they see on TV. If I'm ever allowed back into the fold, I'll be one of those characters who returns from the dead to shock everyone and foil their schemes.

The only kid who doesn't treat me like a ghost is Darren Tran. His locker is two down from mine. I almost jump when he says hello to me.

"Hey, you started the reading for English class yet?"

"No," I say, grateful to be acknowledged. "Have you?"

He pulls the book from his locker. Something called *Childhood's End.* "It's not bad," he says. "Never thought we'd be reading sci-fi in English class."

Darren is also a ghost here at Brandenburg High, which is why he's talking to me at all. It's more of a racial thing with Darren, though. He's from the only Vietnamese family in town, which shows how whitebread this place is. Like everyone else, I've pretty much ignored Darren since he moved here. Now that I'm ostracized, I'm getting a taste of my own medicine.

The bell rings, and Darren joins the flow of traffic in the hallway. He doesn't appear to hold a grudge, even though he has every right to. He just seems happy to have another outcast to talk to. I get it.

I go home after school and watch reruns of *Star Trek.* After dinner, I turn on the lights in the garage and work on the car. Swapping out new plugs, I find a spider living inside the distributor cap. It crawls away the minute I pop it open, which is a good thing because he would have fried the next time I tried the ignition. The radiator gets flushed, the coolant changed. I buff the chrome from nose to tail, but all of it is pointless. The Galaxie 500 is a dead dream. What the hell was I thinking?

I've written two letters to George, but they end up tossed in the wastebasket. The third time, I lay down in the back seat of the Galaxie and prop the notepad against my knee. My guts spew out onto the page, but I don't care and I seal it in an envelope before I second-guess myself. I bike across town. Now that summer is over, everyone's back to routine and the boys in the muscle cars resume their prowling up and down the same dull strip, looking at the same dull faces. I keep an eye peeled for the red Dodge Charger that tried to run me over, but I don't see it anywhere. In fact, I haven't seen it since I let the air out of its tire at the truck stop.

Trying not to get my hopes up for a new letter from George is impossible, and the bubble of anticipation in my chest is ready to burst. I get to the gatepost, eager to slide out the loose brick, but the stupid thing won't budge.

Somebody mortared it shut.

PROM KING

THE INTERIOR OF the Galaxie smells like musty floor mats and sun-bleached vinyl. I like the smell. Lately, I hang out in the car instead of my room. It feels safer. There's nothing in the old Ford that pushes books off shelves or scratches my skin in the night. The back seat is long enough to stretch out on. I could sleep out here if I wanted to. There's more than enough room to fool around, too. That idea conjures up George, pushing everything else aside. I think about the two of us lying on this back seat, talking in the dark. And then fucking and sleeping and talking some more. The hollow ache under my breastbone is so deep that I want to cry. But when the pain fades, I miss it and want it back. I didn't know I was such a masochist. It can't be normal, feeling this way.

I spend an unhealthy amount of time daydreaming. What else do I have to do? I don't have any friends now. I daydream that the car is working, tuned up and raring to go. George is beside me. We blast across the bridge and onto the open road, away from this awful place. At night we park on the side of the road and make a campfire, sleep in that big back seat with the doors locked. In the morning, we get back on the road and just keep driving. Our destination is beside the point.

All of this gets scribbled down on the notepad I've brought into the car with me. Another letter to George, even though the hiding spot in the gate has been sealed off for good. *I know you won't read this*, I scratch out in my crappy penmanship. *It's a one-way conversation, but you're the only friend I have now. Is that ironic or just funny? Neither, I guess. It's just fucking sad.*

Who bricked up the hiding spot, her or her father? I tell her about the zoo at school and how I'm a ghost that no one sees. The social hierarchy is weird. Popularity is like a finite resource, and there's only so much of it at any one time. Like squeezing a balloon, it bulges out in some unexpected spot. As I'm shoved to the bottom of the pecking order, Kevin's popularity rises in direct proportion. Even Eric has more friends now.

I understand now why you hate them all, I write. I hate them, too.

I tell her about Kombat Kevin. Despite his rise in popularity, he's struggling at school. He always has. He backtalks his teachers and gets sent to the office. He gets in fights and bullies the minor-niners. Kevin White has gone full Rambo too, wearing all camouflage and old police boots. The dumbass even wore his big Bowie knife to school. He got sent home for the day. If he keeps this up, he'll be expelled before Halloween.

The letter should end here, but my pen keeps scratching and words keep spilling all over the page. I tell her the terrible thing I've been keeping from her, the events of that awful night. It's a cowardly move, confessing on paper, because I have no way of getting this letter to her. But it's all there. Evidence, I suppose.

A knock on the window, knuckles on glass. Dad motions for me to roll down the window. The glass squeals as I crank the handle.

"What are you doing?"

I flip the notepad face down on the seat beside me. "Nothing."

He leans on the windowsill. "Funny place to do your homework."

"I like it in here."

He surveys the interior, nodding his head along like he approves. "How's school?"

There is only one answer to this eternal question from every adult. The school could be on fire and my answer would be the same. "Fine."

"You keeping up so far? Homework and stuff?"

"Sure."

He nods some more. "Everything okay otherwise?"

Red flags go up. Dad doesn't chitchat. He gets an answer and moves on, end of conversation. There must be some bad news he's dancing around. Did he lose his job? Did Grandma Jean kick the bucket?

"Yeah. Everything's fine."

Normally he'd be satisfied with this vague response, but not today. He swings the door open and slides into the driver's seat. One elbow propped over the back, he looks at me, but he's stalling.

Shit. This is serious. Maybe Liz left. She finally couldn't take anymore shit from her stepson and packed her bags.

"Anything happen at school?" he asks. "Somebody picking on you or something?"

I wish he would stop dancing around and just say it. This phony heart-to-heart, father and son bullshit is getting old. He's been watching too much TV.

"Am I in trouble or something?"

"No, no." The vinyl beading on the seat is loose. He toys with it. "It's just, well, you seem kind of down. I mean, more than usual. I just thought if there's something on your mind, we could talk."

This isn't what we do. Liz put him up to it, prodding him to go find out why his son is moping around with a hangdog face. No wonder he's acting so spastic. Uncharted waters for both of us.

The afternoon we got home from the funeral parlor, the two of us just sat in the living room and didn't say a word. We didn't even turn on the TV. He loosened his tie, I let mine flop to the floor. The sunlight in the picture window faded as that shitty day drew to an end. He asked if I was hungry. I said no. We didn't speak another word until the next day.

The Prewitt men don't talk. We unbutton collars, we stare at the same spot on the carpet for hours, but communicating is not something we do. So, yeah, this is Liz's handiwork. I guess she's concerned.

He's fiddling with the heat vent now, sliding it back and forth. "I'm just worried. We've been down this road before, you know. I hope we don't have a repeat."

"What road is that?" I don't mean to sound scornful. It just comes out that way.

He flicks his gaze at me for a moment and then tries the push-buttons on the radio. The last button sticks and can't be pressed. "The rough patch you had," he says. "The garden shed, the vandalism. Remember?"

"I remember."

He pulls the cigarette lighter out, looks at the heater end. Puts it back. "If we're headed for another phase like that, then we need to course-correct. Get you back on track. Steady keel and all that."

Nautical terms. The old man's always wanted to get a boat. I've never even seen him swim.

"You never talk about her," I say.

The look on his face slides right off, giving way to a blank nothingness. "I thought you liked Liz."

"Not Liz."

He turns, faces front and grips the steering wheel in the correct ten-and-two positions. Staring at the back of his head, I notice his hair is thinning at the crown. "It's complicated," he says quietly.

"Is it?"

He eyeballs me in the rearview mirror. "Hey. I loved your mom."

Silence floods into the interior, suffocating us. He pushes the door open, causing the dome light to come on.

"It's getting late," he says. "Time to hit the sack."

I don't want to go, but I don't argue with him. I can't tell him that something keeps visiting my room at night, knocking books from the shelf. I do as I'm told.

I keep the bedside light on for a long time, reading the Lovecraft book George gave me. One story gets under my skin, about a scientist who invents a device that allows him to see a translucent, alien dimension that overlaps our own reality. The sight of these horrific creatures almost drives him insane and he realizes, too late, that the device works both ways. The alien hordes can see him too, and a bloodbath ensues.

Unnerved and confused, I turn out the light, but a sudden noise clatters softly all around me in the dark. I turn the light back on. The plastic stars have fallen from the ceiling. Every last one. The dusty constellation lies scattered all over the bed as if a hand swept them all away.

Grabbing my pillow, I get the hell of that room, out to the garage and into the back seat of the Galaxie. I lock the doors. It can't get me in here.

The phone rings late Friday. Liz hollers my name. It's Kevin, she says, holding the receiver out to me.

I consider hanging up, but I'm curious. There's no chitchat. He gets straight to the point.

"I'm having a party," he says. "You should come."

I already know about Kevin's party. Darren told me about it two days ago, but I play dumb. "When?"

"Now. Come on over."

Click.

I hook the receiver back onto the cradle, wondering if it's a set-up. An ambush where I'll get treated to a blanket party. That's where you pin some unlucky asshole under a blanket and everyone puts the boots to him. That way the target never knows who's doing the stomping. I decide to go anyway. It's not like I got anything better to do.

Kombat Kevin has really climbed the ranks at school. The last-minute invite is his way of lording it over me, inviting me back into the tribe, but only at his benevolence. Does this mean my exile is over? I'm excited to see friends, to get back to being normal. This shunning crap has been lonely.

Kevin's place is over in the grimier part of town, near the old canning factory. A shabby two-story house of cracked pebble-dash and fried roof shingles. The front door is wide open, leaking loud heavy metal into the night. Sabbath. People from school are scattered over the yard. More people inside, barking over the music or huddled around the stove doing hot knives. Being invisible, I squeeze through the crowd without getting jumped or trapped under a blanket, work my way to the backyard.

Someone started a fire in the big brick barbecue. The family dog darts through the crowd. A girl from my grade squats over the grass with a green complexion, her hair held up by a friend—the first puker of the night. I don't see the host anywhere, but Eric's sitting on the picnic table nursing a purple vodka cooler. I'm relieved to see him, but his expression is indifferent when he spies me.

I play it cool with a simple nod. "Quite the party."

He doesn't motion for me to sit or even look at me. "Yup."

"Are Kevin's parents out of town?" I'm struggling to make small talk—with Eric, of all people. "There's no way his mom is okay with this. She won't even let us into the house."

Eric watches the crowd. "His dad split."

"Again?" I had no idea. "Why?"

Eric shrugs, reaches into a pocket. "Who knows? Kevin said he just packed a bag and drove away." There's a pack of cigarettes in his mitt. He takes one out, lights up. This is new.

I scan through the people crowded into the narrow backyard. Not one of them is wearing camouflage. "Where's Kevin?"

"He's got a lot of new friends now." There's an edge to his tone that makes me look at him twice. Is Eric being frozen out, too? Maybe the newfound popularity has gone to our host's head? Eric guzzles his purple cooler and keeps talking. "I wasn't sure if he was gonna invite you."

"He called last minute. I think there was a message in that."

"I told him to invite you. Didn't seem right."

That knocks me back. I struggle for something to say. "Thanks."

"Not sure if you deserve it." He takes a drag on the cigarette like he's been smoking his whole life. "That was a pretty shitty thing you did."

I let the comment stand without a reply. Eric's still sore about being lied to. He has every right to be. And I'm tired of being friendless.

"I don't get it, Mark." He shakes his head sadly. "How did you even meet her?"

No point fudging the truth here. It's not like this could get any worse now. "I felt bad about what we did to her. So I went to apologize."

Eric squints, puzzled. "What did we do?"

My memory is jumbled up, forgetting that Eric wasn't there when it happened. He had left before everything went so wrong.

"The ambush with the firecrackers. George had her eardrum blown out."

"George?" he says. His mouth pops open. "Oh, shit. Is she really a he? Like that chick in *Sleepaway Camp*?"

"Hilarious."

He scratches his head. I can almost hear the gears grinding between his ears. "So you go apologize and end up banging her?"

"It's not like that."

He wants to provoke me. Fair enough. Does he want an apology?

Eric takes another drag, blows smoke at me. "Did you even think how badly that would look on me or Kevin?"

"I didn't think about you at all."

"Why am I surprised?" he says. "You've always been a selfish prick."

More people spill out of the house and into the backyard. Someone tries to feed beer to the dog. A drink gets knocked over. Someone lets rip with a rebel yell. A girl makes her way across the grass toward us. Rochelle Atkinson is in our history class. I'm wondering what she wants when she hops onto the picnic table and sits next to Eric.

"Can I bum one?" she asks.

He offers up the pack. He even lights it for her. "Did you just get here?"

Rochelle waves the cigarette dramatically. "Dawn made us late. As usual."

She doesn't say hi or even nod in my direction. Eric is weirdly calm around her, which is outright baffling. He used to break out in hives at the thought of even talking to girls. It's like everyone is a pod-person now. Aliens.

Rochelle takes the cooler from his hand and guzzles down the rest of it. "Whoops," she laughs.

"I know where there's more," he says.

Off they go, winding their way through the crowd and into the house. I go back to being the invisible man, marooned in the middle of the party. There's barely any elbow room now. Empty beer bottles clog the picnic table and I grab one just to hold on to so I don't look like even more of a loser than I am. Not that anyone sees me. It's a security blanket, I guess.

On the far side of the yard, I spot Todd the Clod with two of his meathead friends. I don't see Stacy anywhere. Maybe they broke up again. Todd and his friends laugh and shove each other, and that's when I spot Kevin. He's in thick with the senior goons, guffawing with laughter and trading shoulder-punches. I've underestimated his meteoric rise through the ranks—prom king in the making. How he would hate that nickname. There's a lull in their antics and when Kevin looks my way. I give him a nod. He pretends not to see me and then the goons huddle in again, blocking him from view.

The party drags on. Kevin remains with his new best buds, and Eric doesn't come back. Another person ralphs and a shoving match breaks out between two apes. The usual drama. I elbow my way back through the house to the front yard to fetch my bike. Somebody rolled it into the ditch.

The voice comes from behind me. "You splitting without saying goodbye?"

Kevin in all his combat glory stands in the grass, swaying a little. No smile.

I haul my bike out of the mud. "Why did you ask me to come if you were just gonna ignore me?"

"You fucked up, Mark. We gotta take this slow."

I watch him, trying to gauge how much he's had to drink. "Take what slow?"

"You know what these people are like," he says, chucking a thumb back at the party. "They spook easily. Right now, you're a leper. So we need to bring you back slowly."

The benevolent ruler. I look up at him. "Eric said your dad took off. Is that true?"

"Eric's an idiot." He turns, spits into the grass. "You still sniffing around that witch?"

I throw a leg over the bike and point the wheel toward the street. I let the question drift away unanswered.

"Jesus. You're your own worst enemy," he says. "I'm trying to save you from yourself. Leave the freaks alone and be patient. I'll ease you back into the fold, and everything will be cool. Okay?"

"I see. When's that gonna be?"

Kevin scratches his chin. "Thanksgiving. Christmas, maybe."

I want to come back with something snappy, but all I can think of is "Ho-ho-ho." Too lame so I say nothing and coast away.

Kevin says something, but I'm too far down the block to make out what it is.

OFF SEASON

THURSDAY, WE CLOSED up the ice cream stand. Just me and the owner. Two days of rain and he called, said it was time to shut her down. One last shift, he said. But we had to do it after dark.

Mr. Dutton is the mysterious owner of the Dairy Scoop, my boss at the RV Emporium. Dutton has a lot of strange ideas about business, politics, and polygamy. In that order. He didn't want anyone to know that he owned the ice cream hut because he claimed the association would hurt sales.

"People won't accept two sides," he told me back in June when he asked me to run the Dairy Scoop. "They'll assume the product is inferior because they won't believe an RV man can sell ice cream. So. we'll keep this secret for now."

We meet at sundown and start closing up the hut for the season. Maybe for good, Mr. Dutton adds. Ice cream sales were lousy all summer and this little venture has left him in the red. He suspects word got out that he's the owner as we unplug the refrigerator unit and haul out tubs of unsold ice cream. I don't have the heart to suggest that the product he sold was third rate, so I just nod and agree with him.

Peeling the lid off a full bucket of melted orange sherbet, Mr. Dutton scratches his head. "Maybe I picked the wrong flavors?"

I don't want to salt the wound over his failed business. "Maybe ice cream isn't as popular as it used to be."

He tips his hat at the untouched bucket of ice cream at his feet. "Who doesn't love orange sherbet?"

"Tastes change, I guess." That's the best I can come up with.

We carry on, dumping rancid cream into the sewer grate and hosing out the buckets. Pulling the cord on the cash register, I ask if he'll open the Dairy Scoop again next summer. He scans the flimsy plywood walls and the slimy floor.

"I doubt it. This may be the end of my summertime snack experiment."

It feels like a funeral, this dismembering of the business. Shitty as it was, I kind of liked it here. Once the bins are all removed from the cooler, I take a cloth and scoop up the brittle corpses of wasps left in the corners. I flick them out the window and glance up at the Palisades across the street. The glass booth is occupied by someone I don't recognize. Stacy quit after Labor Day, her replacement a total stranger to me. It's another kick to the balls that summer is dead and the world just rolls on like nothing happened. Mr. Blurton, the owner of the Palisades movie house, is perched on a ladder, swapping out the letters of the marquee. *Ernest Goes to Camp* is debuting this Thursday. *RoboCop* has come and gone. I missed it completely.

A mist of water fills the hut as Mr. Dutton hoses the sticky sludge from the floor. The spray gets dangerously close to the wall socket and I consider pointing this out to him, but I figure he knows what he's doing. Wouldn't that be a laugh if we both got electrocuted in a freak ice cream accident?

"How's school?" he asks, hosing the slime out the door.

My answer to this question is always the same because the asker doesn't really want to know, and the askee can't be bothered to answer truthfully. Screw it.

"It sucks," I say. "Big time."

Dutton isn't taken aback by this. "No argument there. You struggling to keep up?"

"It's more of a social thing," I say. "Everyone hates me."

"People can be nasty, especially at your age. You know what you ought to do?"

There's irony here in taking advice from a guy who believes he should have the legal right to have multiple wives and doesn't care who knows it. But I'm honestly curious, so I ask what I ought to do.

"Stop giving a shit," he says.

"Excuse me?"

"Don't waste your time on what people think. It's got nothing to do with you."

I should have known this would veer off into Crazytown. "Uh, it has everything to do with me."

"Wrong. Folks are going to think whatever they want. There's nothing you can do to change that, so don't give them the satisfaction." He turns off the tap. Water drips all round us inside the hut as he continues. "You think I don't know what people say about me behind my back? That I'm crazy or off the wall? Should I change just to make them like me? Hell, no. Opinions are like assholes; everyone's got one, and they all stink. You'll drive yourself crazy trying to make people like you."

I have the weirdest urge to write this down so I don't forget it. Mr. Dutton seems pleased with himself. Unscrewing the hose, he waves me to the door. "Go unhook the shutters out front. Then we'll seal this up tighter than King Tut's coffin."

"Like the tomb of a lost pharaoh," I add. My eyes feel glazed over.

"Today, Mark."

I hustle outside to unlatch the heavy shutters, but I stop cold at what's smeared on the pavement. Folds of brittle gray paper lie scattered about, along with the exposed honeycomb matrix of the larvae—the wasp nest, knocked down and stomped on. The tiny white domes of the eggs have ruptured, revealing the unhatched embryo wasps. White and translucent, aborted into ghost insects before they were even born.

There's no mystery about who knocked it down. The dumbass responsible has left a swastika spray-painted on the plywood wall.

"Mark, what's the hold-up?"

Mr. Dutton comes around the corner, his jaw dropping at the Nazi symbol on his ice cream stand. He doesn't notice the wasp nest at his feet. When he turns my way, his face twists into a funny look.

"Easy, son." he says. "Why are you crying?"

Embarrassing to be caught out like that, I don't even know why I got so upset. It's just a stupid wasp nest. Mr. Dutton gives me a lift home, and I walk in the door feeling drained from my crying jag. The last thing I want to do is talk to anybody, but Liz is in the kitchen and she's grinning and twitchy like she's about to have a conniption fit.

"You're home," she says, clapping her hands. "Yay."

"I'm kind of beat. G'night."

She blocks my path. "Not so fast, mister. Your dad wants to talk to you."

Groan. "Can it wait?"

"Nope. It's a surprise." The grin on her face is stuck on high-beam. Something weird is going on. "He's in the garage. Go on."

Liz follows me out the side door. My brain is sorting through what kind of surprise she means, and it locks on the worst possible scenario. She's pregnant. Dad is waiting with a homemade sign that says something cute about becoming a big brother. Grandma Jean was right, after all.

God, kill me now.

The garage door is closed, light filtering through the greasy window. Liz is bouncing around, urging to me hurry up, so I pull on the roll-up door. The hood of the Galaxie is up and Dad's leaning into the engine. He straightens up at the rattling clack of the door.

"Look who's home," Liz announces.

"About time," Dad says, wiping his hands on a rag. "I was afraid I'd get stuck doing this alone."

Thankfully, there's no sign or balloons. Just the old man, elbow deep in the engine. "What's going on?"

"Got you a little something." He nods at grease-damp box on the floor. "Check it out."

Inside the cardboard box is a greased metal cylinder with a levered arm. A fuel pump.

"Holy shit."

"Language."

I turn the piece over, test the pump arm. It's old and coated with oily grime, but it's a match. "Where'd you find it?"

"Scrapyard over in Greeneville," Dad says. "Buddy of mine goes there all the time for parts. I asked him to keep an eye out for old Galaxies or Fairlanes. He found one."

I'm blinking in disbelief at the piece, then up at Dad. Not only has he found the one crucial replacement part, he's got his hands dirty removing the old pump from the engine. My throat clenches up so fast I'm afraid I'll start crying again.

Liz is grinning like crazy, but her eyes are glassy. "How sweet is your old man?"

"Enough with the old man business," he says. "What do you think?"

I answer as honestly as I can. "I don't know what to say. Why did you get this?"

He shrugs, scratches his chin, shrugs again, stifling off his own emotions. "I just wanted to cheer you up. That's all."

"Thanks." There's so much more to say, but this is the best I can manage right now.

"Oh," he says, an afterthought. "We're also gonna have a baby."

Remember that scene in *Raiders*, when the giant stone comes rolling down on Indiana Jones? That's what this moment feels like—an unstoppable force about to crush me.

"Stop," Liz says, swatting his shoulder. "He's pulling your leg."

We get to work removing the power steering pump just to get at the fuel pump. I scour off the old gasket until it's clean and the new pump goes in. When it's done, Dad tells me to hop in and give her a try. The key is slippery in my sweaty hands as I turn it. The starter cranks, but the engine won't fire. The disappointment is crushing.

Dad waves at me to stop. He thinks we just need a little kick to get it going and pours a little gasoline straight into the carb. He gives me the signal and the engine burps, rolls over, and fires into life. The rumble of the 354 echoes off the close walls of the garage, and I can't remember hearing anything so sweet. There are high-fives, a few laughs, and even a quick hug as we watch the engine shimmy under the hood. But even with the garage door wide open, the exhaust chokes us out, so I dive back into the cab to shut it down.

Dad lowers the hood and has to slam it twice before it latches. There's a dark smudge of grease on his chin, but the smile is bright and honest.

"The beast lives," he says. "How does that feel?"

"Like Christmas morning." That makes him laugh. I bop his shoulder. "Thanks, Dad. I mean it."

Neither of us want the waterworks to start up, so we just stare down at the car. There's a mess of tools and debris on the floor, alongside the corroded carcass of the extracted fuel pump.

He pops the rag from his back pocket and wipes his hands. "Can you take care of this mess? I'm bushed."

He says goodnight and turns for the house. He stops for a moment, like there's something else to say, but then he chuckles and goes inside.

When the tools are put away, I'm tempted to start the Galaxie up again just to hear the engine run. But it's late, and Dad will be in bed by now. I'm still floating in giddy shock when I go to scrub my hands at the kitchen sink. The dark grease makes the print of each fingertip stand out like something from a police file.

"I heard that engine roar," Liz says, carrying teacups to the sink. "That must have felt pretty good, huh?"

"It did." I make some room so she can empty the cups into the sink. "I can't believe he did that."

She scoops the wet tea bags out of the trap. "I think it's easier for him to show you how he feels, rather than to say it. You know what I mean?"

"I guess."

"Now you get to be cool," she says. "All your friends will want rides. Especially the girls."

It's almost funny. I respond with something like a grunt. It's not a laugh.

Liz scrutinizes me for a moment, deciphering what the grunt is about. "I haven't seen Kevin or Eric lately. You guys still buddies?"

My gut instinct is to lie and say everything is fine, but that's not what comes out. It's like a knife to a sack of corn; it spills out all over the place. I tell her about being shunned at school, about being invisible. And there's no way to explain that without spilling about George. The mess of it is everywhere, but Liz doesn't interrupt or ask a question. She just listens as I blubber it out.

"She came looking for me, and I denied knowing her. I just threw her to the wolves. I can't stop seeing the look on her face at how I betrayed her."

Liz pours a glass of water, hands it to me. "Sometimes we do things we don't understand."

"That's just it. I know why I did it. I didn't want anyone to know about her because I didn't want to be a loser. But it happened anyway." I gulp down the water, surprised at how dry my mouth is. "So, there won't be any cruising with friends. There are no friends left."

"That's tough," Liz says. "I'm sorry."

I refill the glass. "Why did I do that to her? She didn't deserve that."

"High school is vicious. That's just the way it is. We all do cruel things and then when it's all over, you ask yourself what it was all for."

I should be used to being surprised by her. But I'm not. "You were cruel?"

Her gaze goes long, like she's gone back to that very moment, whatever it was. Then she shakes herself out of it as if it's too painful to look at straight on. "Everyone gets treated harshly. There's nothing remarkable in that. But when you're cruel to someone else? You learn something about yourself you don't ever forget."

She says goodnight and pads out of the room. I sit there with a stupid look on my face. It's hard to imagine Liz being cruel to anyone.

KISSING TOADS

THE ENGINE IDLES too fast and stalls out at two different intersections. My ears burn when the car behind me honks, but once the Galaxie is in motion, I take a meandering route to school, out on the country roads and let the damn thing fly. The engine hums beautifully on an open stretch of road. It likes speed. There's a slight shimmy to the wheel if I push it over 60 mph, but correcting the alignment can wait for now. Something unfamiliar creeps through me as I turn back toward town, something so sweet that I don't recognize it at first—total bliss. By the time I roll into the school parking lot, I feel weightless with it. I'm drunk with joy, until I have to squeeze the beast into a parking spot. This damn car is huge.

There's no insurance on the Galaxie. That was my third thought after waking up this morning. The first was "the car runs," followed by "I am SO driving to school today." The insurance thing is a minor detail. Still, I waited until Dad and Liz both left for work, stalling for time until they drove away and then sprinted for the garage. I'm aware of how stupid it is to drive without insurance. Bill Prewitt has drilled into my head exactly how monumentally screwed I would be if caught by the local PD. My justification is twofold. One, the route to school is only a quarter of a mile on quiet streets. Two, I'll be home long before Dad and Liz return from work. They'll never know.

So, for the first time in my life, I cruise to school in style. I park the beast without bumping into anything and climb out with a gigantic shit-eating grin on my face. I can't help it; I'm that blissed out.

Crickets.

No one notices the sleek shark of Detroit manufacturing or the person driving it. Serves me right, I suppose. I wanted to look cool, to cheat my way back up the social ladder, but absolutely no one looks my way.

Nothing changes. I sit alone at lunch, shame-faced over my attempt to claw my way back into everyone's good graces. It would be funny if it wasn't so pathetic. But the punchline comes after the final bell rings and I walk back out to the parking lot. The left headlight on the Galaxie has been smashed. Kicking the broken glass away, I look around for the guilty party, but no one glances this way.

Why am I so desperate for their approval? Why would anyone think this car is cool? If I stop to think about it, there's only one person whose opinion matters. And she'll never see the car now.

I dig all the cash out of my pocket, but it's not enough to buy a replacement headlamp. If I pass a cop, he'll pull me over for driving with a busted headlight. Then I'll be in hell.

"It lives." Kevin's drawl, behind me. He looks the car over, kicks the tire.

Eric stands back, looking uncomfortable. He looks that way all the time now.

Kevin points to the shattered headlight. "You should get that fixed."

"I don't know," I say. "I kinda like how it looks now."

He leans on the car, drumming his fingers on the roof. "So you finally got it on the road, huh? Now that summer's over. Good timing."

Sometimes I can't figure Kevin out. He's either a psycho or a manipulative genius. It's a thin line, I suppose. I lock eyes with Eric, then turn back to Kevin. "You guys want to go for a ride?"

Kevin leans into the open window, scans the dashboard. "What's that smell? It's like something crawled under the seat and died."

"Your mother. I had to wipe the seats down after."

Eric's giggle is killed by Kevin's withering look. I take out the keys and reach for the door, but Kevin doesn't move out of the way.

"Where you off to?" he asks. "Gonna cruise up and down the main drag? Blast some shitty AM radio out of those crappy speakers?"

Crazy ideas can be thrilling. This one makes me giddy. "Think I'll drive over to the Farrow's house, take George for a ride."

"Jesus, Mark," he says. "That bitch really put a spell on you, didn't she?"

I turn the key and fire the engine, but the rumble is so loud it drowns out my reply to Kevin. "As a matter of fact, she did."

The Galaxie eases out of the slot and then I stomp the gas, wanting to peel out in that angry way you see in the movies. But the engine stalls out on me, and it takes three tries before it fires up again.

I was joking about taking George for a ride. I said it just to annoy Kevin, but the idea sits in my gut and stirs the butterflies around. Without thinking, I hang a left at the bridge and rumble down Merrily Road instead of driving home. The gateposts come into view and I maneuver the wide Galaxie through the narrow space, almost shearing off the side-view mirror. The tires crunch over the pea gravel and the Farrow house looms up through the windshield. In an upstairs window, I spot a curtain pushed aside.

Am I really going to do this? The question is moot because I'm already bounding up the porch steps and banging on the front door. This is the stupidest idea ever, but what have I got to lose? Even if her father answers the door with the business end of a twelve-gauge aimed at my stupid face, at least I'll have tried. Anything would be better than this slow process of dying every day.

I wait, I bang again. There's a click of a lock turning, but no shotgun, no angry father. It's Claudia, and she is not happy to see me.

"Are you insane? You can't be here."

"I need to see George."

"She doesn't want to see you. Now leave before Mother hears you."

I catch the door before she can close it on me. "Claudia, just get her, please. It's important."

"No—"

A voice calls from inside the house—the matriarch of the Farrow clan. "Claudia, what is all the fuss?"

Claudia steps out of the way, and Mrs. Farrow fills the doorway. Her eyes are venomous, but not surprised. Maybe Tilly sensed I was coming and tipped her off.

It takes all I have to be calm in this moment, to not sound crazy. "Mrs. Farrow, can I talk to George?"

"Ah, the white knight to the rescue. You've come to save the princess from her wicked mother, have you?" Her gaze settles on the strange car in her driveway. "I suppose that is the gallant steed, yes?"

I don't want to admit it, but she's right. This little fairy tale rescue has been bubbling in my brain the whole way here. And just like that, she snips it dead.

"I just want to talk to George. That's all."

Her eyes narrow to pale blue lasers. "You know that is not going to happen, Mr. Prewitt. If you don't leave immediately, I will call the police."

I wedge my foot against the door before she can slam it shut. "What are you afraid of? Why do you keep them all locked up like this?"

She's quick. Her foot comes up fast and stomps down hard, driving a sharp heel into my foot. I stumble back and the door slams so hard it rattles the leaded glass.

Great job, tough guy. You just got your ass whipped by someone's mom. My foot hurts so bad I wonder if there's blood welling up in my sneaker. I hope it leaves a smear of gore all over their stupid porch. Stymied, I limp down the steps. That's when I hear the click of the door latch.

And there she is, walking out the door past me and down to the driveway. She opens the passenger door, looks at me. "Let's go."

Mrs. Farrow is on the porch now. The steel in her eyes is gone, replaced with panic. "Georgia Marie, get back in this house right now!"

"We're just going for a drive," George says. "We won't be long."

The passenger door *thunks* home. I lurch for the car like Frankenstein's monster and slide under the wheel. Thank God the car fires on the first try. I slide the stick into gear, but I misjudge the width of the gates, swiping the side mirror. It dangles like a dead limb.

I check the rearview mirror, expecting to see Mrs. Farrow chasing after us, hurling stones at the car, but she's not there. I don't even look at George until we're two blocks away. When I do, a powerful zap runs all the way through me, seeing her on the passenger side of the Galaxie. How many times have I pictured this moment?

George doesn't look at me, her eyes on the road before us. She's wearing a black sweater that's too big for her. There's a hole in the elbow. Those clunky nun shoes and the same flat hair that hides her face. Her lip is a little discolored, but the swelling is gone.

"You okay?" I ask.

She won't look at me. Did I think this would be easy?

"George, what happened?" She flicks a glance at me. I tap my lip. "How did you get hurt?"

"Kissing toads."

A joke. Maybe there's hope. We drive on, the steering wheel slick under my sweaty hands. I need to pull over. But where?

Her arms are folded, impatient for something. She opens the glove box and looks at the owner's manual, a few loose lug nuts. She closes it back up.

I take a breath. "I'm sorry," I tell her. "For what I did to you. For being a coward like that."

It sounds meaningless in the confined space of the car. Hollow even. But it makes her turn and look at me. I can see her eyes.

"I didn't know something could hurt that bad," she says before looking back to the oncoming road. "It was educational."

It's hard to tell what's thumping harder, my brain or my chest. "Why did you come to the Palisades that night?"

"To see you, dummy."

"But you were upset. Your lip was swollen up. What happened?"

George sinks down in the seat, but doesn't respond.

"Did your father hit you?"

She cracks a knuckle. "Mother found your letter in the gatepost."

"How did she find it?"

"She has her ways," George says. "Where do you think Tilly gets her abilities from?"

"Did she hit you?"

She says nothing, eyes on the road ahead, popping knuckle after knuckle.

All this time, I thought her old man was the dangerous one. My heart foams over with an abrupt need to protect her, but it's useless and wasted. How do I protect her from her own parents?

"I'm sorry."

Her feet come up, planting those ugly shoes against the dashboard. "Tilly said you would do something cruel."

The Galaxie keeps drifting to the left. The alignment again. "She predicted it?"

She chews on a fingernail. "They both warned me not to go. Tilly said you would hurt me."

"What I did was shitty. You didn't deserve that."

She stops biting her nail. "Why did you?"

Sweat beads down the back of my neck. I don't have the brains to explain what I did. Not the way it needs to be explained. "All the wrong reasons."

The car drifts left again. I turn onto Marina Avenue, which bends and twists as it follows the river. We're aimless at this point, tourists in our own town.

The dark hair drapes over her face when she turns my way, one-eyed, like a cyclops. "What's school like?"

"Quiet. I have no friends." I muddle an explanation about being a ghost, about being invisible.

Her mouth tilts. Almost a smile. "You're like me now."

"I guess I am."

The air pressure inside the car shifts. The windows are down, but I feel like there's more oxygen to breathe. We make another turn onto another empty street. George watches the houses pass by. A dead squirrel lies flattened in the middle of the road, baked in the sun. It piques her interest until it fades away in the rearview mirror.

She turns the radio dial, thumbs in the push-buttons. "I like the car."

"You're the first person to ride in it." I smile at her, but she's too busy pushing buttons to notice.

"The radio doesn't work."

"There's a lot of things that don't work."

"Are we going somewhere? Or just driving around?"

My eyes go to the gas gauge. A quarter tank, enough to just coast for a while. "Can I show you something?"

She leans her head back against the seat. "Sure."

NANCY

CALVARY HILL IS tucked out of sight behind a wrought-iron gate that's never locked. There's no parking lot, just a strip of unpaved shoulder for cars to park. There are no other cars here today. We leave the Galaxie near the entrance and walk through the tombstones.

"Some of my family is buried here," George says.

News to me. I've never seen a tombstone with the name Farrow. "Where?"

"Near those weeping willows." She motions to the northeast section. The oldest part of the cemetery. "Liesl is buried there."

That takes the wind out of my sails. "Do you want to go visit?"

"Not today."

The grass is lush and needs mowing. Plastic flower petals tumble over the lawn, blown from their little vases by the wind. We wind our way south-southeast, to the newer section of the graveyard. The tombstones here are still shiny, the inscriptions sharp and clear. We veer off the path, past polished stones that glint in the sunlight, and stop before a black marble slab that bears a certain name.

NANCY BERNICE PREWITT

Beloved daughter, wife, and proud mother

1948 - 1984

George studies the inscription. "This is what you wanted to show me?"

"Yes."

She contemplates the black stone. "Why?"

"I don't really know." It's an honest answer. Maybe this was a dumb idea. "I haven't been here since the funeral."

"I like the name Bernice," George declares.

She sits down in the dry grass, so I sit down next to her. It's like a picnic, but there's no basket or gingham blanket. Just cold slabs and dead people.

"I guess we have something in common," she says. "Here in the cemetery."

I pick up a stray fake flower. The stem is plastic, the petals a cheap fabric bleached out by the sun. "Near the end, my mom got mad that she wouldn't be around for the big stuff: graduation, college, whatever. She wouldn't even get to meet the first girl I fell for. She said it wasn't fair."

She turns away, so I don't catch her expression. Her hands fidget, cracking knuckles again.

"You wanted me to meet her."

"Is that stupid?"

The breeze dies, and everything goes quiet. I twirl the plastic flower in my hand—a cheap and ugly thing. There is a weight to this moment, like an ending to something. Like this is the last time I'll ever see George Farrow. It might be if I can just force myself to say what needs to be said.

I toss the stupid flower away. "There's something I need to tell you."

Her shoulders droop like she's deflating. "Don't. Please."

She thinks I'm going to tell her that I love her. "You don't even know what I'm going to say."

"Just don't," she says. Her voice is raw. "I wouldn't know what to do with that. Okay?"

My hands are useless now that the flower is gone. I pull at the dead grass. She's wrong—about what she thought I was going to say.

"Sit here." She pats the mealy grass beside her.

I scooch closer and she links her arm through mine. We huddle tight like it's a cold day, but the September sun is relentless.

Her voice is barely a whisper. "I missed you."

She doesn't look away, doesn't hide behind her hair. Her neck cranes, and we kiss. My bones turn to slush. Neither of us are great at this. Our teeth clunk together, and our lips mash without grace. We come up for air. A glance at Nancy's tombstone leaves me awkward and flushed. "Can we go back to the car?"

The back seat of the Galaxie is huge. Dangerously so.

George is all angles, sharp elbows and pointy knees. Those ugly shoes finally come off, one sock stays on. Her skin tastes salty, and I want to swallow her whole. I never knew you could be this close to another person. I want to melt into her and never let go, never let this feeling end. It's like jumping off a cliff blindfolded.

More clothes slip to the floor mats, nothing left now. We come up for air. Up close like this, her eyes are huge and distorted.

"Should we be doing this?" she asks.

"I don't know," I whisper back. I want to. I really, really want to.

We fumble on, clumsy and shy, eager and hungry. Neither of us really knows what we're doing, but that doesn't stop us from trying.

Then George freezes up. Her muscles go rigid like someone slid ice down her back. "Wait."

We hold our breath. I'm straining to hear footsteps on the gravel outside the car, but it's not a noise that stops George. It's that hippie smell, strong and musky. It's in the car with us, fogging the glass of the windows.

We tug our clothes back on and sit up straight like scolded children. We stay like this for a long time, holding our breath until the patchouli smell fades and the fog evaporates from the windows. Through the glass, we watch sparrows dip and spin through the trees, always in a rush.

"What if we just left?"

She rests her head against the seat. "And go where?"

"Anywhere that isn't here. I have some money in the bank. We can fill up the car and just drive away, never look back."

"We could be criminals like Starkweather and Fugate, killing and fornicating our way across the country." She slips her bony hand into mine. "We could go to Providence."

"Why Providence?"

"My aunt lives there. The one I told you about, with the bomb shelter. There's a university there. You can get a job while I go to school."

The sun cuts through the glass, making the interior of the car too hot. It's an afternoon for daydreaming, so we just lie back and indulge in petty fantasies for a while.

She props up on one elbow, looks at me. "Have you felt anything weird lately?"

"Everything is weird now."

"I mean, since the seance," she says. "Something else slipped through because it wasn't closed properly. Nothing has gone right since then. Have you felt it?"

If it was anyone else, I would sneer at that question. "Late at night, my room gets really cold. And I feel like someone's watching me."

She lays her head back down. "Tilly thinks something bad is going to happen."

"Like what?"

"She can't see that part. She just feels the aftermath of it. Pain and tears."

Another bird flits past the window. A drop of white hits the glass. I wonder what time it is.

"We should go," I say.

The ugly shoes slip back on. We climb back into the front seat.

I reach for the key. "Did your parents really confiscate your spell books and stuff?"

"All of it."

"Are they going to give it back?"

"It doesn't matter now. I don't need those books anymore." Her mouth tilts into a weird grin. "I'm crafting a new spell. One that will punish this whole town."

Punish? The implication sounds biblical. "What does that mean?"

"You'll see."

This isn't a joke, but she clocks my concern. "Don't worry. I'll give you some warning so you can escape first."

We drive back into town. All the talk of running away dries up like the sweat on our skin. It leaves a smell behind, but that's all. Her hair is messy, not so flat now. I tell her I like how it looks. The fact I can make her smirk that way is like a drug. An overdose would be lethal, but I wouldn't care.

Rumbling back over the trestle bridge, I hang a left onto Main Street to cruise the strip just like every other asshole with a car in this town. George hooks an elbow out the window and watches the storefronts go by, all these people that she hates stepping out of shops or walking their dogs. A kid on a skateboard, a woman looking at a flat tire.

The Palisades movie house comes into view—on the opposite side is the ice cream hut, shut down for the season. And right beside it are two figures on their bicycles—Batman and Robin. I slow the car and look right at them. George does too. Shock registers on both their faces as we roll past them. Eric's mouth hangs open in disbelief.

But Kevin? Kombat Kevin looks ready to explode.

I offer a very smug and self-satisfied wave and then drive on.

FULL RAMBO

"PAYBACK," DARREN SAYS. "That's what I heard, anyway."

This is the scuttlebutt in school—hard to take seriously. Gossip flows like water, following the path of least resistance to drown the gullible.

"Are you sure?" I ask.

Darren shrugs. "He said he was going to teach those witches a lesson. For trying to steal one of his own."

Darren Tran, my only friend at school now. Students cram the hallway between classes, but neither of us make an attempt to be discrete. That's how invisible the both of us are. We talk, ghost to ghost.

I shut my locker, snap the lock home. "Did you hear Kevin say this?"

"No," Darren replies. "But Don Gorvin heard him bragging about it. He said Kevin's gone a bit nutso."

The bell cuts us off, but Darren's warning keeps ringing in my head the rest of the day. I hear it confirmed by other people. Not that anyone tells me, but I keep my ears open. The advantage of being a ghost.

Kevin's become something of a ghost himself. He doesn't show up for any classes, but I see him skulking around school—out in the smoking area or down in the machine shop. Yet, when I go looking for him, he isn't in either of those places.

But I do spot Eric, sitting alone near the parking lot, head down, writing in a notebook. He doesn't look up when I approach.

"Have you seen Kevin?"

His eyes come up, not happy to see me. "No," he says, and goes back to work.

"Did he skip today?"

"No, he's here."

Eric doesn't bother to look up again. I sit down next to him. "I heard he's talking shit about the Farrow sisters."

"Who doesn't talk shit about them?"

He's got a point. "Something about teaching them a lesson. What does he mean?"

"That's just Kevin. You know what he's like."

"Is he gonna pull another stunt like with the firecrackers?"

"Why don't you ask him?"

"I can't find the guy. He's pulling his ninja shit."

Something isn't right here. Eric keeps his head down—alone, doing his homework. Red flag. Normally, Eric is never more than five paces from Kevin's side.

"Why aren't you hanging out with him?"

"I got work to do."

"Did you guys fight?" It happens from time to time. Kevin and I went three weeks once without talking. Eric and me, a week and a half. I nudge Eric's arm to claw his attention away. I lower my voice. "Hey, did he go off the deep end again?"

He scans the yard, but no one's looking this way. "It's bad this time."

"How bad?"

The pen resumes scratching at the paper. "He's gone full Rambo."

"Shit."

I sneak a peek at the page Eric's working on. Why did I assume it was schoolwork? It's all doodles—a few dicks and boobs, but mostly guns and samurai swords. Kevin's influence is all over the page.

Eric closes the notebook, grabs his bag. "I gotta go."

Kevin stays vanished the rest of the day, but the rumor mill becomes a flood and everyone is waist deep in it. The Farrow's car will be firebombed. Molotov cocktails are ready to be tossed through their windows. The family cat will be nailed to their front door. The Farrows don't even have a cat, but the stories just keep piling on. By the time the bell rings, there's talk of a lynch mob marching on the Farrow house with pitchforks and torches like something out of a Frankenstein movie.

My bike's locked up in the rack. There was no way I could risk taking the Galaxie to school again. I've got ten bucks in my pocket to buy a replacement headlight from Tony's Auto Garage on the way home. Pulling the bike from the rack, I finally spot Kevin. He's in the student parking lot with Todd the Clod and some other senior clowns. Todd's car, a turd-brown Chevette, has both doors open, music blaring from the stereo. He *would* listen to Bon Jovi.

I hesitate over what to do, but I'm feeling suicidal and walk the bike across the parking lot. Todd spots me first, and nudges Kevin.

"Dude, your girlfriend's here," he says.

Kevin turns, disappointment drooping his face.

"Got a minute?" I say.

"For you, Mark? Anything." He steps away from the car with its grinding volume. His heavy army boots clomp against the pavement like they're weighted down.

"Are you planning some stunt on the Farrows?"

He shakes his head. "Jesus, Mark. You really drank the Kool-Aid with that bitch, haven't you? When are you gonna wake up?"

"Tell me you're not planning something."

Kevin looks back at his new friends. "And here I thought I'd get an apology."

"For what?"

"You really hurt my feelings, man," he says. "You promised the first ride in the Galaxie to me and Eric. And you go give it to that freakshow?"

He's right. That was always the plan. I keep my tone as friendly as I can. "Look, just leave George and her sisters alone, okay? She didn't do anything to you."

"But she did, Marko. Don't you get that? She stole our best friend. That witch swooped in and took one of our own. Filled his head with a bunch of nonsense. And now he's crawled so far up her skirt, he can't tell when someone's trying to help him."

"Do you hear yourself? This isn't some revenge movie you're in."

Kevin takes my arm, not harshly, and says with all sincerity, "It's okay, buddy. We're gonna bring you home. Deprogram you. You'll thank me when it's all over."

He saunters back to the Chevette and one of the goons cracks a joke that I can't hear. Todd just glares at me like he's waiting for an excuse to kick my ass. Stacy told me about his hair trigger, so I coast away before something sets him off.

The paperback is old, the spine cracked. The cover shows a saucer-like spaceship hovering over a city. The alien Overlords, when they reveal themselves to humankind, look like demons. *Childhood's End*—we're reading it for Ms. Treblinski's English class.

The back seat of the Galaxie isn't the best place to read, but it's the only place I want to be right now. It is distracting, though. My brain keeps slipping back to the memory of George folded into me, our skin sweating against the vinyl. The way her hair smelled or the press of her hand against my face, all damp and hot. There's a ghost of her here in the car with me, and it's carving out a hollow space in my chest. It's confusing, feeling horny and sad at the same time. Is this really what people go through? I've always had a disdain for sappy love songs, but every one that bleeds through the radio makes sense to me now. It's like I've caught a fever I can't shake. Nothing is normal anymore.

It's hard to concentrate with all this gooey stuff sloshing inside. I keep having to read the same paragraph over and over, so I don't notice the creeping chill until I shiver. The mercury has dropped in a way that is not at all normal. The windows fog up, and there's an abrupt shift in my mood. The longing in my chest is flattened by an overwhelming sense of misery.

It's back.

I sit up. The light in the garage goes out. There's a click, and the radio turns on, tuned to a station I don't recognize. A smug evangelist sermonizes about the Soviet threat and the end of the world. He calls it a reckoning. The missiles will burn away the wicked, leaving only the righteous behind. The truly faithful will be immune to radiation poisoning. Which side, he wants to know, will I stand on when Judgment Day comes?

Something clammy fingers the back of my neck. I leap off the vinyl, but there is nothing there.

The dead sister is in the car with me. Door locks won't keep her out. She wants to punish me. My first instinct is to say that I'm sorry, but what would contrition mean to a lost soul? It doesn't change the past. A sour smell wafts up inside the car. It reeks like exhaust fumes, but the car isn't running. The garage door is down, the side door closed.

She'll make it look like a suicide. Another heartbroken teen who offed themselves for love. How dramatic. How boringly cliched.

The door locks *thunk* home and refuse to budge no matter how hard I pull on them. I crank the window down and crawl out, slumping onto the cracked concrete floor. I can feel a breath on my neck as I tug on the garage door until it rolls up. I cough and hack until the night air clears out my lungs. I expect to see her ghostly shape sitting behind the steering wheel, but there's nothing. Just the car in the narrow space of the garage, no exhaust fumes, no phantom sister in a green sweater with a red Soviet star on the front.

I know why it wants to kill me.

The sound of gravel, sharp and crunching. There is someone here after all, but the lonely figure in the driveway is flesh and blood. More blood than usual.

"Eric?"

Backlit by the streetlight, walking his bike because the front wheel is bent all to hell. There's blood on his shirt.

"Jesus, what happened to you?"

There's more blood running from his nose. One eye is purpled and puffy.

"I always make excuses for him," Eric mutters. "Why do I do that?"

Tears along with the blood. Eric wipes them away quickly, as if these are the unsightliest blemishes on his pummeled face.

I approach him with my hands up, the way you would with a suicidal jumper. "Eric, what the hell happened?"

His laugh is high. "I fell down some stairs."

"Who did this to you?" It sounds stupid the moment I say it.

He looks down at the bent front wheel. His bike looks like a horse that needs to be put out of its misery. How far has he dragged it like this?

"Even when he pulled some crazy shit," he says, "I made excuses for him. Why? I must have rocks in my head."

There's no way Kevin would do this. That's going too far, even for him. I can't help assume that there's a logical explanation until I realize that I'm doing exactly what Eric just said, making excuses for him.

"Why did he jump you?"

"Because I said no."

This makes sense. "No to what?"

"He said we were just gonna prank them. You know, like burning a bag of dogshit on the front step or something. He said we were just gonna teach them a lesson. But when we got there, he and his goons pull out spray cans and rocks to throw through the windows."

My knees go wobbly. I know the answer but ask anyway. "Prank who?"

"The Farrows. They started smashing windows and Todd whats-his-name had a gas can. I told Kevin to stop. That's when he lost his shit."

Even Kevin isn't that crazy. This is followed by a second thought: George wasn't wrong about the townspeople wanting to hurt them. Kevin just proved her right.

"He went nuts." Eric dabs at his nose, looks at the blood on his hand. "So I ran. Last I looked, something was on fire."

Everything slows down and I'm drifting outside my body again, unable to square what Eric is telling me. I feel the way he looks—punched stupid.

Eric tugs himself away, lifting the front end of the bike to roll it home.

I need to get my feet back on solid ground. "Wait. We can't just let him do that."

He yanks his arm away, keeps walking. "I'm done. Let it go."

"Eric, come on."

"You think I'm going back there?" He spits a bloodied gob onto the pavement. "I thought you should know. I'm done with both of you."

The back wheel of Eric's bike must be bent because it squeaks as he rolls it away. Even after he's swallowed by the darkened street, I can hear the rhythmic screech of the tire.

I'm still standing under the piss-yellow streetlight, not knowing what to do, when a grinding noise rips out from the garage. The tumbling purr of an engine with a new fuel pump firing on all cylinders. One cyclops headlight pops on, hazing my eyesight. Something has decided for me.

A SPELL TO END ALL SPELLS

THE GALAXIE IS still new to me, and I'm new to it. The steering is loose, still pulling left, and I get a hard lesson when I hit a curve too fast. The rear end fishtails off the pavement onto the shoulder, and there's an angry buzz of gravel firing inside the wheel well. The Ford comes within an inch of landing in the ditch before the car rights itself and jerks back onto the blacktop. I'm lucky there's no other traffic on the road.

Swinging onto Merrily Road, I see an evil glow rising from the dark treetops ahead. The sour smell of smoke is sharp on the night air. I leave the car at the curb and run through the gates toward the blaze of the fire. Not the house, one of the outbuildings. The garden shed is all pumpkin orange and honey yellow as the fire swallows up the tinderbox structure.

The blaze is keeping the parents busy. Mrs. Farrow stands in the grass in a silvery kaftan, spraying the garden hose at the flames. Mr. Farrow flails a wet burlap sack at the smoldering grass to prevent the fire from reaching the house. He curses a string of obscenities at the flames as if to scold them into retreat.

The house is untouched by the fire but brutalized in other ways. Four windows on the main floor are smashed, another on the second floor. Someone has destroyed the wicker furniture on the porch, and the screen door hangs limp from one hinge. And there's the graffiti—a swastika, and also the word "witch." Black spray paint leaks down the clapboard like dripping blood.

The sisters have retreated to the gates, well away from the fire. Claudia's eyes are bald with horror. Tilly is crying, her arms wrapped around her older sister. George is not with them. She isn't anywhere. I run to them, asking what happened, but the Farrow sisters turn on me. Claudia's fists are brutal and fast, knocking me flat. Tilly kicks me with her hard-soled shoes.

I yell at them to stop, that it wasn't me who attacked them. My ear gets boxed one last time before they let up.

Claudia spits on me. "I always knew you'd turn on us."

I scramble to my feet, swearing to God I had nothing to do with this. The sisters don't believe me. Why would they? Kevin's stunt has proved that they weren't paranoid after all. Their hatred for us is justified.

"Where's George?"

Claudia hovers over me, her fists still clenched. "She's gone."

"Gone where?"

"She went to cast her spell," Tilly says. "She's going to make everyone pay for what they did."

Jesus Christ. "What spell? Where did she go?"

"She wouldn't tell us," Tilly says.

A loud pop sounds from inside the shed. God knows what just exploded in there. The three of us watch the fire.

"Did you call the fire department?" I say.

Claudia shakes her head. "They won't come out here."

"Just call them for Christ's sake."

Tilly looks to her older sister. Claudia nods, and Tilly runs for the house.

"Claudia, what is George going to do?"

"Tilly already told you. She's gone to cast her spell."

I'm running in circles here. "What does that mean?"

She brushes the soot from her hands. "She took a can of gasoline and left."

My heart snags on something sharp. This is way bad. "What is she going to do with it?"

"She didn't say."

"Where did she go?"

"I don't know!"

My questions are cut short by a blast of cold water to my face. The mother has spotted me, turning the hose in my direction. She calls me a bastard and a vandal and now the father is coming on fast. So I run.

The engine wails as I stomp the gas pedal and double back toward town, eyes peeled for any sign of her. The streets are dead, the town tucked in for the night. Not a single neighbor of the Farrows comes out to see what all the commotion is about. I don't hear any sirens. Maybe Claudia was right about the fire department. The firemen will carry on with their card game and mosey on over in the morning to kick through the ashes of the Farrow house.

The train tracks *thunk* loudly under the tires. Elm Street is empty of souls, as is King and Chestnut. Not even a stray dog is out. She can't have gone far lugging a can of gasoline with her. Did she take the bike?

I steer the car toward Main Street. Where else would George go? If she's going to start a fire, she'd go there. I need to find her before she does something stupid.

The single headlight picks out three figures on the road ahead, none of them George. It's Kevin and his new friends sauntering down the middle of the street like they own it. It's an open invitation. I mash the accelerator to the floor and the steering wheel shimmies as I pick up speed. I picture a smear of bloodied camouflage splattered on the front grill.

The car is loud, giving them plenty of time to duck out of the way. I get a glimpse at Kevin as I roar past, and the shock on his stupid face is extremely satisfying. How much more gratifying would it be to hear his bones break against the bumper, the wet thud of his carcass rolling under the wheels?

The car drifts to port again, almost shearing the side of a parked car, when an image pops into my vision—the blueprint on George's desk. A pet project she told me. Something special. Now it becomes obvious—George plans to burn down the Palisades.

Main Street is a ghost town, empty of souls. I slow the car, scanning the main drag for movement. That's when I hear the abrupt clamor of breaking glass. Like magic, she materializes, hurling a brick through the plate-glass window of the ticket booth.

I jump out of the car, holler at her to stop.

George Farrow turns in my direction. I'm expecting to see rage or tears or gnashing teeth, but there isn't any of that. Instead, there's a weird calm to her. A determination.

Then she smashes another window. Glass explodes around her as it hits the sidewalk.

"Stop." Panic ripples my voice. I'm the one who's hysterical. "What are you doing?"

At her feet is a dented can of gasoline. She picks it up. "Vandalism, arson. And, fingers crossed, mass murder."

The lid spins off. She splashes gasoline through the broken theater windows. The smell of it sours everything around us.

"George, stop. You can't just burn down everything."

"Yes, I can." She raises a hand, warning me away. "Stay back, Mark. I don't want to splash gas on you."

I scramble for some way to make her stop. "This is crazy. Why burn the movie house?"

"You know why."

The fuel is everywhere, splashing over the sidewalk, her shoes.

"I'm sorry they went after you. It was just Kevin and his goons. They're idiots."

"I told you they'd come for us. Did they expect us to just take it?" She works her way through each broken window, splashing the gasoline inside. "They need to be taught a lesson."

She won't be talked out of this. What do I do, tackle her? "Burning the theater down won't solve anything. It won't make things right."

"It's the only thing these people will understand."

The noxious fumes shimmer the air, already giving me a headache.

"So this is your big spell, starting a fire?"

"No. This is just the start. The spell is in the bones of this building."

Has she lost her marbles? She doesn't look crazy. No tears, no rage.

"Bones?" I'm stalling. "That doesn't make sense."

She backs away from the building, trailing a thin line of gasoline on the sidewalk behind her. "Do you know how old this building is? All of these buildings are connected through the shared attics and basements. If one burns, they all burn." She flings the jerrican at the cinema where it takes out more glass. "This whole block will go up in flames. When the wind picks up, the whole stupid town will burn, too."

"George, please. You can't do this."

"We have to do this," she says, suddenly implicating me in her plan. "There's no other way."

"This won't solve anything!"

She looks disappointed in me. "Mark, think about all the books you've read, all the movies you've seen. What's the only true way to destroy evil?"

I take a step toward her. "Those are just stories."

Like magic, a box of matches materializes in her hand. Her hand was empty, then it wasn't. "You burn it out."

She rummages the box as if searching for just the right match. I should slap the matchbox out of her hand, pin her to the ground before she sets off an inferno. I do neither of these things. And then it's too late because a new voice rises at our backs.

"Looky here, the happy couple."

Kevin has arrived.

GASOLINE

KEVIN WHITE BECAME my best friend in the summer before seventh grade on a tedious August afternoon. I was wading in the creek, turning over rocks to find crayfish when I notice this strange kid watching me.

"You want to go to the bridge and smash stuff?" he said.

I immediately said yes, as if I'd been waiting for someone to ask me that question all afternoon. No greeting, no introduction. We walked the bank until we slipped into the shade of the trestle bridge. There was tons of stuff to smash there. The bridge had long been a nocturnal dump site for unwanted appliances, old car parts and broken tools. There were always bottles or mirrors to smash, sometimes ceramic lamps or cast-off dishware. The best were fluorescent lights, the long tubes that became lightsabers in our hands. They would explode on impact, spewing out a chalky dust that we were too stupid to realize was poisonous. Sometimes we'd push a discarded stove down the bank to watch it splash into the river or construct a crude ramp to launch old tires into the muddy water. One time we found a paper bag with seven shotgun shells in it. Kevin had the brilliant idea of cutting open the wadding to get the gunpowder out and light it up. It stank up our clothes and singed our eyebrows.

Mindless mayhem and pointless destruction—it was the basis of our friendship. As long as it was loud and possibly life-threatening, we ate it up and came back for more. That was the best summer—before Mom got sick. Before I knew the world could kick you in the nuts so hard you'd never want to get up again.

It was kid's stuff, and that stuff doesn't last. Or it shouldn't, anyway. Smashing stuff eventually lost its luster for me, but not for Kevin. He still lives for it. Somewhere along the way, we stopped being best friends. I just didn't inform Kevin of that fact. I guess he knows now since I tried to run him over.

It takes him all of three seconds to put it together. The broken windows of the Palisades and the sour stink of gasoline everywhere, the matches in George's hand—that's why he's grinning now. He's all in.

"Is this what we're doing?" he laughs. "Setting the town on fire? Let her rip, Georgie!"

From bad to worse we go. I hate playing the monkey in the middle—George on one side, holding the match, and Kevin on the other, twitchy and eager for destruction.

"Kevin, not now," I warn him. "Stay out of it."

"You really hurt my feelings, Mark, trying to run me over." He looks sincere as he says this. He has a knack for this, luring you in close so he can strike. "And yet, here I am still trying to save you. That's what friends do."

George strikes the match, flings it at him. The gas is everywhere, but the flame snuffs out at Kevin's feet.

"Too bad Mark missed," George says, shaking another match from the box. "Roadkill suits you."

Kevin laughs. It's all a joke to him. "Marko, I don't think your girlfriend likes me very much."

This isn't happening. I want to kill Kevin. I want to slam his skull against the pavement. "Why did you trash her house? What is wrong with you?"

"She stole my best friend," he says. "Am I supposed to just take that shit? I'm trying to help you, dumbass."

George sneers at that. "No, you aren't. You just want to punish him."

"Do you hear this?" Kevin says to me. He shakes his head. "Wake up, man. She's turned you stupid in the head. She's evil, just like the rest of them."

This needs to stop before it turns way bad. "Kevin, listen to me—you have to leave. Quit the Rambo shit and go home."

"Marko, it's okay. I'm not gonna give up on you. I'm the one who saves you from yourself, remember?"

George sneers at that. "He's lying. He just wants to control you."

"Sister, are you gonna torch this place or what? Get on with it!" He turns back to me. "Dude, you'd be dead if it wasn't for me. Or in a wheelchair, pissing your PJs."

When he takes a step toward her, I block his way. Which is suicide, because Kevin's about to go off, and it's going to be painful.

But there's no punch, no kick to the nuts. Kevin seems genuinely hurt. "That's how it is, huh? Her over me?"

"Kev, please. Just go home."

The hurt in his eyes falls away, replaced by something colder. A grin aimed right at me. "Did you tell her?"

"Shut up."

He looks at George. "He didn't tell you, did he? About how your sister died."

That knocks her back, confusion behind the fall of her hair. I shove Kevin away, tell him to shut his trap, but he won't listen.

Matches spill from the box in her hand. She looks at me. "What's he talking about?"

"Lisa," Kevin butts in. "She died in a car accident, right?"

"Liesl," she corrects him.

"Yeah, her," Kevin pushes me out of the way, moves toward George. "Do you know why she crashed her car? It was me and Marko here. We did it."

Her eyes bounce from me to Kevin and back again, desperate for the truth. Or a denial. It's hard to tell.

I tell her he's full of shit, that he's a liar, but it sounds unconvincing even to me. Her hands are trembling. "Mark?"

Kevin loves to brag about doing crazy stuff, and he's on a roll now. "We used to have these Roman candle wars, right? Shooting fireworks at each other across the street. It's crazy. And one night, we're blasting at each other when this car comes ripping around the corner, gets caught in the crossfire. This shitty Datsun gets seriously strafed with pyrotechnics, but a few of them go through the windows, and that shit ricochets inside the car like crazy."

I jump the son of a bitch to shut him up, but I could never take Kevin in a fight. He's too fast, sends me sprawling over the pavement. He keeps talking. I used to wonder what it would feel like to be buried alive. Now I know.

"Mark and me, we ran and didn't look back. Heard it on the news the next day. Car crash on Cedar Avenue, straight into a brick wall. One fatality—Lisa Farrow."

"Liesl," I say, but no one hears me.

George has gone scarily pale. Her lips move, but I can't hear what she's saying at first. "Tell me he's lying."

I can't. I can't even speak, let alone lie.

"Mark? Tell me he's lying."

Kevin just laps it up. He feeds on mayhem, so he twists the knife further and looks up at George. "Why do you think he became friends with you? The guilt's been eating at him ever since, the pussy."

All the matches spill to the ground, save for the one in her hand. Her guts have just been punched in, but the sheet of horror on her face slips into something terrible, something frighteningly powerful. The sharp smell of sulfur cuts the air. The match is struck, and she throws it on the gasoline.

NERO

EVER WONDER WHY they're called Roman candles? Because the Emperor Nero burned the early Christians alive to light the streets of Rome. The poor saps were slathered with pitch, hoisted up on poles, and set ablaze. I don't know if that really happened, but that's what the fireworks are named after.

The rockets we had that night were cheap, bought off a guy who sold them out of his trunk. A Roman candle is basically a cardboard tube packed with black powder, a lifting charge that propels the pyrotechnic star, and some delay charges. Getting hit with one hurts. The magnesium burns through clothes and scorches the skin. It's dangerous if you get one in the face. But that didn't stop us from re-enacting the siege of Stalingrad across an empty street. We had six candles between us, enough to fill the square with smoke and red explosions. Eric got one in the stomach and surrendered, crawling off somewhere to cry.

Kevin and I kept at it, lighting up the street like a war zone. Kevin was in his glory. Neither of us heard the car coming. It was just there, as if by magic, hurtling around the corner at top speed. A crappy Datsun with Bondo patches on the fenders. The windows were open, radio blaring, as it roared through our field of battle. Two separate rockets flew straight into the Datsun and ricocheted around inside the cab. I didn't get a look at the driver, but I remember the scream.

Kevin didn't waste a second, yanking me away and pushing me down the alley. We booked it the hell out of there and didn't stop until we got to his place. I threw up on the front lawn.

"Don't say shit," he wheezed. "I mean, never." Then he went in his house and closed the door.

It wasn't until the next day that I realized what we had done. It was on the radio—car crash, one fatality, the name withheld. I ran to Kevin's house, scared out of my mind. We had to go to the cops, tell them what happened. He refused, said we'd be screwed if the cops found out. We swore ourselves to secrecy.

The next day, they released the victim's name on the radio—Liesl Farrow, age seventeen.

That was the cap to my Summer of Doing Dumb Things—we killed someone. We caused Liesl Farrow to crash her car, ending her life. Events rippled out in a chain after that. The Farrows withdrew into grief and pulled their children out of school. An already eccentric family became even stranger and more reclusive, which further poisoned local sentiment against them.

I'm pretty sure I'm going to Hell. And right now, I'm about to get my first taste of hellfire with the match George tosses onto the fuel. It arcs through the air like a tiny falling star, one last Perseid, and lands on the gas-drenched pavement. We're all going to die.

Nothing happens.

The flame winks out, leaving a wisp of smoke curling in the air. Apocalypse averted. Kevin's jaw is like mine, flat on the ground. George scrambles for one of the lost matches, eager to get the spell right this time.

That's when the light hits us. We're blinded by it, hands up to shield our eyes. I'm convinced the gas really did ignite and we're all dead, faced with that bright light you hear about it with near-death experiences. But it's not the afterlife calling. It's the Galaxie 500.

Did I leave it running? I must have because it's rolling forward, blinding us with its one headlight. There's no one behind the wheel. It must have slipped out of gear. The idle is too high, setting it in motion. The Galaxie lumbers up over the curb and trawls right for us like a smooth gliding shark.

It rolls over the spilled matches, denying George the tools of her spell as the bumper pushes her back. It nudges me and Kevin, pushing all three of us against the wall. Kevin's hollering at Eric to knock it off. He thinks our friend is behind the wheel, but the car is clearly unoccupied. George is yelling too. She's raging at her sister to butt out, but she's not addressing Tilly or Claudia.

She means Liesl.

When Kevin realizes there's no one in the car, he turns all kinds of pale. The ghost of Christmas past has finally come for him and me.

George bangs her fist against the hood, screaming at her sister to stop. The engine revs up, pinning us harder against the brick. I think my leg is going to snap from the pressure.

Her skinny knees slip out of the trap and George scrabbles around the back of the Galaxie. She's still screaming at her sister, but I can't make sense of what she's saying. She finds another match and strikes it. Gears shift and the car rolls back, knocking her out of the way. Too late. The match is tossed, and this time, it lights the fuel. A line of flame snakes across the pavement to the broken windows. Whoosh.

A shock wave of heat knocks me flat. I hug the cracked sidewalk because I don't want to die, not like this. I don't look up until I hear the screaming.

It's Kevin, rolling on the ground as fire ripples up his back. He becomes the Human Torch, and his screams are so awful they don't even sound human. I jump on him to beat down the flames, but the fire eats my hands and now I'm screaming, my palms already blistering. Kevin rolls onto his back, snuffing the flames. Hellfire erupts over us as the Palisades goes up in flames.

I see George staring up at the fire, but I can't tell if she's mesmerized in triumph or horrified at what she's done. The fire drips off the building and onto the sidewalk, the car. The Galaxie is burning, flames blistering the paint and eating its way into the interior. It's already too far gone. How much gas is in the tank? Enough to kill us all.

I'm clotheslined at the throat, cutting hard into my windpipe. It's the dead sister, I'm sure of it, come to exact her revenge. It's caught me by the shirt collar, dragging me away from the fire. The fabric strangles my throat and doesn't stop until I'm hauled around a corner and out of danger. George kneels over me, breathing hard from saving my stupid life. She turns my hands up to see the blistered palms.

She shakes me awake. "Mark, look at me. Don't pass out."

She looks kind of savage, all crazy hair and black pupils. I want to tell her something, but all that comes out is the hacking of a two-pack-a-day smoker.

George freezes up, her grip crushing my wrist. Then I hear it too—sirens. She looks at me, then out to the street. And then she's gone.

The pain makes me cross-eyed, rendering everything blurry. Every sound is baffled like I've got cotton in my ears. George reappears out of nowhere, yelling at me, but I can't understand what she's saying. She's gone again.

When the Galaxie's gas tank finally blows, it flattens my eardrums into a high-pitched ring. And then everything goes dark.

OFFICER FRIENDLY

A RED STROBE light cuts through the smoke. There's a lot of muffled noise. A fireman is kneeling over me, checking my hands and asking my name.

"George?" I don't see her anywhere in all the smoke.

The firefighter mistakes this for an answer. "George, you're going to be okay," he says. "Do you know who this is?"

There's a lump sprawled on the ground beside me.

"His name's Kevin."

My oldest friend is face-down on the pavement. I can't tell if he's conscious or even alive. His back is so burned up I can't look at it. Two paramedics rush in with a stretcher. When they lift Kevin, he screams.

The smoke stings and I can't stop blinking, can't think straight. Kevin was on fire. That's how my hands got burned. But how did he end up beside me?

George. She must have dragged him here the same way she hauled me away from the fire. Even after what he did to her.

The fireman waves a hand before my face. "George, we're going to get you on your feet. Ready?"

Strong hands prop me up like a limp dishrag and walk me toward the pumper truck on the street. There's water everywhere, reflecting the flashing red lights on the trucks. It hurts to look up, but I do it anyway. The Palisades is a scorched ruin, as are the two buildings on either side. The water cannon pushes back the flames rippling from the blown-out windows. Greasy black smoke bubbles into the sky like poison.

The Galaxie squats before the burning building, a black silhouette against the orange light of the flames. Nothing left but charred metal and smoking rubber.

Second-degree burns—that's what the nurse at the hospital tells me. Both hands are red and bloated with blisters, the right worse than the left. I won't be writing letters anytime soon. A blister pops as the nurse cleans the wound, and hot fluid runs through my fingers. It stinks. She wraps both hands with gauze, rendering me a double-amputee. How am I supposed to pee with these oven mitts on?

I'm walked out to the waiting room, told my parents are on their way. The hard shell seats are uncomfortable and no matter which way I sit, I can't avoid the stench of smoke. It's soaked into my clothes and my hair, ash clotted in every pore.

Dad shows up, inspects my bandaged hands and asks if I'm okay. We drive home in silence. Liz is in the kitchen when we get home. She cries when she sees the mummy-hands. Dad assures her I'm fine. The questions start. How did the fire start? How did I get hurt? Who else was involved?

My eyes fall to a crack in the linoleum floor. I'm too numb to even understand what he's asking me. This only makes him angrier.

He paces the floor, stepping over the crack I'm staring at. "I thought we were done with this stuff? The burning shit for attention."

I tell him I'm tired, that my hands hurt. Liz intervenes. She finds some Aspirin and tells me to go to bed. We can figure it out tomorrow, she says.

Dad asks if I need help. I lie, say I'm fine, but getting undressed is impossible with these useless paws. I give up and just lie down in my reeking clothes. I stare up at the clean spots of ceiling where the plastic stars used to be. I keep seeing the image of the Galaxie rolling up the curb to mash us against the wall. I must have left it running. The wonky transmission slipped a gear and the high idle caused it to rumble forward. There wasn't any ghost behind the wheel.

That's what I'm telling myself, despite the lump in my jeans pocket. It takes forever to wriggle them out, but there they are—my car keys. It's all that's left of the Galaxie now.

A hand on my shoulder shakes me awake.

"Get up," he says. "We need to talk."

A police officer sits at the kitchen table. Liz and Dad across from him, looking uncomfortable. There's a plate of danishes on the table like it's a social visit.

"Good morning, Mark," the officer says. "How are you feeling?"

I look at my mitts. "Okay."

Dad pulls out a chair. "This is Officer Reeves. He has a few questions about last night."

"Are you hungry? Do you want some coffee?" Liz makes a fuss until Dad shoots her a cold look. She folds her hands in her lap and stays quiet.

The gauze on my hands is dirty and frayed. The officer makes a whistling sound. "That looks pretty serious. How bad is it?"

"They said it'll take a couple weeks to heal."

"I guess you'll get some time off school, huh?" Officer Reeves spoons sugar into his cup, stirs slowly. "How did you get hurt?"

A thousand lies ping-pong through my brain, but none of them make sense. "Kevin was on fire. I tried to put him out."

"I see." The spoon clinks against the cup. "You and Kevin are buddies, right?"

"Since seventh grade," my dad adds proudly. Which is strange, because he's never liked Kevin.

The officer glances at him without smiling.

Dad shuts up.

There's a pin on Officer Reeves' tie—green enamel, shaped like a shamrock. Is he Irish or just superstitious? I'm unable to focus on anything but this shamrock tie pin. "How is Kevin?"

"He'll be in the hospital a while yet. His injuries are pretty serious." Officer Reeves finally stops stirring and lays the spoon aside. "So which one of you started the fire?"

Dad acts shocked, but it's so forced it's laughable. Liz is genuinely upset.

I'm sweating for a way out of this when I realize I don't have to lie. "Neither of us started it."

He's displeased with this answer, but not surprised. "The fire chief said it's a clear-cut case of arson. The jerrycan was still there, right next to your car."

Dad growls at me to answer the police officer.

I wish I could fold my arms, but that hurts too much. My hands flop in my lap, and I just sit here like a dummy.

"A lot of this doesn't make sense," the officer continues. "Why burn your own car? Why was it on the sidewalk?" He lifts his cup and makes a slurping sip. "Both you and Kevin White have a history of arson, correct?"

Dad bristles, but the cop shuts him down with a glance.

Kevin and I got caught once burning down a shack near the creek. We weren't charged because we were minors, but Officer Reeves knows all about it.

He leans closer, like it's just the two of us in the room. "Was someone else involved? One witness reported seeing a girl smashing the windows of the movie theater. Did you see this girl?"

Liz's eyebrows shoot up. "That doesn't sound like something a girl would do."

Officer Reeves looks at me. "Was there a girl there, Mark? Did she start the fire?"

Dad snaps his fingers, the idiot. "That girl. The strange one."

"Who?"

"One of the Farrow girls," Dad says. "Mark was spending time with her. God knows why."

"The Farrows out on Merrily Road?" Officer Friendly perks up, eyes darting between me and Dad. Fishing for a lead, he's snagged one he likes. "What's her name?"

The room turns cold. No one else notices. They're too busy waiting for me to answer.

"George."

"George?"

"Georgia."

"I see." Reeves sets his cup aside like he's ready to do business. "Was Georgia Farrow there last night? Did she start the fire?"

"No."

He doesn't like this answer. The pleasantness in his face drops away. "That family is odd. Lord knows we've had our dealings with them." He leans closer to me. "I need you to think hard about this, Mark. Was that Farrow girl there last night?"

The chill is getting worse. She's here, watching over her sisters again, just like Tilly said.

My voice cracks when I open my trap. "I started the fire. I smashed the windows at the Palisades and splashed the gasoline around. Then I lit it up. Kevin tried to stop me, but he caught fire. I tried to put him out."

It all comes spewing out like that, gift-wrapped. Dad hits the roof and Liz insists I'm delirious, that I don't know what I'm saying. The cop keeps asking questions, but I can't answer them because I'm crying like a fucking baby.

PROVIDENCE

OFFICER REEVES SAYS I will be formally charged with arson. A court date will be set. He tells Dad that I can stay under his supervision for now but warns that this may change. He suggests calling a lawyer, thanks Liz for the coffee and leaves. Dad flips his lid, raking me over the coals for what I've done. He runs the full gamut, from shaking his fist in my face to breaking down in tears and asking God where he went wrong with me. Liz stays quiet. She knows this isn't her fight, so she remains sidelined until Dad exhausts himself.

He wonders how disturbed I am. He fears I'm psychotic. He wants me to see a therapist, if, he adds, we can afford one after the lawyer bills. The expense side of it sends him into a new tailspin. A couple of times I think for sure he's going to knock my head into the wall. If Liz wasn't there, he probably would. I might even welcome it.

Eventually he throws up his hands and says he's going to lie down. He asks Liz to call his office and tell them he's sick. She makes the call, stretching the phone cord to its max as she moves about the kitchen. She brings me a cup of coffee and points to the danishes on the table. "Eat something," she mouths.

I pick at one of the pastries to make her happy. I don't have much appetite.

When she hangs up the phone, Liz sits down and wraps her palms around her coffee mug. Her hands are always cold. "So, you burned down the theater, huh?"

"And the department store. The Chinese restaurant, too."

"Seems odd." She blows on the coffee, takes a sip. "You love the Palisades. Did you plan on torching the Galaxie too, or was that just an accident?"

She's fishing.

I shrug. "None of it was really planned."

Liz watches me pick the pastry apart. I can't even look her in the eye. She's more of a detective than Officer Friendly is. I guess she thinks I'll break if she keeps staring at me. She's not angry the way Dad is. But she's patient.

"Being loyal to your friends is admirable," she says. "Up to a point."

"Isn't that what friends are for?"

Her hand folds over my wrist. "Mark, you shouldn't be the scapegoat here. It's not fair."

"I'm not doing anything. I did something bad. That's all."

My hands are useless. There's pastry crumbs all over the gauze.

"We should change those bandages," she says.

The hospital sent me home with fresh gauze. Liz tears open the package with her teeth and then starts unwrapping one of my mitts.

"You don't have to do that. It's gonna be gross," I say.

"I've seen worse."

It's repulsive. The skin is red and puckered with blisters.

To her credit, Liz doesn't flinch. When both hands are freed, she throws out the old gauze. "We'll let this air out a bit."

Some of the blisters have popped, leaking fluid between my fingers. I drop my disgusting hands into my lap so Liz doesn't have to look at them.

"I saw this movie once," I tell her. "This guy, he's a famous pianist, he loses both hands in an accident. Then a surgeon transplants new hands onto him, but these hands belonged to a murderer, right? And the hands want to kill again."

"I saw a movie like that once," she says. "Except the guy loses his legs, and the new transplants are from a dead tap dancer."

She can be pretty funny and I laugh, even though it's the last thing I want to do right now. Liz reaches into her bag for her cigarettes and lights up. I guess she doesn't care if Dad sees it. Smoking is nothing compared to the catastrophe I've created.

She blows smoke up at the ceiling fan. "Reeves said the fire could have been a lot worse."

"How so?"

"No wind last night. He said that even a small breeze would have spread the fire, burning down the whole strip."

My hands stink like the flesh is rotting. Maybe it's gangrene.

Liz unfurls a roll of fresh gauze. "I guess someone upstairs was watching out for us," she says, stubbing the cigarette out on the plate.

For a moment, I consider telling her about Liesl's ghost, but decide to keep my mouth shut. She'd think I'm crazy.

Unfurling the roll of fresh gauze, she says, "Let's wrap those hands up."

"You don't have to. It's gross."

"I don't mind. Let's see them."

I lift my revolting hands onto the table, and she starts rolling the gauze over them. "You never mind anything," I say. "Even when I'm mean to you, you don't mind. Why?"

The gauze slips. She wasn't expecting that. "Guess I'm a glutton for punishment," she says, dismissing it with a joke.

"I'm sorry," I tell her. "About everything."

This she dismisses, too, saying something about water under the bridge. A moment later we hear Dad holler from the other room about smelling smoke in the house.

The hospital is across town, a small white building with a statue of Saint Michael at the entrance. I can't ride my bike with these stupid hands, so I go on foot. No car, no bike, just a loser on the sidewalk while every other kid is at school.

Except Kevin.

The nurse at the reception desk consults a chart, but she isn't sure if Kevin White is allowed to have visitors. I wonder if Officer Reeves has been here. The nurse checks with another person behind the desk and then rolls her chair back.

She gives me his room number. "But keep it brief, okay? He needs to rest."

I called Eric's house this morning, hoping to catch him before he left for school. His mom answered. She did not sound friendly. Then Eric came on the line.

"Hey," I say. "I'm going to the hospital later to see Kevin. Want to come?"

"I'm busy."

"Come on. We'll go cheer him up."

The line goes quiet for a moment. "Why would you go see him?"

"I don't know. He got burned pretty bad."

Eric sighs. "I'm gonna be late for school."

"Yeah, okay. I'll tell him you said hi."

"Don't." He's emphatic on this point. "I never want to see that asshole again."

So I'm on my own, following the yellow line on the hospital floor to room 310. I hate it here. The orange line on the floor leads to the palliative care unit. Nancy was there for two months, until she wasn't. The nurse who treated my hands last night passes me in the hall and stops to ask how I'm doing. She checks the fresh bandaging, and then gets called away.

I wonder if any of Kevin's new friends have gone to visit him. Hard to imagine Todd the Clod taking time away from his precious girlfriend to visit the hospital.

I find the room, but I don't even recognize Kevin at first. There's just this lump on the bed, face down. His hospital gown is open, exposing his back to the air. It looks like a war zone, mottled pink and wet in some places, angry red in others. Some of the flesh is just dead, gray skin. I have to look away before I lose my breakfast. The back of his head is burned as well, the hair scorched clean off. His face is turned to the wall.

He looks dead. What if he died just now, while I was following the yellow line? I honestly don't know how I'd feel about it.

"Who's there?" He doesn't raise his head to see who it is. It must hurt too much to move. "I hope you brought more painkillers," he barks. Even his voice sounds charred.

"Hey." I have to force the words out. "It's me. Mark."

"Hey, buddy." His tone lifts immediately. "About time you came to visit."

I look at my shoes. "Yeah, well."

"Do you have any idea how boring this place is? I didn't think you could die of boredom, but not anymore."

I can't tell if he's messing with me. All I see is the back of his red scalp. "You look like hell."

"No shit. Don't worry, it's not as bad as it looks."

How does he know what it looks like? Did someone hold up two mirrors so he could see his scorched flesh?

Ragged coughs break up his speech, like he still has smoke in his lungs. "Is Eric with you?"

"He couldn't make it."

His ribs move up and down as he breathes. The flesh looks like it's still cooking.

"You in a lot of pain?" Stupid question, but I'm at a loss for small talk and my nerves have shriveled up.

"They're keeping me pretty doped up."

"Silver lining, I guess."

"Hey, you know what I keep thinking about?" he asks. "That scene in *RoboCop*, when the guy gets drenched in toxic waste and he starts melting and shit? Then Robo-dude hits him with the car and he just splats all over the windshield. Remember? Shit, that was funny."

He doesn't remember that I missed the movie. I guess the pain meds have messed up his memory. No sense bursting his bubble.

"Yeah. That was wicked."

I pull the chair over and we talk about movies for a while. With his face to the wall, I'm left conversing with the back of his red scalp. We run through our favorite gross-out special effects like when the severed head in *The Thing* sprouts crab legs and scampers away or watching Seth Brundle slowly rot to pieces in *The Fly*. This kills about half an hour. Neither of us mention how he got injured or the fire at the

Palisades or George. I don't know if he's avoiding this or if he's too doped up to remember. Does it matter? The conversation dwindles down to nothing, and the room grows quiet. From the hallway I hear another patient moaning in pain.

He coughs. "I hate hospitals."

"Everyone does."

This is as close as we get to discussing what happened or why he's here. It fizzles quickly.

"When I get out of here," he says, "we should do some target shooting. When was the last time we did that?"

He doesn't remember target practice in Eric's backyard a month ago. I wonder how permanent his memory loss is? Maybe the last few weeks have been erased forever.

"We can set up some army men in the dirt hill and replay D-Day," he says. "Remember how much fun that was?"

It was a lot of fun, back when we were twelve—before anything changed or became complicated. We talk for a while about how satisfying it was to hit the mark and watch a plastic soldier go spinning off into the dirt.

A nurse glides into the room and says it's time for Kevin's medication. She smiles at me, politely nodding at the door.

I get to my feet. "I gotta split. Rest up, man."

"I'll be out of this dump soon," Kevin says. His speech becomes slurred, like he's swallowing down raw eggs. "Get your gun loaded and we'll storm the beaches."

I nod, even though he can't see it. "Goodbye, Kevin."

In the hallway, I retrace the yellow line, knowing that target practice will never happen.

I think about Kevin and his burned-up skin on the walk home. It's hard to hate him after seeing the state he's in, but I know we won't be friends anymore. I'm not sad about this. I'm sad that I'm indifferent to it. It means nothing to me. Maybe it never did.

I tell myself I'm just taking a long walk, but I know exactly where I'm going—across the tracks, and down to Merrily Road. I'm not going to pull anything stupid like bang on the door again. I just want to walk by the house. That's all.

The place looks like hell, what with all the broken windows and spray-painted swastikas. The garden shed is a mound of soot and half the lawn is scorched black. But that's not what troubles me about this vista. There's a moving truck parked in the driveway. Men in coveralls carry furniture up the loading ramp into the back of the truck. Mrs. Farrow is on the veranda, cigarette in hand, scolding the movers to be careful. Her husband loads suitcases into the back of the station wagon.

Cold panic cuts right through me. The Farrows are leaving.

I stand by the gate, unable to venture any further. I'm like a vampire whose invitation has been revoked. Maybe it's one of George's witch bottles, placed here to keep me out. I sweep the yard, but there's no sign of the sisters. I glance up at the small attic window, expecting to see the moth-eaten curtain flutter, but it remains still. I guess the ghost is packing her bags, too.

She appears a moment later, coming down the steps and crossing the yard. George stops on her side of the gate. There's an invisible force-field in play that neither of us can cross.

"What's going on?" I ask.

"Moving day."

"Where?" I'm already filling in the answer—a rented house nearby, a hotel room across town, somewhere temporary while the house is repaired.

"Providence."

A sharp kick to the guts. It's where she wants to attend university. "That's really far away."

"We'll stay with my aunt…the one with the bomb shelter. Until we find a place of our own."

"Are you coming back?"

"Why would we come back?" Her tone is sharp. She looks down, kicks a pebble. "You know I hate it here."

She's wearing sneakers instead of those ugly black shoes—white deck sneakers. They look new.

"Were you going to leave without saying goodbye?"

George watches the movers hauling boxes out of the dilapidated house before turning back to me. She squints against the sunlight. There's something weird about her hair. It's all lopsided like she took scissors to it.

"Did you get burned?"

She runs a hand through the cropped side. "A little." She nods at my mummy hands. "Is that serious?"

"It's fine," I tell her. "Kevin's in the hospital. His burns are really bad."

Her face sours. "I don't care."

"Then why did you save his life?"

She looks down, but there are no more pebbles to kick. "The spell didn't work."

"It sort of worked. The Palisades is gone."

"None of it ever worked," she says. Her eyes keep darting around, refusing to lock onto mine. "I just wanted it to."

The clock is running out and I need to tell her, but I can't get it out. Too chickenshit, like always. I need to stick my fingers down my throat and just vomit it out. When I finally tell George that I love her, it sounds corny and fake. Insignificant.

She winces like someone stuck her with a pin. She won't look at me and the moment grows sickly and uncomfortable. Her hands fidget, desperate to be put out of this misery. It takes forever for her to look me in the eye. "I can't say it back to you."

"Yes, you can."

"You killed Liesl."

It's a fight to keep my hands at my sides. I want to take hold of her and tell her that I know she feels the same way. I need her to admit it. But doing that would make everything worse, so I keep my hands to myself.

She says, "You can't just say that and expect everything to be okay." Her eyes are red. She wipes at them impatiently. "Love isn't some dumb fairy tale."

"I know it isn't." I hate the sound of my voice right now, so needy and desperate. "But it doesn't change how I feel about you. I need you to know that."

Her shoulders drop, no fight left. She shifts her weight from one foot to the other. She becomes impatient with my neediness, bored with my dramatic declaration, and in her impatience I see my mistake. Why did I assume that she feels the same way? I'm no one special to her. I'm just the only friend she's ever had.

Her mother's voice booms across the yard, telling George to get a move on.

She says she has to go.

"Write to me."

She stops.

Her mother keeps hollering at her.

I'm clawing at a life-preserver here, but I don't care how desperate it sounds. "Write to me when you get settled in. I like your letters. I still want to hear from you."

She brushes the hair out of her eyes. "Mark, what's the point? I'm never coming back here."

"You've got my address, right?" I don't wait for an answer. There's a pen in my backpack, notepaper. I scribble down the address and press the note into her hand. "Take it. Please. Just let me know how you're doing."

She folds the paper twice. "Okay."

Neither of us says goodbye. George looks back at me only once as she crosses the scorched lawn to rejoin her family. I should leave, but I just stand here like a gawking ape, watching them—a dumb townie they'll never have to see again. The family piles into the car, and I watch the station wagon rumble past me. The Farrow sisters are in the back seat. George sits in the middle, head down and slumped into Claudia's shoulder. I can't see her face. Tilly is rubbing her back. Claudia looks at me as the car rolls past. Her hand rises, and she flips me the bird, and then the Farrow sisters drive away.

HOMEOWNERS MAKE EERIE DISCOVERY
—Brandenburg Bugle

Owners of a historic home in Brandenburg were shocked to unearth strange containers that experts have identified as 19th century "witch bottles." According to experts, these talismans were often hidden in homes to ward off evil. Sarah and Patrick Stedman, who purchased the house four years ago, have unearthed twelve of these rustic folk charms while renovating the historic house on Merrily Road. The homeowners plan to showcase the historic artifacts in a place of prominence once the renovations are complete. "We want to honor and respect the people who placed these objects so long ago," said Mrs. Stedman. "Partly for its historical value, but also because we don't want to invite any bad voodoo."

THAT ARTICLE FIRST ran in the local newspaper back in late September. It was picked up by the Associated Press and run nationally during the lead up to Halloween. Liz clipped the article and showed it to me when I visited her two weeks ago. I had a good laugh over it and shared with her the secret of this strange archaeological find, how George Farrow had buried these charms when she was a kid, and not, as the experts suggested, a witch from the 19th century. Liz found it funny, remembering the strange girl who lived in that house twenty years ago.

The house sat empty for years after the Farrows moved away. In time, it became the local haunted house, and teens would dare each other to venture inside to look for ghosts, but the spirit that once rattled in the attic had left along with the family. The property changed hands a few times, but little was done to repair the place. It wasn't until the Stedmans bought the place that a full restoration of the house began. That's when they found the witch bottles.

George never wrote, in case you were wondering.

I used to check the mail every day, waiting for a letter from her. There was a brief period where I couldn't check, because I was serving a four-month stint in juvenile detention for arson. When I got home, with two years' probation on my heels, I went back to checking the mail every day. No letter ever came.

My school year was junked, and I had to repeat the grade while my friends all moved on. Not that I had any friends at that point. I was the arsonist kid who burned down the movie theater, more of a pariah than the Farrow sisters ever were. I was radioactive.

I still checked the mailbox daily, wondering whatever happened to George or why she never wrote.

During my last year of high school, I went to look for her. I figured she would be starting her first year of university. That meant Brown, the university in Providence where the Farrows had gone. I bought a bus ticket to Rhode Island and roamed the campus looking for her. No luck. I went to the registrar's office, but they wouldn't let me check the enrollment list. A student working in the office took pity on me and discreetly searched for the name on the list. There was no Georgia Farrow enrolled there.

Did she go to a different school? Maybe she didn't pursue it at all, but that seemed unlikely. She'd been so keen on going, to find that life she knew was waiting for her. The next two Septembers I called the registrar, but no one under that name was ever enrolled there.

So, I moved on. I made it out of Brandenburg, but only as far as Chatham. Dropped out of college after one year. Met other girls, all of whom shared a certain dark intensity. Like Zoe, who was doing her thesis on folk magic in American literature and was big into the tarot. Or Lucinda, a photographer who wore only black and had seen every vampire movie ever made. Writers who made their own clothes or artists obsessed with the occult.

See a pattern? I was chasing the shadow of George Farrow for a long time, without even realizing it. When I finally did, I made a conscious effort to avoid the dark brooding type completely.

That's how I met Becky. She was athletic, easy-going, and very social. Everyone loved Becky. She spent her free time volunteering at different women's shelters. We found a place together six months after our first date and even got engaged, but never picked a date. Lasted seven years, and then it ended bitterly. I suppose all relationships do.

I found myself drawn back to the dark intense type again—artists interested in the paranormal or psychics obsessed with true crime. Chasing George again, but nothing serious came of this, so I gave up. I've been on my own for almost two years now. That sounds dramatic, but it's fine. I'm okay being alone.

Dad died the week after my 31st birthday. He adored Becky. I guess it was a blessing he wasn't around to witness the break-up. Liz and I remain close. We're family now. She's still in the same house in Brandenburg. I helped her remodel the kitchen after Dad died. I drive back there to visit all the time, and to this day, I still ask if there's any mail for me. It's a running joke between us now. On the first anniversary of Dad's passing, we opened up a bottle of scotch he'd been saving for a special occasion. Grandkids, Liz admitted. We sipped the scotch, and I told her what really happened that night the Palisades movie theater burned—the only time I ever spilled the beans about that incident. Liz wasn't surprised. She had always suspected it had something to do with George. She also knows that the letter I'm waiting for is from the strange girl who used to live on Merrily Road.

When the scotch was all gone, I told her about Liesl Farrow's death. About how Kevin and I caused that poor girl's accident all those years ago. That was news to her. If she condemned me for that act, she kept it to herself.

Kevin survived his burns. He became a successful contractor and even went on to join the Brandenburg town council. He left office in disgrace three years ago when he was caught embezzling public funds to build a lakefront cottage. We haven't spoken since that last time in the hospital.

Eric and I remain good friends. He's married now, with two kids who inherited his lanky genes. Eight years ago, he opened Brandenburg's first comic book shop that has since done surprisingly well. I helped him out with some initial seed money, so now we're business partners too.

I still think about George. Sometimes, late at night when I've had too much to drink, I play the "what-if?" game—which is never a good thing to indulge in. All the same, I still wonder where she is and what happened to her. Is she happy? Did she ever find the life she felt was waiting for her? I know I didn't. Life is all detours and unplanned side-adventures. Does anyone's life turned out the way they imagined it would at sixteen?

Reading the news article about the witch bottles brought it all back. It took me by surprise, how powerful and raw it still felt. Is it normal to be wistful about something that happened so long ago? Or has nostalgia tinted the memory of it into something more romantic than it actually was? No one stays in love for this long, do they?

Love is a fairy tale, George told me once. It just wasn't a very happy one. Hard to forget a sentiment like that. I believed it too, all this time. Maybe that's the reason I'm on my own now.

I continue to believe that until I stop by the old house to visit Liz again. This time, there is a letter waiting for me.

ACKNOWLEDGEMENTS

Writing can be a lonely business, but looking up from the page, I see a lot of people lending a hand in ways both big and small. All of it is crucial.

Thanks first and always to Monique for her love, inspiration, and wisdom. And patience! Love and thanks to Ginger and Ruby who never fail to inspire me in the strangest ways.

Barrels of appreciation to Jennifer Barnes and John Edward Lawson for inviting this book into the kennel at Raw Dog Screaming Press. You've been awesome to work with.

Huge thanks to Becky Spratford for all the support. I'm truly grateful for that, and for the introduction to Jennifer, which got us here!

Thanks to Kealan Patrick Burke for his brilliantly gruesome cover.

Huge thanks to Brian Francis for his friendship and early feedback on this story. Means the world to me.

To Mom, for everything. To the horror community at large for being so welcoming and for the support when things went screwy with this book. I love you weirdos!

Lastly, I want to thank Jeff McFarlane, my best friend for about three decades. A lot of this story is about you, even though you won't ever get to read it. You are missed.

ABOUT THE AUTHOR

Tim McGregor is the author of *Taboo in Four Colors*, *Lure*, and *Hearts Strange and Dreadful*. A former screenwriter and current HWA member, Tim lives in Toronto with his wife, two kids, and one spiteful ghost. He can be reached at timmcgregorauthor.com

CPSIA information can be obtained
at www.ICGtesting.com
Printed in the USA
BVHW032349290123
657426BV00014B/62